The Devi

Chaos of the Covenant, Book Three

M.R. Forbes

Published by Quirky Algorithms

Seattle, Washington

This novel is a work of fiction and a product of the author's imagination.
Any resemblance to actual persons or events is purely coincidental.

Copyright © 2017 by M.R. Forbes

All rights reserved.

Cover illustration by Tom Edwards

tomedwardsdesign.com

The Devils Do

CHAPTER ONE

"THERE IS A PLACE OUTSIDE of this one," Jequn said. "It is the beginning. It is where the Seraphim were born. It is where the One resides. It is called Elysium."

"Whoa, whoa, whoa," Gant said. "Hold on one second. A place outside of this one? You mean a parallel universe?"

"We've already established that," Bastion said. "You were too busy solo sieging a starship to keep up with current events."

Gant glared at Bastion. "At least I was doing something useful. I'm willing to take bets Queenie was doing everything for you."

Bastion smirked. "Not everything." He opened his mouth to make another comment.

"Are you going there?" Abbey asked.

He closed his mouth.

"I don't mean a parallel universe," Jequn said. "Not exactly. Elysium is the home of the One. It is the root of all living things. It is the origin of all."

"What? Wait," Gant said, again. "The origin? There are a bunch of theories about how the universe came into being. Big Bang, Oscillating Universe, Hologram, Simulation. Which one are you referring to?"

Jequn looked confused. "First, there was the One. Everything followed after. All universes originated from Elysium."

"Eternal Inflation?" Gant said. "Multiverse? I can accept that, I suppose. When you say the One, I assume you mean God? If he was the first, where did he come from?"

"Gant," Abbey said.

"What?" Gant replied. "I think it's a fair question."

"I don't think it's relevant to our current situation."

"Someone claiming direct access to God isn't relevant?"

"You're still assuming the One she's referring to is God," Benhil said. "It's all a matter of perspective."

"How do you mean?" Gant asked.

"If the individual you most look up to can do all of this cool shit, and you don't know any better, you're going to call him God, too, right? Could be he is. Or it could be he's just another alien with better tech. Maybe Elysium isn't the first. Maybe she just thinks it's the first because she doesn't know any better, and neither do we. Maybe this One was a nobody where he came from, and he decided he wanted to be all powerful, so he left his universe and started a new one. The Trickle Down Theory of Universal Evolution." He smiled. "I just made that up, but you can use it if you want to."

"A multiverse of gods?" Gant said. "I can get behind that. But the first one still had to start somewhere."

"Unless the whole thing is one big loop," Erlan said.

"What a mind frag that would be," Bastion said.

"Can you all shut up and let her speak," Abbey said, finally intervening. "Those details don't matter. God, The One, Nephilim, Seraphim, Ophanim, Watchers, Converts, angels, demons, blah, blah, blah. They're all just labels for things. None of it changes the reality of our situation. You know, the one where some hyper-powered asshole is trying to subdue the civilized galaxy."

"I like labels," Bastion said. "They make it easier to know what to hate."

"What's a Nephilim?" Pik asked, wandering onto the bridge.

"Where the hell have you been?" Bastion asked.

The Devils Do

"Went to Medical to get some pain meds." He held up his limp glove. "This fragging hurts."

"We can get that fixed on Machina Four," Benhil said. "You'll love the results."

Pik's eyes landed on Dak. He grunted. "Another Trover? I don't feel special anymore."

"Dak," Dak said, putting his palm up and out toward Pik.

Pik approached him, pressing his hand to Dak's. The other Trover's hand was at least six centimeters larger, a fact which wasn't lost on Pik. He grunted again. Then he smiled. "Welcome aboard."

"I don't know what just happened there," Bastion said.

Abbey sighed loudly. "Can we please just get back on topic?"

"Sorry, Queenie," Pik said.

"Jequn," Abbey said.

Jequn nodded.

"Wait," Pik said. "What's a Nephilim?"

Abbey glared at Pik. "Really?"

"Nevermind."

Jequn started speaking again. "As I was saying, Elysium is the beginning. It is the first universe, where the One made his home and created his first subjects, the Seraphim, of which I'm a descendent. Of course, we didn't always know the One created us. Some of us worshipped many gods. Some of us worshipped one, but not necessarily the One. Most of our focus was purely on science and technology, learning and discovery."

"There's nothing wrong with that," Gant said.

"There is," Jequn countered. "We grew, we learned, we evolved. In time we gained the stars. We settled hundreds of planets in Elysium. We had problems. There were wars. There was death and destruction. There was chaos. It lasted for thousands of years."

"That sounds familiar," Gant said.

"And then it ended. The years of violence made us long for peace in ways we never imagined. We learned other ways to settle our differences. We learned to accept one another. We became peaceful. We all worked together. When we came together in harmony, that was when the One made himself known across Elysium. He had a plan, and we were part of it. We had always been part of it, but he was waiting for us to be ready. We learned that he had been there with us the entire time, guiding us like a parent guides a child. Letting us trip and fall, but ultimately picking us up."

"What kind of plan?" Bastion asked.

"He came to us. He presented us with a contract. A Covenant. He wanted to fill all of the universes he had made with life, and in exchange for our help, he would ensure the eternal survival of our kind."

"What did you need that for?" Benhil asked. "It sounds like you had it pretty sweet already. No more war. A benevolent god."

"He offered us enlightenment. And besides, we wanted to help. We agreed to the Covenant. The first of his Prophets appeared on our homeworld of Earth. He provided us with specifications to build a temple to the One."

"Wait," Benhil said. "Your homeworld is called Earth, too? What are the odds of that?"

"Clearly, it isn't a coincidence," Gant said. "Shut up." He glanced at Jequn. "Go on."

"We didn't understand the nature of the technology we were creating, but we followed the schematics, and we made the One a home."

"You're saying this One of yours had no physical form?" Abbey asked. "He didn't speak for himself?"

"Correct. He chose a Prophet from each of our worlds. We knew the Prophet was true because he spoke of things we didn't understand. Science and mathematics and technology that we had yet to discover. Through them, he showed us the secrets of the universe he created for us. When the temple was completed, a great light filled the sky and then settled within what we had built. The following day, the first of the Shards appeared. The following month, the first of his ships rose from within. One year later, we began to build the gate."

Abbey's eyebrows raised at the word. "Did you say gate?"

"Yes. The Elysium Gate. It was made to transport the Shardships

The Devils Do

and their crews throughout the many universes that the One had made."

"Was a gate built on the other side?"

"It wasn't necessary. The ships were never intended to return to Elysium. Why?"

"I lifted some data from Eagan Heavyworks. We found a schematic. It was badly damaged, but it was a technical diagram of a gate."

"The Shards traveled through the Elysium Gate. Each Shardship had a crew of close to ten thousand Seraphim. Our mission was to travel to the planets in the universes, find those that could support life, and plant seeds among them. Single celled organisms that would evolve based on the planetary climate. The Gant. The Trover. The Atmo. They came from these seeds. All life forms did, except for one."

"Humans?" Bastion asked.

"Yes. Humans too were a seed, but they were not the same stem organism as the others. They were taken directly from the genetic code of the One, and engineered to evolve in his exact image. Like the Seraphim, humans were intended to be peacemakers in the universe, even if it took millions of years for you to evolve to the same place we have reached. Such is the patience of the One."

"But something happened," Abbey said. "I know that much. There was a rebellion."

"There was an engineer on the Shardship named Lucifer, who was responsible for helping to prepare the seeds. When he learned that the Shard had made an organism that would evolve in the exact image of the One, he became enraged. Had the One not made the Seraphim? Were they not his chosen? He began to believe that the One was using them, and that when their task was done they would be abandoned and replaced by humankind.

"He wanted to prove his theory, so one day he approached the Shard and asked him why they couldn't go home. The Shard replied that the fate of the Seraphim was to be without a home and that we had agreed to this when we accepted the Covenant."

"When Lucifer informed the others of this reply, many dismissed him. They believed the Shard meant the Seraphim would one day be raised up to a higher place of being, in brotherhood with the One, as had been promised. But where the others saw salvation, he saw further imprisonment. Over time, he grew certain that the One had indeed fooled them, and that the Seraphim were nothing more than slaves to his grander designs. He worked tirelessly to convince others of his lies."

"And then they turned on the Shard?" Bastion said.

"Yes. Lucifer and his followers formed their own sect. They called themselves the Nephilim. They began secretly altering some of the Seedships and outfitting them with the necessities to survive away from the Shardship. We later discovered that they were also modifying and taking seeds. In public; however, Lucifer apologized to the Shard and went out of his way to be the ideal follower and crew member. He excelled in his work and spoke to the Shard daily about how to improve and become closer to the One.

"One day, the Shard gathered the Seraphim to speak to them on the progress of their work, with Lucifer standing beside him in a show of unity. The Shard had only just started to speak when Lucifer withdrew a weapon he had made. A weapon! There had been no tools of violence in Seraphim culture for thousands of years.

"He drew it from his clothes, held it up, and then plunged it into the Shard's side. He shouted at the other Seraphim as the Shard fell to the floor. 'Do you see your god? Do you see that he can be killed so easily? Is this a true god, or are we slaves to superstition?' The fighting began immediately. While the Nephilim were outnumbered, they all had weapons, and they didn't hesitate to use them. Many were killed as they made their escape. They fled the Shardship, vowing to free their brothers and sisters of their slavery no matter how long it took. That was the beginning of the war."

"Where does the Blood of Life fit into that?" Abbey asked.

"The Blood of the Shard," Jequn said. "That's what it is. The key to the everlasting. Human legend has placed it as something called the Holy Grail. Thraven's power. Your power. It isn't magical. It isn't mystical." She glanced at Benhil. "You weren't completely wrong with your trickle down theory."

"Ha!" Benhil said.

"The Shards are physical representations of the One. The power of the One is contained within them, also as a physical manifestation. Their power comes from machines. Molecular machines."

"Molecular machines?" Gant said. "You mean like an atomic engine?"

Jequn smiled. "An engine is a simple thing. The machines within the blood of the Shard are infinitely complex. A work so intricate that only the One could have created them. Self-healing, self-replicating, able to store and disburse massive amounts of energy in multiple forms. The Shard called them naniates."

"Naniates?" Gant said. "What does that mean?"

"I don't know. He said they were the pinnacle of his creation, made to serve him in his work."

"Then Lucifer didn't just kill the Shard; he also took his blood?" Abbey asked.

"Yes. Lucifer stole a prick of blood from the Shard to prove that he was not a god, but a being just like us. That was when he discovered the naniates."

"And it proved his point," Gant said.

"He came to see everything as deception."

Abbey reached inward, feeling for the Gift. It had been nearly silent since they had gotten off Anvil, a surprising change after it had literally been burning on top of her skin. She wasn't sure what to think of the idea that the grittiness she had tasted in Emily Eagan's blood was a congregation of atom-sized machines. And that she had billions, if not trillions of them running through her body right now. They weren't dormant either. According to Thraven, they were changing her. Altering her. To what end? And why?

"Emily Eagan claimed she was a true Nephilim," she said. "Whatever that means. She said she needed human blood to keep the Gift strong."

Jequn nodded. "The Seraphim are very much like the One, but not identical. Not like humans. You are made in his exact image. Your blood is the environment the original naniates were designed to function in. While they can survive externally for a time, the blood is their food. Their fuel. Without it, the naniates will stop functioning. The Nephilim won't die, but they will lose control of the Gift. Believe me; they don't want to lose control of the Gift."

"I can imagine," Abbey said. "You have a Gift of your own. You healed Bastion with it."

"Yes. I accepted the Blood of the Shard six months ago to help the cause. But accepting the naniates isn't without consequences."

"What kind of consequences?" Abbey asked.

"We gain some of the power for a short time. Less than the Nephilim. Much less. Then we go mad. Then we die. We don't partake of the Blood of the Shard unless we must."

"Wait," Bastion said. "You just said-"

"That I accepted the Blood of the Shard," Jequn said.

"Knowing that it will kill you?"

"Yes."

Bastion whistled. "I don't know if I would ever do that."

"Thraven said the Nephilim turn into violent monsters without the second half of the Gift," Abbey said. "He claimed that's what happened to Lucifer. He told me that's what will happen to me. Based on what you're saying, it seems that the Nephilim must have developed an immunosuppressant of some kind so that they could survive indefinitely with it. But since I'm human, shouldn't the naniates be compatible?"

"If the Nephilim naniates respond to a suppressant, they have to be different from the Seraphim version," Gant said. "It makes sense that Lucifer might have re-engineered them to be different."

"Or perhaps the naniates have evolved to better survive in their changing environments," Jequn said.

"You say that as if they're alive," Abbey said.

"They're machines, but they react as though they're alive. They respond to chemical changes in the bloodstream, often triggered by an emotional stimulus."

The Devils Do

"The Gift responds to anger and hate," Abbey said. "I don't think your Shard was angry all of the time."

"He was never angry. He forgave Lucifer for his misguided thoughts before he died."

"How do we know any of this bullshit is true?" Benhil said. "No offense, but we're going on what, exactly? The testimony of a woman that looks like she just fell out of a gypsy trawler? Queenie, do you really believe this?"

"I don't need to believe it," Abbey replied. "I need to understand it." She paused, thinking. "You have the Blood of the Shard, but no way to prevent the madness?"

"Yes. That's why we don't all use it. Only those who volunteer. I expect to survive two more years, at most."

"But you're so young."

"And stronger because of it. This is war, Queenie. Sacrifices must be made."

"I don't understand what happened to the Nephilim?" Bastion asked. "You said they were kicking your asses. Between that and the Gift, they should be running the show out here, not building a fleet to take control of the galaxy."

"The Focus," Jequn said.

"What is that?" Abbey asked.

"The tomb of the Shard. The place where his remains are kept. He told us how to build it before he died. It contains what was left of his blood, along with the naniates that survived within. It is our only truly effective weapon against the Nephilim. We used it on Drune to prevent the *Brimstone* from hitting your ship, redirecting their attacks."

"I knew that had to be more than dumb luck," Bastion said, shaking his head. "Son of a bitch."

"How did the Focus help you defeat the Nephilim?" Abbey asked, still trying to keep the discussion on track.

"We used it to destroy ninety percent of all life in the galaxy."

Bastion stopped laughing. "Excuse me? What?"

"The Nephilim came to depend on the naniates. Not only internally to maintain the strength of their Gift, but externally as well. Over the course of the First War, they learned to harness the power of life and twist it to their needs."

"Like the Brimstone," Gant said.

"Yes. An incredible power source, with humans as the catalyst. The ships aren't the only weapons the Nephilim created that depend on the Blood of the Shard. There are monstrosities that have yet to return to this galaxy. Things I hope we will never see."

"This whole thing is so messed up," Pik said. "But why is everything Terrans this and Terrans that? What about Trovers?"

"The naniates are poison to Trovers," Jequn said. "If one entered your bloodstream, it would kill you within minutes."

"Ouch," Dak said.

"But why all living things?" Gant asked. "Why not just Terrans?"

"We couldn't affect specific kinds of life. Only all life."

"What happened to the Nephilim?" Benhil said.

"Without humans to feed the naniates, they were forced to retreat. They abandoned this part of the universe. It wasn't long before they started blaming one another for the loss and began to fight among themselves. Between losing their blood supply and the fighting, a great deal of their technical progress was lost."

"That explains why they built the *Fire* and *Brimstone* in Republic space," Benhil said. "They needed the humans to power it, as fragged up as that is. I wonder how many people died while they did the R&D on these things?"

"I wonder how many people the Crescent Haulers delivered to them?" Bastion said.

Gant hopped onto the side of the command station. "So while the planets in the galaxy were repopulating, the Nephilim were warring with one another somewhere beyond our galaxy?"

"Yes."

"What the hell were the Seraphim doing? It sounds like you had thousands of years to rebuild."

"Nearly ten thousand years," Jequn said. "We tried. But between

The Devils Do

the war and the use of the Focus, we were down almost ninety-five percent of our original population. The Seraphim who remained clean of the Blood did reproduce with one another, and later with human counterparts, but it hasn't been easy for many reasons, including the Nephilim. They retreated after we used the Focus, but they never left completely. While they waited for the stock to replenish, they visited Earth and took what they could. They've been abducting humans for thousands of years. We did our best to try to prevent it, but we weren't powerful or numerous enough. We still aren't."

"That's awesome," Bastion said. "Just fragging awesome. So what you're saying is that if we're going to survive, we have to fight these assholes ourselves?"

"Pretty much."

CHAPTER TWO

A SILENCE FELL OVER THE bridge as each of them tried to absorb the weight of the statement. It wasn't every day someone told you monsters were real and they were coming to get you.

"Okay," Bastion said, breaking that silence. "Let me try to sum this all up in case anyone got lost." He paused to fill his lungs with air. "Assholes from a parallel dimension allegedly decide to come here and make some intelligent life, which turns into us. In the meantime, there's a mutiny and a rebellion, and a Seraphim named Lucifer, which also happens to be Satan in our religious culture, who kills the Shard who is kind of like God and steals his blood and wants to eat said tasty little morsels like yours truly. But the supposed good guys killed everything first to keep that from happening, except now it's ten-thousand years later and they're hungry, so they came back to eat us all. Oh, and bonus points to them for using us as fragging fuel for their new, indestructible starships."

"They aren't indestructible," Erlan said.

"What?" Bastion replied.

"The ships. They aren't indestructible. We destroyed one off Anvil."

"Well, good for you, Nerd. Let's forget everything else I just said, then. It's all good. We're all fine. We took out one of their ships." He lifted his hand. "High-five!"

"Lucifer shut it," Abbey said. "You sound like Jester."

"Hey," Benhil said.

"I think Jequn made it pretty clear that they didn't come back to eat us. They came back to use us."

"Oh. That's much better. For what?"

"To rebuild their military and provide a power source for an Elysium Gate. Thraven said he wants to go back home and finish what Lucifer started. The Nephilim want to kill the One."

"That doesn't sound good," Bastion said.

"Under any circumstances," Abbey agreed. "Thraven called us Lessers. He thinks of us as tools or slaves. Not only because of the naniates. I'm sure a few billion individuals doing involuntary labor for them wouldn't hurt either."

"They're going to need a massive force even to consider challenging the One," Jequn said. "Hundreds of ships. Thousands. Even that won't be enough. It is a fool's errand."

"What if they had the Focus?" Abbey asked.

Jequn froze. "I don't know. It shouldn't work for them, but if they've managed to twist the naniates?"

"Where is it now?"

"I can't tell you that."

"Can't or won't?" Gant said.

"Can't. I don't know where it is. Even if I did, I wouldn't tell you. We need your help. Yours especially, Queenie. But that is our best and last defense against Thraven and the Nephilim."

"Understood," Abbey said. "Especially after Fury pulled that bullshit and went off with that bastard. I should have seen it coming."

"You used the Focus on Drune," Bastion said. "It had to be there, right?"

"No," Jequn said. "We had a Node on Drune, but not the Focus itself."

"Node?"

"The Shard once used them to transport himself between the Seedships and the Shardship, regardless of distance. After his death, we learned to use them to transfer the power of the Focus. It's also how Phanuel and I came to Anvil. Only those with the Blood of the Shard can use it."

"But what were you doing on Drune in the first place?" Abbey asked.

"Other members of the Ophanim met with Ursan Gall's engineer, Yalom. They convinced him to abandon Thraven's army and tell Mamma Oissi what he knew. She sent him to Drune. We had forces there, watching and waiting. When we heard what happened on Hell, we were hopeful. We've known for a long time that the only chance we have in this fight is to use the enemy's strengths against them. Their Gift." She waved at the bridge. "Their ships. But gaining that position has been difficult until now."

"You said ships," Gant said. "Plural."

"I know Thraven is building more of them."

"They need to be destroyed, not commandeered. You understand how they function, right? Those are living, breathing, humans in the engine room."

"We don't have a choice."

"There's always a choice," Gant said. "If we destroy the ships, it'll stop them in their tracks. The Republic fleet has to be strong enough to take out the four that are left, especially with our help."

"We only have two torpedoes," Erlan said. "And we've taken a lot of damage."

"We can get the damage fixed on Machina Four. Queenie, you're a Terran. Tell me you don't agree with this."

Abbey looked at him. She could see how much he wanted her on his side. But he only had half a view of the fight ahead of them. She had felt Thraven's power. They needed to find a way to counter it. If that meant keeping the ships instead of destroying them?

"It would be temporary. Only until Thraven is gone."

"Queenie, go down there with me. See it for yourself. You won't-"

The Devils Do

"No," Abbey said, more forcefully than she intended.

Gant shook his head and made a light sound her translator registered as disappointment. "You know I'll follow you anywhere you go. But I don't agree with this. For the record."

"I know," Abbey said.

"Speaking of choices," Benhil said. "I'd like to choose to be somewhere else."

"Did we recover the Fire?" Abbey asked.

"No."

"Then I still need you. Jequn, where do General Kett and his mainframe fit into all of this?"

"General Kett fell in love with and married a Watcher. He knows about the war between the Nephilim and the Seraphim. He's been raising an army to join the fight."

"The Republic Council branded him a traitor," Benhil said.

"Thraven's Council, you mean. Do you think he's a traitor?"

"I never did," Abbey said. "There was always something off about the way he was removed from authority."

"General Kett has been working to enlist the soldiers loyal to him to the cause, and then get them to safety by providing transportation. But since the location of his base must remain secret, it had to be done in a way that would not threaten its security. The mainframe Thraven wanted you to break is a part of that system.

"This is how it works: First, the mainframe is delivered to the Crescent Haulers. Then the Haulers pick up the soldiers. They connect the mainframe to their onboard systems. It takes control of the FTL drives and brings the ship to Kett's location without allowing the vessel's computer to store the position. The soldiers and equipment are offloaded, and the software sends the Haulers back to the origin. It's a spatial blindfold of sorts."

"Except the Haulers work for Thraven," Bastion said.

"No," Abbey replied. "The Devastator was contracted to work for Thraven. The Haulers as a whole are supposed to be neutral. Besides, if they can't gather any positioning data, it wouldn't matter. If the planet is Etype, there are a thousand possibilities. If it isn't, there are thousands more. But why didn't Kett's mainframe in question make it to its destination? And how did Thraven know it was missing and what it contained? There are countless ships crossing the galaxy every second of every day."

"It's possible that we too were betrayed," Jequn said. "Our carrier was assaulted, the mainframe taken."

"If the attackers were working for Thraven, he wouldn't have needed to send Coli and his team to retrieve it."

"Unless his real goal was to get a Breaker involved," Gant said. "Someone who could help him crack the code."

"But why throw me in Hell?" Abbey said. "Why give me the Gift? He could have waited it out and let me keep working on the mainframe aboard the Nova."

"The Gift would make you easier to control," Jequn said. "Imagine you took your findings to the Council. While Thraven controls the majority, he doesn't have everyone, and you can't unshoot a gun. They would have known. They would have been curious. This way, everything remained secret. All it cost the Republic was a platoon."

"Except the Gift made me harder to control."

"He underestimated you."

"Good."

"Every downfall begins with a single error in judgment. A single mistake. Thraven is not the One. He cannot be perfect. You're his mistake."

"I'll make sure to remind him of that the next time I see him, which might not be too long from now since we're planning a trip to Kell. I don't suppose you have any more Watchers you can throw at him as a distraction?"

"General Kett ordered me to help you."

"Just you?"

"For now."

Abbey didn't like the sound of that.

"What about those threads you're wearing?" Bastion asked. "That isn't a lightsuit."

The Devils Do

"No." She held out her arm and pinched the material of her suit. "This one is based on a Seraphim design. Lighter weight, but more resistant and stronger than a battlesuit. I have something else." She reached to packs on her hips, withdrawing a pair of thin rods. With the flick of her wrists, they spread into a pair of fanlike blades. "These are called Uin. They are the weapon of choice for the Ophanim. Well, in conjunction with modern ballistics." She smiled. "As you know, guns have a limited effect on many of the Nephilim."

"Those are nice," Bastion said. "Better than a katana any day."

"You'll have to show me how to use them," Abbey said. "If I can get a pair somewhere."

Jequn snapped her wrists again, and the blades folded up. She handed them to Abbey. "Take these. I brought them for you."

"Thank you," Abbey said, accepting the weapons. She put one into a tightpack and held the other up. It was a small seamless box when closed.

"Make a motion like you are throwing it to the ground," Jequn said.

Abbey did. At first, it felt like the Uin would simply fall out of her hand and onto the floor. Instead, it snapped open, a handle extending and wrapping itself around her palm as it spread and became a blade. Now she could see the separate pieces, each so thin the whole thing was nearly seamless.

She waved it in the air a few times. It was light, too. Graceful.

"It isn't much of a stabbing weapon," Jequn said. "Cutting is preferred. But it is much sharper than any standard issue knife. Once you have a greater aptitude, you'll be able to control the deployment of the separate pieces, such that you can hold and fire a gun and keep the Uin in hand at the same time."

"Sounds fun," Abbey said.

"What do you need it for?" Pik asked. "You have claws."

"You can never have too many weapons," Abbey said.

"You're the weapon we've been waiting for," Jequn said. "The weapon we need."

Abbey reversed the throwing motion, and the Uin folded up. She tucked them into tightpacks and then let her eyes travel across the bridge, pausing on each of the individuals gathered there. In the end, it didn't matter if she believed in the One or Elysium. It only mattered that their place in the universe was being threatened, and through whatever twist of fate or bad luck or mistake, she was one of the individuals responsible for doing something about it. She had never backed down from a challenge before, and she damn sure wasn't going to start now.

She wasn't letting her team off the hook, either.

"Well, Rejects, it seems like it's time to do some more evil."

"So nobody else has to," Bastion said.

"Hell, yeah," Pik added.

"Hell, yeah," Abbey replied.

CHAPTER THREE

THE SHUTTLE EASED ITS WAY across the downtown traffic, taking advantage of its cargo to use one of the reserved flight lanes en route to the Pentagon.

Captain Olus Mann observed the maneuver from his seat in the rear of the transport, smirking slightly at the move. There wasn't all that much above-ground traffic left in D.C. these days. But the pilot had an excuse to hit the VIP lanes, and he had used it.

Olus didn't expect to be a VIP for much longer. He was scheduled to meet with General Omsala in ten minutes, a meeting he had prepared for with guns and armor, not documents and words. He knew from Thraven himself that Omsala was loyal to the Gloritant, not the Republic. He knew he was heading for a face-to-face intended to at best discredit him, and at worst apprehend him.

He was betting on the worst.

He was ready for it.

He looked down at the Pentagon as the shuttle made its approach. The building had been torn down and reconstructed a few times in its long history, each time growing a little higher and extending a little deeper. Each time gaining more glass and metal and less drab stone. Each time retaining its original, symbolic shape. As the center of military operations for the entire Republic, it was intended to evoke the military history of the

United States, while also evoking the future as a combined power. Not just of Earth, but of all of the planets under the Republic flag.

He thought it was effective.

The shuttle slowed and descended, landing in a specially marked spot only VIPs could reach from the air. Olus could see the thick form of Omsala as they got closer, surprised the Fizzig was waiting for him outside. Earth's gravity wasn't the most forgiving for the race's dense bones and thick, heavy skin. The General was making a statement. Asserting his power, and by extension Thraven's power.

He would see about that.

The shuttle's landing pads tapped lightly on the ground, the craft dipping and settling. The hatch opened and a ramp extended to the surface. Olus stood, straightened his suit, and moved toward it, sticking his hands in his pockets to make himself more casual. He was going to make a statement, too: None of this scares me, so save your bullshit and get to the point.

"Captain Mann," Omsala said as Olus emerged from the shuttle.

Two guards, Olus noted. Both in lightsuit. They wouldn't be a problem.

"General," Olus said, saluting lazily.

Omsala grunted before returning the salute. Olus was being disrespectful, and they both knew it. So what?

"How was your trip to Feru?" Omsala asked.

"Uneventful," Olus replied. "Although it is disappointing that I didn't get a chance to speak with Mars Eagan again. I had a lead I believed she could clarify for me. I'm afraid I'll be starting back a few steps."

"You have a gift for understatement, Captain," Omsala said. "Mars Eagan is dead. So is Emily Eagan. But I'm sure you already knew that?"

"Of course. It's my job to know. The fugitives from Hell. My people tell me they're calling themselves the Rejects." Olus smiled.

"I've informed the Council of the events. They're eager to hear more about your exploits, and what you've learned regarding the attack on Eagan Heavyworks."

"That's why I'm here. I figured it would be more efficient to deliver my report in person so that I could respond to any questions the Council might have."

"Are you sure that's the only reason?"

"For now."

General Omsala began walking back toward the building, each of his steps heavy and strenuous. He didn't complain at all, even when his breathing started to become labored.

The strain vanished as they entered the building, the regulators in the floors averaging out the gravity differences to even the field. Olus could feel the slightly lighter pull enough that he adjusted his gait to compensate, taking longer, bouncier steps.

"I received a report on my way down that there may have been a conflict in the Fringe," Olus said. "My sources said Anvil was under attack. It turns out that one of our fleets was also assaulted near Anvil. Another patrol confronted by the *Fire* and four other ships like her."

"I've read the same reports, Captain," Omsala replied. "Do you have a theory? Your Rejects again, perhaps?"

"One crew of fugitives against a planet? I don't think so."

"But who would have done such a thing, do you think?"

"That's the question of the millennia, isn't it?"

They entered a tube, heading up to the tenth floor of the building. Omsala led him toward his office, the guards staying close.

"The Committee believes they are part of a larger contingent from the Outworlds, one that intends to push us into war and let us beat one another up for a while. Then they'll move in like vultures to snatch the remains."

"An interesting theory," Olus said. "But why attack both Outworld and Republic assets simultaneously if that's the case? Your larger contingent is making enemies of two very major powers."

"We haven't corroborated the attack on Anvil as being related to the *Fire* and Brimstone," Omsala replied. "The Outworlds have attacks like this too often to be surprised. It's the downside of being so loosely controlled."

"Those attacks occur one hundred percent of the time on planets with populations of less than two hundred thousand."

"I suppose there are always outliers."

They reached Omsala's office. The door opened ahead of them, and the General led him in. He had a sparse desk at the back of the room; a second desk positioned caddy-corner to it. A young human woman was sitting in it, doing something on her terminal. She stood and saluted when she saw them.

"General," she said.

"At ease, Vee," Omsala said.

The door closed behind them.

"You don't know Vee, do you, Captain?" Omsala said. "Corporal Vee, this is Captain Olus Mann. Captain Mann, my assistant, Vee."

Vee saluted. Olus saluted back. "A pleasure," he said, turning back to Omsala. "What happened to Yellin?"

"She was killed in the same accident that took General Soto's life. A tragedy, to be sure."

"Should I leave the room, General?" Vee asked.

"No, Vee. The Captain is accustomed to my assistants. Aren't you, Olus?"

Olus smirked. This wasn't the first time he had been to Omsala's office to discuss things. Meeting with members of the Committee was part of the job. That Yellin had been killed and replaced with Vee? He trusted that about as far as he could throw the General.

Omsala circled his desk, sitting in a wide, thick chair specially designed for his frame. Even so, it creaked under the pressure of his reduced-gravity weight while his skin spread around it.

"General Soto assigned you with figuring out who took the *Fire* and *Brimstone* and getting the ships back," Omsala said.

"She did," Olus agreed.

"Yet we have no progress in that regard."

"We have quite a bit of progress, General," Olus said. "As you well know. The question is, what are we going to do about it?"

Omsala huffed, Olus' translator suggesting amused respect. "You don't waste time, do you, Captain?"

The Devils Do

"You've wasted enough of my time already," Olus said. "So yeah, let's just cut through the bullshit and get down to the real business."

"Very well. I have two options, Captain. You know what they are. My concern is that your people in the OSI won't accept either of them."

"That's what happens when you build a web of respect over a number of years," Olus said. "People learn to trust you. There was a time when I believed the Committee had the Republic's best interests in mind. But did it ever? I'm not sure now. My people have the Republic's best interests in mind, and there's nothing you can do to change that."

"I wouldn't be so sure about that, Captain." Omsala leaned forward in his seat. "I respect you for coming here. I imagine you had to know you weren't going to just walk out."

"I needed to be here as much as you needed me here. I need information that my people don't have direct access to. Information that would get them killed. I won't ask them to do anything I won't do."

"But you will," Omsala said.

Olus saw Vee in the corner of his eye. She was pretending to be working at her terminal. She glanced at him, a slight smile tugging at the corner of her lips.

Timing was everything.

"Will I?" Mann said. "I don't have a problem killing traitors. Even in a hardened building."

"Even if you were able to make good on that threat, it won't do any good. You don't know how deep this goes, Captain. And I'm not talking a few years."

"Did you know what was going to happen on Feru?"

"No. But I knew something was coming. You can be part of the past, or you can be part of the future. I've seen the future, Olus. I know where I want to be next year. Do you?"

"Yes," Olus said, putting his hands in his pockets again. "I'm going to stop you."

Omsala smiled. "You and what army? Your Rejects? No. Sorry, Olus. If your goal is to see how much of the Republic Armed Services is in the Gloritant's pocket, you're going to be in for the shock of your life. You don't have a friend left on the Committee, and the Council will be dealt with soon. A few more accidents and the balance of power will have turned completely. Now, you're going to resign. We're going to record it and send it along with our pick for Director of the OSI. Then you're going to disappear. Whether that disappearance includes your loss of the ability to breathe depends on your resistance to the idea. So, what do you say, Captain?"

"What can I say?" Olus said, pulling his hands out of his pocket. He held out his right hand, raising his middle finger. "How about that?"

Omsala grunted again. "The fearless Killshot." His eyes shifted to Vee, widening when he saw the knife sprouting from the woman's eye. "What?"

"Sleight of hand," Olus said. "And good aim. I realized on the way here that you don't need to cut off a Venerant's head to disable them, only kill them. Destroying brain function is enough to keep them in line."

Omsala tried to stand, to reach for the panic button that would summon the guards outside. Olus slipped a hand under his jacket, producing the gun and pointing it at Omsala.

"The knife is too light to get through your fat ass," he said. "Bullets, not so much. Touch that button, and I put a slug in your head."

Omsala paused and looked at him. Then he leaned forward again.

The noise of the shot was suppressed, preventing the guards outside from hearing it. The force of the bullet through the thick Fizzig skull was enough to change Omsala's direction, and his hand landed next to the button even as he slumped out of the chair and fell to the floor.

"I've decided," Olus said, circling the desk. "I like you much better this way."

The Devils Do

CHAPTER FOUR

OLUS STOOD WITH HIS LEGS straddling Omsala's body. He pulled one of the buttons from his jacket, attaching it to the General's terminal. Then he leaned over, lifting the heavy Fizzig and getting him back in the chair. He ducked behind him as he activated the terminal, placing Omsala's meaty hand on the palm scanner and positioning his head for the eye scanner. The terminal accepted the inputs and unlocked.

Olus looked over at Vee, checking on her. He wasn't completely sure that she was a Venerant like Emily Eagan, but the fact that the muscles in her hands were expanding and contracting and making her fingers wiggle was enough of a reason to believe she was. Either way, she wasn't innocent. She also wasn't about to lock him in place.

He pushed the chair away from the terminal, and Omsala with it. He could see the data flowing in front of his eyes, passing from the micro-extender to the TCU, and from the TCU to the lenses he was wearing. He had access to everything. Had the General been as stupid as Ms. Eagan and left evidence of his relationship with Thraven? He hoped so.

He navigated through the terminal, into Omsala's personal account. He scanned it quickly, using tools stored on the TCU to send a query, looking for Thraven's name, for Emily's name, and for Iti's name. He didn't get any hits on the first two. The third turned up a few messages centering around her untimely death, the accident, and Omsala's assumption of her assignment to find the *Fire* and Brimstone. It was painful to read, but it also wasn't anything incriminating.

His eyes passed to Vee again, just to be sure. She was still static, the end of the knife poking out of her eye. It had been a long time since he had used that trick. He was glad he hadn't lost the muscle memory or his aim.

He was still for a few seconds while he considered the problem. Omsala had claimed the Committee was already compromised, but the Council was still in play. The members of the Council were all elected, and they had three years left on their terms. The only way to replace them would be to kill them, assuming their secondaries were on Thraven's side. If that happened, he would be able to tear the Republic apart from the inside, reallocating funds, repositioning units, and subtly destroying the Republic's ability to defend itself. It would take more time to claim victory, but he had a feeling Thraven was patient.

He had to figure out who on the Council was still loyal to the Republic. He might not be able to prove anything, but he had some ideas on how to deduce that information. He resumed his search, using each of the Council member's names to guide him. Major alterations to Republic policy required three-quarters affirmation. That meant that at a minimum there were eight members of the Council who Thraven hadn't reached. By checking Omsala's communications with them in turn, he quickly built the list of suspects.

Eight individuals. He couldn't protect them all. Not on his own. He had to at least warn them, and get them surrounded with those he could trust. His team at the OSI. He memorized the list and backed out. Then he turned back to Omsala's corpse. The General had been careful not to speak to Thraven through official channels. That didn't mean he wasn't speaking to him. He was sure to have a private, portable communicator somewhere on him.

Olus checked his wrists first. Then his ear. Then his collar. Then the shirt below his jacket and his buttons. There were so many styles of communicators, including implants. He hoped it wasn't an implant. It

The Devils Do

would make the search so much messier.

He patted Omsala down, grateful when he found the device tucked into the General's pocket. It was an older, card-based model.

It was blinking.

Olus didn't hesitate. He pulled the extender from the base terminal and stuck it to the communicator. He didn't waste time breaking into it. He only needed to check one thing right now.

It was sending, not receiving.

"Damn it," Olus said. "We have to do this the hard way, don't we?"

He shoved the card in his pocket, pulling a different weapon from his pocket. An edged wire. An assassin's tool. He couldn't leave the Venerant alive to hunt him.

He approached her, getting behind her and putting the wire over her head. He looked the ends in his palms a couple of times, and then pulled, using the enhanced strength of his suit to help bring the wire into the neck, through the bone, and out the back.

"Not so hard to kill after all," he said. Only because he had caught her off-guard.

He dropped the bloody wire and then straightened his suit, heading for the door.

It opened ahead of him. The two guards who had been with them before were gone, replaced with a new pair in unmarked black lightsuits.

Inside the fragging Pentagon?

He stepped to the side as the first soldier fired, the bullets whipping past him and shattering Omsala's desk behind him. He didn't give the man a chance to recover, kicking the gun with enough force to tear it away from his grip, bringing his other knife to his hand and driving it hard into the soldier's neck, above the armor of the suit. He gripped the body, turning it in front of him at the same time the second guard started shooting, the bullets tearing into his shield, the range allowing them to go through. He could feel the localized stings as his suit caught the remaining energy and prevented the slugs from reaching his flesh.

He shoved the body forward and into the second guard, who tried to move aside. Olus followed close behind, grabbing the soldier's hand and pulling it up, kicking him in the gut, turning him and kicking him in the back of the knee, the force breaking his leg. He ripped the rifle from the soldier's hands, turning it and shooting him once in the back of the head.

He looked down the corridor. The two original guards were on the ground, dead. He glanced up at the cameras positioned there. A small jamming button was attached to them. They were the kind an assassin would use.

An assassin like him.

He wasn't surprised. He had known this wasn't going to be pretty. He had to get out and turn off Omsala's distress beacon. Thraven's forces could track him until he did.

First, he had to get out of the Pentagon.

He dropped the rifle and tidied himself up again, walking down the corridor as though everything was fine. He reached the intersection and then turned right and headed for the tube. It was coming up as he neared, and he looked through the transparency in time to see a pair of guards rising to meet him. They were each in a Republic MP lightsuit, not blacksuits. He stuck his hands back in his pockets, standing in front of the tube to wait.

It stopped and opened. The guards walked out. Their weapons were holstered.

"Sir," one of them said, noting the hardware on Olus' chest. "We got a signal that two of the cameras are offline up here."

Olus smiled. "I don't know. I was just in a meeting. I'm heading down to the cafeteria to grab a bite."

"Have a good day, sir," the soldier said.

"You, too," Olus replied.

He slipped into the tube, counting in his head. He had about forty seconds before the two guards discovered all of the bodies.

What would they think of the soldiers in the black lightsuits? It probably didn't matter. Thraven's cronies would make those corpses disappear.

The tube reached the bottom floor. Olus stepped out. He could see right away that the transport he arrived in was gone. He would need to

The Devils Do

procure his own transportation.

He knew where to find it. He crossed the open space quickly, still counting down. He wasn't going to make it.

He was on three when the guards at the front of the building stiffened up. A few seconds later, one of them turned around, finding him.

"Sir," the soldier shouted. "Sir, hold up, please."

Olus stopped. He didn't want to kill the soldier, and he didn't want the soldier killing him.

"Is there a problem, Private?" Olus asked.

"Sir, there's been an incident on the eighteenth floor. Private Galal said he passed you near the tube there."

"What kind of incident?" Olus said.

"General Omsala is dead," the soldier replied, just as a soft tone sounded. "There's the alert now. We're putting the building on lockdown."

"Of course you are," Olus said. "Sorry about the headache, Private, but I have to go."

"What?"

The Private didn't have a chance to react. Olus' fist caught him in the temple, knocking him to the ground. He reached the door and put his hand on the biometric scanner. Omsala hadn't revoked his clearance before their conversation. It was a stupid mistake.

"I'm getting too old for this," he said as he bounced down the stairwell. "Why couldn't all of this shit happen after I was gone?"

He went down four of the twenty underground levels. It was as far as these stairs would go. The deeper floors were beyond even his clearance level, home to emergency bunkers and backup systems to keep the Republic Armed Services functioning in the event of a catastrophe. Instead, he arrived in an underground garage, one most of the building's employees didn't even know existed. It was filled with unmarked cars, each resting on small skids to lift them up for easy entry. He went to the nearest one, putting his hand on the side of it. It read his credentials and unlocked.

There was a second stairwell on the opposite side of the garage. The door to it opened at the same time Olus climbed into the car, a squad of soldiers in black pouring into the space.

"Too late," Olus said, tapping the controls for the car.

The Presser coils beneath the vehicle made a sizzling noise as they came to life, the electric motors emitting a soft whine. The skids retracted, and Olus guided the vehicle forward, accelerating toward the currently closed exit.

The soldiers began shooting, the bullets pinging against the armored shell of the car. Olus guided it with one hand, using the other to reach the gate controls. He pressed his hand against the screen to enter his credentials, unconvinced the system would let him through.

"Come on," he said. "Come on."

The gate started to open.

"Thank you," Olus said, guiding the car through. He increased the throttle, pushing it to full as the car entered the long tunnel that would lead to a hidden surface exit three kilometers away.

He sat back in his seat, giving himself a second to relax.

He wasn't safe. Not yet. Not until he disabled the beacon. At least he was clear of the Pentagon.

It was a start.

CHAPTER FIVE

"Are you sure you want to see this?" Gant asked.

"You were the one who suggested I should," Abbey replied.

"I was trying to make a point. Once you've seen it for yourself, it's going to haunt you."

"I've got plenty of other things haunting me right now. What's one more? I need to see it."

Gant moved aside, allowing Abbey to reach the door controls and open the hatch into the engine room. It slid aside, and she walked forward without hesitating, bypassing the main terminal and heading for the secured door beyond.

"I don't want to see it," Dak said, standing outside.

"You don't have to," Abbey replied. "But you do have to unlock the terminal. You said you know the code."

"Yeah."

He entered the room, making sure to keep his head down. Abbey paused her advance to watch him. He activated the terminal, big fingers slowly typing in the codes to unlock the security on it.

"There you go, new Boss," he said as the projection changed, providing a full control interface.

"Open it," she said.

"Do I have to?"

"Yes."

He put his hand up and tapped an icon in the projection. A soft hiss followed from the door ahead of her, the compartment adjusting pressure or something. Then it slid away.

It had been silent before the door opened. Not now. Abbey set herself and moved forward, forcing herself to confront the truth of the Brimstone's operation. In her entire life, she would never have imagined the horror of what Gant had described, or that it would be a real and viable means to power a starship.

And other things, according to Jequn. What kind of things? She didn't want to know. She hoped never to find out.

She let her eyes sweep the room. She felt her heart begin beating faster, thumping hard in reaction to the visual data her brain was receiving. She could hear the soft moans, the pained breaths. The smell was nearly unbearable.

"Whew," Dak said. "The smell."

She could hear him gagging behind her.

"Close it," she said. "I'll knock."

The hatch slid closed behind her.

She moved forward. There wasn't much space in the compartment, but she had to see it all. She had to surround herself with it. She had made the decision that if they captured any more of the ships they would keep them. She couldn't be that callous about it. She couldn't be that cold. Maybe they called her the Demon Queen, but she hadn't changed into a real demon yet.

She moved to the device in the center, leaning over and looking into the clear tubing where the darker blood flowed. She couldn't see individual naniates, but she could imagine them in there, trillions-strong, flowing throughout the vessel. What kind of properties did the machines possess? Were they intelligent, or did they react purely based on inputs? What were their weaknesses and limitations? Gant had been immune to them, as though they were afraid of him. What did that mean, if anything?

She stood up, turning and looking at one of the humans attached to the wall. A woman. Her eyes were closed. Her chest rose and fell lightly. She looked almost peaceful. Abbey's eyes dipped to the tubes running into and out of her body. One was clear. The nutrients that kept her alive. One was slightly yellowish. The waste being drawn out. One was red. The blood.

"Can you hear me?" she said softly. "Can any of you hear me?"

She watched them. They didn't react to her voice or her presence. She moved deeper into the space. The machine in the center of it was larger than she had expected, a mostly rectangular shape that continued to the rear of the compartment. There had to be at least five hundred bodies in here. Probably more.

She closed her eyes. She was getting nauseous. This wasn't right. None of this was right.

She turned around, heading back for the exit.

Something grabbed her shoulder.

She turned, wide-eyed, looking at the human positioned against the wall, bound by the hardened shell that glued them there. He had worked a hand free and used it to reach out to her. His eyes were open, looking at her.

"Help me," he said.

Abbey's whole body began to shake. The Gift came alive within her, reacting to it. She stared at the man, into his eyes. She saw a light reflected there. It was the same light she had seen when the Gift had tried to wrest control from her.

"Help me," the man repeated.

Abbey could feel the tears begin to stream from her eyes. She was strong, but she wasn't this strong.

She pulled herself away from him, rushing to the hatch. She pounded on it until Dak looked up and quickly activated the controls to open it. She fell through, stumbling to her knees on the other side.

She heard him one last time as the hatch slid closed.

"Help me."

Then she vomited.

"Queenie," Gant said, coming to her side.

"I barfed, too," Dak said, joining them.

Abbey leaned over the floor, her whole body convulsing. She stayed that way for a few minutes, trying to reconcile what she had seen, trying to calm the Gift. What did it want from her? Why had it reacted that way?

She pushed herself up, sitting with her back against the door. She reached up, wiping the tears away. She looked over at Gant, his concerned expression nearly cutting through her horror and getting her to laugh.

"You were right. I shouldn't have come down here." She banged her head against the hatch and squeezed her eyes closed.

She knew they were fighting monsters. This was a step beyond.

"We're going to destroy them, right?" Gant said. "The ships on Kell. The Brimstone, when the time comes?"

She opened her eyes to look at him again. "I don't know."

"What do you mean, you don't know?"

"This sucks, Gant. It really does. But we need the Brimstone. We may need those ships. You heard Jequn. The Seraphim are almost gone. They won the war because of a weapon of mass destruction, one they can't use again. If we're going to win, we have to match them."

"We can find another way."

"Come on, Gant. I know you better than that. You aren't a dreamer. You know there's no magic bullet. This is the way right now, as much as we both hate it. And I do hate it."

Gant made a squeaking noise that her translator told her was a sigh. "Yeah. I guess we do, for now. Just tell me we'll keep our options open."

"Of course. In the meantime, see if you can figure out what this setup is, and how it works. Maybe there are schematics in the control system. If we can find a weakness, something that will work to shut this down, an EMP or something, we can end their suffering."

"Aye, Queenie."

"I'm going to have another chat with Jequn. If we're supposed to attack Kell, I expect some more damn help than one Ophanim."

She pushed herself to her feet, refusing to look back into the engine compartment. What was the light she had seen behind their eyes? The one she had seen before. The one Thraven had seemed so intrigued by? It had to mean something. Didn't it?

"I expect to speak to General Kett."

CHAPTER SIX

ABBEY FOUND JEQUN IN THE quarters they had given her, a small but private space close to the Captain's Quarters. They were only a dozen minutes from arriving at Machina Four, and she intended to be on and off the planet as quickly as possible, pausing only to pick up necessary replies and effect important repairs on the Brimstone's systems. Now that she had seen what at least some of those systems were composed of she knew it might get tricky, but enough money would go a long way to keeping any engineers she hired quiet.

In that sense, it had worked out in their favor that they had never actually paid the Crescent Haulers. The two disterium canisters in their possession would go a long way with shrewd bargaining, and what the hell else was Benhil there for, if not to manage those kinds of transactions?

"Queenie," Jequn said, her door opening. "I wasn't expecting you so soon."

"I just went down to the engine room. You should too."

"I know what's down there."

"But have you seen it?"

"No."

"You need to see it. It will change your understanding of what this is all about."

The Devils Do

"Very well."

"Not now. I need something else from you right now."

"Of course. How can I help?"

"I want to talk to Kett."

Jequn looked away. "Queenie, I can't."

"Why the hell not? He wants me to be part of this, he's raising an army to fight, but he won't talk to his supposed prize fighter?"

"It's not that. I mean, I can't. I don't know how to reach him."

Abbey froze. "You've got to be kidding me."

"If Thraven had captured me on Anvil, he could have forced me to reveal Kett's comm codes. It's possible he could have used them to backtrace the signal to Kett's location."

"Do you know how difficult that is?"

"Yes. Difficult, but not impossible."

"So what's the expectation here, Jequn?" Abbey said. "The Rejects are supposed to assault Kell on our own? Half a dozen soldiers versus an entire military installation? You said he was raising an army."

"He is."

"What the frag is it for if he isn't going to help me attack Thraven?"

"His intention is to join the fight, Queenie. His orders were to help you. You need to prove yourself before he's going to commit what's left of the Ophanim."

"Prove myself? Not that bullshit again. Thraven said the same thing."

"The Nephilim's Gift can change you. It's meaningful that you turned Thraven's advances down in a direct confrontation, but now you have to prove that you're worth rallying behind. We'll only have one chance at this."

Abbey clenched her fist. This was ridiculous. The Sylvan Kett she knew was a legend for his ability to do more with less. Not his ability to do nothing.

"And if I'm not? Then what? You'll just keep hiding?"

"General Kett has a backup plan."

"Which is?"

"I don't know. He didn't tell me."

Abbey was silent for a moment, her anger simmering. She was getting sick and tired of being used as a pawn. First by Thraven, then by the Republic, and now by Kett and the Seraphim. She didn't have to do any of this. She could take the Rejects and fly away, disappear somewhere into the Outworlds and let the shit come down wherever it was going to land.

Except there was Hayley and Liv and Gavin. She couldn't abandon them. She couldn't abandon the poor souls suffering in the engine room so that they could shoot around the galaxy. She couldn't abandon the individuals on Anvil who she was sure Thraven had taken. She had joined the Republic Armed Services to protect people. She didn't know how to do anything else.

Whether she was turning into some kind of demon or not, that would never change.

"Then we're doing things my way," she said. "If Kett wants in, he'll get in on my terms."

"What does that mean?" Jequn asked.

Abbey smiled. She had no idea if the Ophanim had access to Kett or not. She wasn't about to give anything away.

"You'll just have to wait to find out. We'll be at Machina Four in five minutes. Meet us in the hangar."

"As you wish, Queenie."

Abbey nodded, turning and leaving the room. Kett had a backup plan? Good.

She had a plan of her own.

The Devils Do

CHAPTER SEVEN

"I WANT TO BE ABLE to trust you," Abbey said.

She was standing at the edge of the docking system. Dak was in front of her. The Trover looked different than he had on Anvil. He had cleaned himself up and changed, putting on a crisp uniform that displayed his rank. She had noticed he had gotten the rest of Ursan Gall's remaining mercenaries to do the same, immediately turning them back into an organized force. Whether or not it was an effective one was yet to be determined.

"I won't lie to you, Queenie," Dak said. "We were mercenaries for a long time before we joined up with Thraven. We worked for money, and that's it. It wasn't a bad life. Now? Ursan's dead. It isn't your fault. I heard you. I know you tried to talk him out of it. He was too far gone, and I blame Thraven for that. The Outworlds? Tro is in the Republic, but my father brought me to New Terra when I was your size. I grew up there, and I'm loyal to it. But I also know it doesn't matter which side we're on. Outworld. Republic. Thraven doesn't give a shit. He attacked Anvil. He attacked Drune. He ordered us to attack a Republic fleet. The more chaos he can create, the easier it will be for him. Frag that."

"Is that your way of saying you're with me?"

"I already told you I was. It's my way of saying you can trust me.

Giving you the reasons you can. I won't turn tail and take the Brimstone. I don't plan to remove the individuals you're leaving behind. I want to help you kill Thraven."

Trovers didn't have well-defined features, making Dak's face hard to read. Abbey watched his body language, instead. She pierced his eyes with her own. Spotting tells was part of her training. She was certain enough he wasn't lying that she was willing to take the chance, and the idea of asking him to prove himself worthy was leaving a bitter taste in her mouth.

"Nerd," Abbey said.

"Aye, Queenie?" Erlan replied from the bridge.

"Commander Dak is going to be in charge of the *Brimstone* while I'm gone. Follow his orders."

"Aye, Queenie."

Abbey looked at Dak again. "Don't make me regret this. If you do, I promise I'll find you."

Dak nodded. "I believe that. On my honor, Boss."

He saluted. A Republic salute. Crisp and sharp. She returned it.

Then she turned to the docking airlock, moving through it and into the Faust. The Rejects were waiting on the other side. Pik, Benhil, Gant, Bastion, and Jequn. She pointed at Bastion.

"You need a new callsign."

"I like Lucifer," he replied.

"In light of recent events, Lucifer is off the table."

Bastion didn't complain. He shrugged. "Can I go back to Worm?"

"You should pick it, Queenie," Pik said.

"Shut up," Bastion replied. "She's going to call me A-hole."

"Or worse," Benhil said. "Go for it, Queenie."

Abbey smiled. "Something appropriate. Let me think. Crybaby? Whiner? Loudmouth?" She looked at him, watching his reaction to each of the names.

"I'm not that bad," he said.

"You do talk too much sometimes," Gant said. "Most of the time. I like A-hole."

"Of course, you would say that," Bastion said. "Fr-"

"Don't," Gant warned.

"Loudmouth is suitable, but too much of a mouthful to say efficiently," Abbey said. "How about Imp, in honor of the first ship you got shot down in?"

"I'll take Loudmouth," Bastion said. "Or we can shorten it to Mouth. That would work."

"You don't get to pick," Pik said. "Not this time."

"Yeah, not this time," Benhil said.

"I hate all of you," Bastion said.

"Good," Abbey replied. "Imp, head up to the cockpit and get us headed to the surface."

Bastion glowered. The others laughed.

"Fraggers," he said, leaving them and heading up the ladder.

Abbey hit the controls for the docking system, closing the airlocks. She turned to Benhil. "You know what our necessities are, right?"

"Aye, Queenie," he replied. "A new hand for the big guy, a hush-hush repair crew for the Brimstone, and an upgrade to our existing arsenal." He smiled. "I assume you want an entire closet full of softsuits? You go through what? Three per day?"

"Give or take. If you can find them in red, I would appreciate it."

"I've been the Machina Four before. I got picked up by the Republic on my way back from here. I know the individuals you want to meet with."

"We need the disterium to go as far as we can take it," Abbey said. "I expect you to haggle your ass off."

"Aye, Queenie."

"Hey Queenie," Pik said. "I just noticed." He pointed down at her head. "Feel your skull. You've got a fuzz coming in."

Abbey reached up, running her hand along her scalp. It had been smooth the last time she touched it. Now she could feel the resistance of new follicles poking up. Had the Gift restored her hair? That was a change she would accept gratefully.

"I wish I could get my locks back," Benhil said, putting a hand on his bare scalp.

"You look good bald," Gant said.

"I do?"

"Sure, why not?"

"Are you screwing with me?"

"Yeah. You're kind of ugly."

"Shut up, Gant."

"I'm only kidding. You look fine. Seriously."

"Oh. Thanks."

"Sure thing, chrome dome."

"Gant," Abbey said.

Gant laughed. "Fine. You're a handsome man, Jester."

"I'm not listening to you anymore."

"It's a head only a blind mother could love."

"Gant," Abbey repeated.

Gant chittered and walked away. Benhil looked annoyed, but Pik and Jequn were both smiling.

"You're fine, Jester," Pik said. "Don't listen to him."

"Yes, I think you're very handsome," Jequn said.

"You do?" Benhil said, looking at Jequn. "Because-"

"I don't like bald men," she said, winking at him and heading for the ladder while Pik roared in laughter.

"She's going to fit right in," he said, still laughing as he made his way past.

"You're going to let them treat me like this?" Benhil asked.

"You wanted to be Jester," Abbey replied.

"Do you think I look good bald?"

Abbey abandoned him, walking toward the ladder up.

"Wait. Queenie. Do you? Queenie? Assholes."

CHAPTER EIGHT

MACHINA FOUR. THE PLANET HAD started its inhabited lifecycle in the Outworlds the same way the first three planets named Machina had - as a rare mineral mining facility owned by one or more of the corporations that had founded the Governance. Like the first three, Machina Four had also been depleted beyond profitability for the corporation, and had since been abandoned by the original owners and left to be settled by whoever wanted to live on a rocky planet with little surface water that was just barely inside the nearest star's habitable zone.

Steel Town was one of the smaller settlements on the planet. It was tucked into a deep ravine where massive crawlers and tunnelers had once collected kilos of rock to sift for valuable particulate, causing the sides to increase in height as mountains of sediment were built up and stabilized around the main dig sites. It was a dirty place by nature, but also a thriving community of tinkerers and mechanics, bot makers, and prospectors. There was still enough valuable source materials left in the surrounding rock for independent operators, just not enough for a large corp to get a decent return on their investment.

The city was directly inaccessible by anything larger than a shuttle, forcing Bastion to land the *Faust* on the upper ridge of the ravine. There were four other starships already parked nearby, all of them a configuration of mixed-use cruisers.

Abbey did a quick scan for the crescent moons of the Haulers as they descended, and then led the Rejects out onto the surface, with Bastion remaining behind to manage their ride. She was sure the word had gone out about the Destructor, and while it might take some time for management to figure out exactly what had happened, she didn't want to be caught off-guard.

They moved on foot from the *Faust* to a small guard station perched on the edge of the ravine. The Rejects had dressed for the occasion, in civilian clothes instead of armor. Abbey had her softsuit on beneath baggy pants and a loose white shirt. She had brought nearly two dozen food bars with her on the trip down and had eaten all of them. The result had been a return of the crawling feeling beneath her skin, a renewal of the Gift. It was a feeling she was growing more accustomed to but still didn't like without the pressure of the suit counteracting it.

Still, she was grateful to be able to down the bland bars instead of requiring an influx of blood. The idea had disgusted her before the visit to the engine room, and now the thought nearly made her puke. Tasting Emily Eagan's blood had been a mistake. At the same time, she knew she might need to do it again before this was over if she was going to have any chance of matching Thraven. Nephilim blood only, and only if there was no other choice.

No humans. Ever.

An overweight Skink rose from a chair inside the station as they approached, joining two older Terran guards on the outside. The Terrans were armed with simple rifles, typical Outworld garbage weapons. They also had them shouldered wrong, making it obvious they never needed to use them.

"Nice collection," the Skink said, looking them over. His eyes stopped on Gant. "You have Gant."

"I'm getting tired of hearing that already," Gant said.

"Gilliam," Benhil said, moving ahead of the others. "It's been a long time. You gained weight."

Gilliam eyed Benhil, trying to remember who he was. "I know

The Devils Do

you?"

"I've been here a few times before. Is Phlenel still in business?"

"Why wouldn't it be?"

"You know Phlenel."

Gilliam laughed. "True enough. Rates have gone up. One thousand per head."

"A thousand?" Benhil said. "To get into this shithole? You can't be serious."

"It is what it is. Pay it or get lost."

"Come on, G. You can't count a Gant as a whole, he's half my size."

"And the Trover is double your size."

"At least," Pik said.

Benhil motioned for Gilliam to move in closer. "How about three thousand, plus three hundred for you to say there were only three of us?"

"Five hundred," Gilliam replied.

"Deal."

"And don't make any trouble."

"Me? Never."

Benhil reached into a pocket, removing a payment card. Gilliam ran his thumb over it, scanning it.

"Welcome to Steel Town," Gilliam said, moving aside. "Lift is through there."

Abbey let Benhil stay in the lead as they headed to the massive lifting platform that had been built into the side of the rock. Gilliam activated it as soon as they were all on board, and it began to descend into the ravine.

"Who's Phlenel?" Abbey asked.

"She's a Hurshin doctor," Benhil replied. "She specializes in dark-med and augmentations. She fixes up most of the idiots who come here to mine for rare minerals and wind up losing limbs to the machines."

"A Hurshin?" Gant said. "I've never met one."

"The Goreshin, the creatures that attacked us on Anvil, are derived from the Hurshin," Jequn said. "That's what allows them to change form."

Benhil turned to Abbey. "I recommend leaving Pik with Phlenel and then heading over to Northside. I have a business contact there."

"Do you know anyone here with insider access to Republic asset movements?" Abbey asked.

"In Steel Town? This is a great place for tangible resources, Queenie. Intel? Not so much."

"Jequn, what about Nephilim? Should we expect any complications?"

"The potential exists everywhere," Jequn replied. "We don't know everyone who may be working for the enemy, and as you saw the Goreshin can pose as standard humans. However, I would say the odds are low due to the nature of the planet."

"Fair enough. That's why we came armed."

"That fat Skink didn't even frisk us," Pik said.

"Why would he?" Benhil replied. "Nobody comes to Machina to make trouble. There's nothing here worth making trouble over, at least until one of the prospectors stumbles on a tract with a high enough recovery density. And I doubt the corp that used to own this place left any of those."

The platform took a few more minutes to reach the ground, finally leaving them at the beginning of a wide street that split the center of Steel Town. Factories and workshops were obvious on the edges of the ravine, and apartments and larger homes were intermingled with storefronts on the inside. The whole setup was primitive compared to more developed planets, but that was more a question of scale. No merchant could turn a profit bringing in non-necessities to a planet like Machina Four.

Benhil led them through the settlement. They drew looks from many of the locals, but they were looks of curiosity, not malice. Steel Town saw its share of newcomers.

They stopped in front of one of the storefronts. It didn't have a sign anywhere to describe what kind of shop it was. Abbey had noticed none of them did. It made sense to her. If you were from the town, you knew what each thing was and where it was. If you weren't, you figured it out quickly enough.

The Devils Do

Benhil approached the steel door. It didn't open as he neared it, so he tapped the control panel on the wall beside it. "Phlenel, are you in there?"

"What do you want?" a clearly synthesized voice returned in clear Terran Standard English.

"I've got business."

Abbey noticed movement above them. She looked up to see the camera pivoting behind its casing and focusing on them.

"You look healthy."

"Pik," Benhil said.

Pik rolled back his sleeve, showing off his missing hand.

"Augmentation then?"

"I came to you because I know you're the best," Benhil said.

"Flattery will not reduce the cost."

Benhil laughed. "I wouldn't expect it to."

The heavy door clanked as it unlocked.

"The Trover may enter with you."

"Shy, isn't she?" Gant said.

"I need this one to enter as well," Benhil said, pointing at Abbey. "She's in charge of payment."

"She may enter with the Trover. You will wait outside."

"It's all you, Queenie," Benhil said. He lowered his voice. "Don't make her mad. She's got hidden gun fixtures inside the walls."

"I don't intend to."

Abbey moved to the door. It was manual, and she pushed it open, letting it swing inward on smooth hinges. The inside of the space was cool and dimly lit. A service bot was standing ahead of another doorway.

"Welcome," it said in the same synthesized voice. "Close the door behind you."

Pik closed the door. Abbey heard it lock again. She hoped Benhil knew what he was doing.

The service bot walked backward on spindly metal legs. "Follow me."

It backed up into the second room. It too was dimly lit. It had a large, adjustable medical chair in the center, and the walls were ringed with bins of components. Abbey could see a second room behind it, also stocked with augmentation parts.

"Trover, sit," the bot said, waving a metal arm at the chair.

"Whatever happened to bedside manner?" Pik said, plopping himself down in the chair. It groaned under his weight before actuators adjusted the configuration to better support his form.

"Where's Phlenel?" Abbey asked.

"I am Phlenel," the bot replied. "I will be with you in a moment. I am reconfiguring."

They waited in silence for a minute. Then Phlenel entered from behind them.

It had taken a human form, her gelatinous body mimicking Abbey, using her as a guide for the shape. It was naked, semi-transparent, and almost ethereal looking. Its internal structure had no bones or organs, but instead consisted of a web of electrical impulses and motion and a cellular structure that was hardened and condensed in places to keep it upright. Abbey couldn't help but stare. She had seen video of Hurshins before, but the real thing was even more incredible.

"Now I've seen you naked, Queenie," Pik said behind her.

"Shut up," Abbey replied. The Hurshin could have taken a generic form. Why had it chosen to copy her?

"I am Phlenel," the bot repeated. Abbey watched part of the Hurshin's internal structure sparkle ahead of the signal to the bot.

It approached Pik.

"Put up your hand," the bot said.

Pik raised his wrist. Phlenel reached out, putting a fingertip to it.

"That tickles," Pik said as the finger began to spread around the site.

"I am taking measurements. What manner of augmentation do you require?"

"He needs to be able to hold and fire a gun," Abbey said. "And something that can take some abuse."

"If it makes me stronger and looks badass, that's a bonus," Pik said.

The Devils Do

"I can make any number of suitable configurations. Each will alter the cost of the procedure. For example, five fingers cost more than three."

"Three should be enough," Abbey said.

"What?" Pik replied.

"It's better than what you have right now, and we aren't rich."

"Okay. How about four?"

"We'll see. I don't need Rhodinium," Abbey said. "But something better than standard."

"Twenty thousand," Phenel said.

"Ten," Abbey replied.

"Twenty thousand."

"He doesn't need a hand that badly. Come on, Okay."

"Yes I do," Pik said.

"No, you don't. Let's go."

Pik grumbled but moved to stand.

"Eighteen thousand," Phlenel said.

"Fourteen."

"Seventeen."

"I know you're good, but I'm not getting ripped off. Hand replacement isn't that complex."

"Fifteen. That is as low as I can go without sacrificing component quality."

"Sit back down," Abbey said.

Pik sat.

"Fine. Fifteen. How long?"

"Six hours. Payment now."

Abbey found her card and held it out to the bot. It scanned it in silence.

"Why did you take my form?" Abbey asked, turning back to Phlenel.

The Hurshin shifted. Abbey knew it didn't see the way other species did. It was in essence one big sensor, able to bounce all kinds of waves off things to build a picture of the environment around it.

"You are different," the bot said. "Interesting. I have never been your kind before."

"I'm a human," Abbey said.

"No, you are not."

Abbey felt her body turn cold. She knew she was changing, but this was an individual that could sense her in ways nothing else could, and it was saying she wasn't human.

"What am I then?" she asked.

"Unique. That is what makes you interesting."

"It's what's inside me that makes me unique. You can't mimic that."

"I am processing. I will interpolate and adapt my form accordingly."

Abbey raised her eyebrow. "How long will that take?"

"Unknown. I must begin the procedure. Return in six hours."

Abbey glanced back at Pik. Phlenel had given him something while she was paying the bot. He was already unconscious.

"See you later," Abbey said.

Then she left.

CHAPTER NINE

ABBEY REJOINED BENHIL, GANT, AND Jester outside of Phlenel's shop, still slightly shaken by what the Hurshin had said. Would it be able to show her the physical changes she was going to undertake? Would she like what she saw? Would she even want to see it?

Thraven had said madness accompanied the change. Violent, unfettered madness. How long would it take? Would she have enough time?

What did enough time mean?

She was herself for now. That would have to be good enough.

"Six hours," she said. "Let's take care of getting a crew out to the Brimstone."

"Do we even know what we need them to fix?" Benhil asked.

"Armor plating, for one," Gant replied. "Surprisingly, there's nothing special about the ship's armor, other than a secondary force shielding that apparently rests on the surface. It isn't as effective as the outer shell, but it does redirect kinetic energy outward."

"Which means what?"

"When it gets hit with torpedoes, the blast radius is expanded to cover a larger surface area, meaning less force to any given point along the surface. It's like a slap versus a punch."

"What good will fixing the armor do if we don't have shields?"

"The naniates are self-replicating," Jequn said. "They will replenish, which means the shields will replenish."

"The armor is the tertiary line of defense," Gant said. "We don't need to repair it, but we do need to shore up life support. The primary system is damaged. We've been breathing on the backup."

"Oh. Yeah, I imagine that's important. My contact isn't a starship engineer, but he can probably point us in the right direction."

"Good enough," Abbey said.

They made their way across the settlement, bypassing the rest of the shops and moving further out toward the surrounding factories and warehouses.

"These were left over from when the corporations were still working the mines," Benhil explained. "A lot of them have been converted to handle parsing for the prospectors. One has even been turned into a hotel. Sam runs a salvage operation. He pulls in shit from all over the galaxy, brings it here, and either melts it down or makes it into something else and then ships it back out."

"Legit or black market?" Abbey asked.

"A little bit of both. He'll give us a good price on the disterium, too."

"Good. I used the last of the money Olus gave us on Pik's hand."

"Like he needs a hand."

They approached the front entrance to the factory. A guard was waiting ahead of the door.

"Is Sam in?" Benhil asked.

"Who are you?" the guard asked. She was young, with short hair and a dirty face.

"An old friend. Go tell him I have disterium to sell."

The woman made a face and turned to the door, putting her hand on the control pad to open it.

"Biometrically secured," Abbey said. "I thought nobody cared about this place?"

"Sam's always been a little paranoid."

The Devils Do

The woman returned a minute later, an older Terran trailing behind her. His face changed when he saw Benhil.

"You," he said, suddenly afraid.

"Hey, Sam," Benhil said, producing his sidearm from beneath his coat and pointing it at Sam.

"Jester?" Abbey said.

"Joker, please," Sam said, putting his hands up. "Don't."

"Shut the frag up," Benhil said, getting angry. "What the hell do I care? You sold me out, you piece of shit. You told the Republic what I was doing."

"I. I didn't. I swear."

"Bullshit."

Benhil took a few steps forward, getting closer to Sam. The guard moved to draw her weapon. He shifted his sidearm to her.

"No!" Sam cried, throwing himself in front of her. "Joker, I swear I didn't."

"Jester, what the frag?" Abbey said.

"Queenie, this asshole is the one who got me sent to Hell. He told the Republic where I was going. I know he did."

"Do you have proof?" Abbey asked.

"Yeah. They showed me the message he sent when they sent me to trial. They used it to convict me. It wasn't enough that I paid him to send some equipment over to Tamaroon, he wanted to get me busted so that he could keep my money and the goods."

Sam froze when he heard that. He put his hands up higher. "Fine. I did it. Are you fragging happy? Just don't hurt my wife."

"What kind of monster do you think I am?" Benhil said. "I don't hurt innocents."

"Is this why we came to Machina Four?" Abbey said, getting angry herself. "So you could shake down the asshole who got you busted?"

"I figured it was as good a place as any. It didn't hurt that I could take care of some unfinished business."

"Olus told me why you were in Hell. You got arrested because you were helping equip the Outworlders on Tamaroon. That's treason."

"The Republic didn't need to be on Tamaroon. They were using them for fragging target practice. My brother was there, damn it. I was trying to get them portable shelters, to give them a chance to hide until it was over." His head whipped toward Abbey. "But they don't put that shit in the reports, do they? They don't give a shit about reasons."

"No, and right now I don't either. Put the fragging gun down. You aren't shooting anyone."

"I spent the last four years in Hell, Queenie. Because of this shit. He keeps his mouth shut, nobody ever knows about Tamaroon. It's easy for you to be cool about Hell, you only spent what? Three weeks there?"

"Six," Abbey said.

Benhil laughed. "He deserves to die."

"No, he-"

Benhil pulled the trigger.

Abbey threw her hand out, feeling the Gift flowing within her. The bullet changed direction, hitting the side of the factory and skipping away. She put out her other hand, sending Benhil back and to the ground.

She was seething. Furious. She walked over to Benhil, standing over him. She pushed down with her hand, and he began to choke, his neck compressed beneath the Gift.

"We came here to get supplies. The *Brimstone* isn't your personal fragging transport. This is a war, damn it. Whether it looks like one yet or not, it is. And it's one we don't win without a fragging miracle or two. And it's one we don't win if my team is going to treat it like a fragging game. I don't need this shit, Jester. I don't need more complications."

"Uh, Queenie," Gant said.

"What?" Abbey said, looking back at him.

He drew back in shock. "You're attracting the wrong kind of attention." He pointed to the side of the factory. The delivery bay doors were open, and a group of workers had come out.

"You should have let him shoot me," Sam said. He was standing again and smiling. "Flappy lips detonate starships, you know."

His form began to change. So did the woman's. They were Goreshin. Children of the Covenant. So were the workers.

The Devils Do

Abbey let go of Benhil, shifting her attention their way. "Of all the damn places on all the damn planets in all the damn galaxy."

"Can't take you anywhere," Benhil said between gulping breaths of air.

CHAPTER TEN

SAM WAS CLOSE TO THEM. Too close. He pounced towards Abbey, claws slashing in a downward cross that would have ripped her chest wide open if they had connected. She bounced back on the strength of her hidden softsuit, her baggy shirt torn in half but otherwise unscathed, the Gift churning inside of her at the ambush.

Sam barely paused, coming at her again, ready for a second try.

His head snapped back as Benhil opened fire, the rounds hitting him square in the face and going right through. He toppled to the ground.

Abbey found one of the Uin in her tighpack, taking it out and flicking her wrist, extending the weapon. She heard hisses as the other Goreshin began charging from across the tract, coming their way. She heard a second hiss when Jequn brought her own blades to hand, bouncing quickly from her position and charging Sam's wife. The woman growled in a mix of anger and fear, caught off-guard by the sudden presence of an Ophanim. She backed away defensively, hoping to buy time until the reinforcements arrived.

Abbey hopped toward Sam, raising the Uin to bring it down in a swift, clean slash across the back of his neck. He jerked suddenly, coming up and toward her, forcing her to spin away as he slashed at her once more.

The Devils Do

"Why don't you stay down?" Benhil said.

Sam spun his way, preparing to charge. Benhil tried to shoot him a second time, but he slipped from side to side, impossibly fast, covering the distance to the soldier in a split-second.

Abbey was right behind him. She dove, grabbing his foot and pulling, yanking his legs out from under him. They fell to the ground together, with Sam scrambling to regain himself as she ran the Uin across his back. He froze for a moment; his spine separated, his legs suddenly not working.

"That's right, die," Benhil said, shooting him again.

Abbey pulled herself forward, neatly slicing off his head. Then she stood up, facing Benhil. "This is your fault," she said, before springing away.

She threw herself toward the larger mass of creatures, eight in total that were nearly on top of them. She noticed Gant out of the corner of her eye, a knife in his grip, spinning lithely as he leaped into one of the Goreshin. He somersaulted in the air to avoid its claws, hitting its chest with the blade and vaulting back off, landing behind a second and stabbing it in the back of the head.

"Jequn," he barked, dropping off the creature as the Ophanim turned, vaulting back and slicing the creature's head off. Gant rolled beneath an attack and grabbed his blade from it, sidestepping a falling claw and slicing into his attacker's forearm.

Abbey waded into the group, spreading the fingers on her left hand, feeling the Gift pooling there, extending from her fingertips to create claws of her own. She used the flat part of the Uin to block an attack, knocking the Goreshin off-balance and raking its face with her claws, tearing its eyes. She spun around behind it, sweeping the Uin through the neck on the other side and removing it from the fight.

Bullets followed, fired from both Jequn and Benhil, the shots targeting the heads of the creatures, the damage pausing them for a few seconds each time while they healed. Abbey charged one of the stricken Children, her blade cutting it apart. She rounded on another, squaring off against it, face to face.

"What are you?" the Goreshin asked, looking at her with fear in its eyes.

"The Queen," Abbey replied.

The Gift was throbbing inside her, regenerated and replenished by all of the food bars she had eaten. She put her hand out, slamming the Gift into the creature, the power bringing it to its knees despite its resistance. She brought the Uin violently around and through its neck.

"Is that all of them?" She heard Benhil say behind her.

She spun on him again. He dropped his gun and put his hands up. "Whoa. Queenie."

"You son of a bitch," Abbey said, still enraged. "You stupid son of a bitch. Give me one reason not to kill you right now."

"Queenie," Gant said.

"I'm sorry," Benhil said. "Shit. Queenie, I'm sorry. I made a mistake. A stupid mistake."

Abbey moved closer. Her head was pounding, her forehead throbbing from the anger. She wanted to rip his head off with her bare hands. She wanted to -

She stopped herself. That wasn't her. She stared at Benhil, taking a few breaths. She looked around. They were alone in front of the factory, surrounded by dead Nephilim.

"How was I supposed to know he was one of Thraven's?" Benhil continued. "There's no way to know. No way to tell."

"Shut up," Abbey snapped.

He did.

"Security had to have heard the gunshots," she said a moment later, beginning to calm somewhat.

"What security?" Benhil asked. "I told you, Queenie."

"What about the fat Skink at the top of the ravine?"

He shook his head. "Gilliam? The only thing he controls or cares about is the ride down. This is a mess we can clean up."

Abbey flicked her wrist, closing the Uin. She put it back in the tightpack. Then she grabbed her torn shirt, pulling it the rest of the way off. She checked her softsuit. At least it had avoided any new holes.

The Devils Do

"I like what this means less than what it was," she said. "Children of the Covenant here means there could be Children anywhere."

"Or everywhere," Gant agreed.

"And we can't spot them ahead of time."

"Now you see why the Seraphim lost," Jequn said. "There weren't as many of them back then. Nowhere near as many."

"How the frag are we supposed to fight this?" Benhil said.

"One at a time if we have to," Abbey replied. She looked at the door to the factory. "No security? Then at least this isn't a total loss. Jequn, I want you and Jester to look around and see if there's anything we can use." She looked at Benhil again. "We can't risk that Thraven knows we're here. Not now. We have to bug out early thanks to you. No time for repairs."

"What about the life support?" Gant said.

"We'd better hope the backup system doesn't break," Abbey replied. "Move it, Rejects. And be careful. We don't know if there are more of them hiding inside."

"Roger," Benhil said. Jequn nodded.

Abbey watched them enter the facility. Gant came to stand behind her.

"Where'd you learn to fight like that?" she asked.

"Why does everybody forget that I'm a trained soldier?" he replied.

"Normal trained soldiers can't fight like that."

"I picked up a few lessons over the years. It happens."

Abbey looked down at him, raising her eyebrow.

"What? It does. Besides, do you think Captain Mann only wanted me for my cute face?" He laughed. "You need to watch yourself, Queenie. When you were fighting, your eyes turned dark red, and I swear I saw ridges along your softsuit, maybe from under your skin. I think the more you use the Gift, the faster you're going to lose it. You're getting more angry more easily. You looked like you were half a second from cutting Jester's idiot head off. Not that he wouldn't have deserved it."

"I know. I can feel it." She shook her head. "But I can't ignore the power. Not when my team needs me. Not when the stakes are so high."

"You were a badass before you had the Gift. You don't need to use it as a crutch. Just remember that."

She nodded. "You're right. Thanks, Gant."

"Anytime." He looked back toward the factory. "Why did you send Jester and Cherub in there alone?"

"Cherub?"

"She's a Seraph, right?"

"Or a descendent of one. So she says."

"She needs a nickname if she's going to be a Reject."

"At the pace we're collecting strays, I don't know if we'll be able to keep up."

He laughed again. "Building our own army. I can live with that."

"I sent them off alone so we could go check out their network. Sam knew who I was, which means he's got a link to Thraven. I'm hoping we can use it to track down the Nova."

"The ship you were on when you got arrested? Why?"

"General Kett wants us to deal with Kell ourselves, before he'll commit his forces to this. Do you know what I say to that?"

"Frag that?" Gant guessed.

"Exactly. The upside of Jester's screw-up is that we just found some extra time. If possible, I want to locate the mainframe, finish cracking it, and find out where Kett is hiding. Then I want to go pay him a visit and make him be part of this damn war."

The Devils Do

CHAPTER ELEVEN

Abbey and Gant made their way through the factory. They moved in the opposite direction from Benhil and Jequn, angling away from the heavy machinery and the warehouse beyond, and toward the administrative offices tucked in the back corner.

The factory itself was warm and damp and poorly lit, and it smelled like the Children of the Covenant didn't believe in using modern toilets. There was a strong ammonia scent in the air, matched with a permeating stench that reminded Abbey of raw sewage. There was no reason for the place to smell so rank, but it did.

"In here, Queenie," Gant said, pointing to a room at the end of a corridor.

Abbey joined him there a moment later. The room had a stack of computers in the corner, and a filthy terminal in the center. There were greasy handprints on the controls, an indication that the station had been used relatively recently. Abbey put her own hand on it, activating it.

It was locked. That wasn't much of a surprise.

"This would be easier with a helmet," she said, opening a tightpack and removing an interrupt disc. She placed it on the terminal, waiting a few seconds for the data flow to stabilize. Then she withdrew a hidden cable from the softsuit, reaching over and connecting it to the disc.

"What is that?" Gant asked.

"The interrupt gives me middleware access to the source layer," she replied. "The cable links the suit's SOC to the middleware. From there, I can use the onboard software Ruby downloaded for me to brute force the security lock and get root level control of the system."

"Learn something new every day."

"This is going to take a few minutes. Keep an eye out for Jequn. I don't want her to know what we're planning until it's too late for her to do anything about it."

"You don't think she would approve?"

"Of us crashing Kett's party? No."

Gant retreated from the room. Abbey watched the projection. She could see a single execution line at the bottom of it. The software entered passwords so quickly it was only showing every ten thousandth or so attempt. She was sure the terminal had a lockout on it, but their classified software didn't give a shit about lockouts. It bypassed that part of the system, letting them enter as many codes as possible as quickly as possible. There were other ways to get into systems like this, of course, and it was always a matter of finding the right balance between time and effort.

She smiled when the terminal unlocked. Nice and easy. She liked it that way.

Of course, this was only the first step. She needed access to whatever network Thraven was using to pass messages. The Milnet, the public Galnet, the Outworld's Syncsys, the Darknet, or something proprietary?

She could have tracked the Nova from the Brimstone's Milnet, but it wasn't the best choice, which is why she had asked Benhil about finding an informant. Any backdoors she knew about in the system were monitored to ensure they didn't get used against them, and would trigger a backscan the moment they were tripped. That would help the HSOC pinpoint the origin of the vector and lead them right to Machina Four. While she was sure Thraven would discover what had happened here within a few days, that was still a lot better than within a few minutes.

The Devils Do

She navigated through the system, her actions slowed by the need to use the projected interface instead of a direct command line. Within a few minutes she had located the network configuration, uncovering the link keys and smiling. Syncsys. She should have guessed.

She opened a path to the softsuit's SOC, checking the signatures on her packages. The latest exploit she had stored was three days old. That was a long time by network security standards, and it meant she might wind up getting backscanned regardless. But only if the Outworlders had discovered the vulnerability. Since the system was more highly distributed among the planets in the Governance, this sort of thing usually took longer to patch and monitor.

There was no decision to be made. She had to use what was available. She executed the network hack from the SOC, watching the commands run across the bottom of the projection.

"Queenie," Gant said, reappearing in the doorway behind her. "They're on their way back. Jester looks excited about something."

"Cut them off, find out what they've got. I need more time."

"Roger."

Abbey turned back to the projection. Her hands moved in a blur at the base of the terminal, entering commands as quickly as she could. She needed to find out what had happened to the mainframe she had captured on Gradin. She knew it had been on the Nova, but was it still there?

She needed reports, messages from someone on the Nova to someone in Thraven's cabal. Who? She had no idea. Unless.

She froze, thinking about it for a minute while she stared at the screen. The mainframe wouldn't be on the Nova. Everything they had taken on Gradin would have been confiscated by the Republic Military Police as evidence. The hardware should have been taken out of play. Except Thraven had a finger on the MPs, and he had access to the mainframe.

Mr. Davis.

The son of a bitch who had sent her to Hell, and looked so damn smug doing it. He was the link between the Nova, the mainframe, Thraven, and her. He was the asshole she was looking for. But was his name really Davis?

She did a query on his name against the private Syncsys messaging service the terminal was connected to. Nothing came back. Frag. She held her face with her hand. She was sure he was in the system but under another name. Someone else then. Who? She would have to connect the dots. She considered the crew of the Nova. Best to start near the top.

She entered the ship's CO, Kyle Ng.

Nothing.

She took out his first name.

A raft of results appeared. She opened the first one, a short message from Gloritant Thraven to Honorant Ng.

She felt a sudden chill. The Commander of the Nova was working for the Nephilim. How many Republic starships did Thraven have under his control?

"Shit."

She updated her query, adding an Earth Standard timestamp range for the days before and after her arrest. Only four messages. She opened the first of them:

Drop complete. Package confirmed. Prepped for delivery.

That was it. The entire message, sent to Evolent Ruche.

Evolent?

She checked the other messages. All of them were to Ruche. She backed out and updated her search, setting a timestamp for after her arrest.

Ruche had been busy. A few hundred messages appeared. She started at the top, pausing when she got to the one that revealed his identity:

Meeting with Cage as expected. Recommend conversion.

Ruche was Davis, that fragger. She clenched her fist, feeling the Gift respond. She took a few breaths. She had to stay calm. Gant was right. It was coming more easily. Almost too easily.

She scanned the other messages until she found what she was looking for:

Transfer complete. Package en route to Earth for processing.

Earth?

The Devils Do

She slumped back. There was no way they could go to Earth. Then again, maybe they wouldn't have to.

CHAPTER TWELVE

"Q̲ueenie," Benhil said as Abbey emerged from the offices and onto the factory floor. "You have to see this."

Abbey nodded, glancing at Jequn. The Ophanim was looking at her curiously. It was clear from her expression that she was wondering what Abbey had been doing.

"You'll forgive me once you do," Benhil continued.

They made their way across the factory, past a row of bots working at the end of a long conveyor belt, past a huge sorting machine and an equally large smelter. The warehouse was at the far end, hidden beneath a pair of large blast doors that were hanging open enough for any individual smaller than a Trover to squeeze through. They went through, entering the large, open floor of the storage area, where a few smaller hoppers sat, half-loaded with goods to carry up the ravine to incoming merchant ships when they arrived. Most of it was blocks of melted down metal and boxes of parts stripped from the salvage.

"I'm not impressed," Abbey said, looking over the stash.

Benhil laughed. "I knew you were going to say that. Forget this section. This way."

He led them deeper into the building. The smell was stronger here. What the hell was it?

The Devils Do

He stopped halfway across the floor. "Wait here," he said. Then he ran to a small terminal base jutting out from the floor near the south end.

"Jequn?" Abbey said.

"I told him to leave it open, but he wanted to surprise you."

"What is it?"

"I'm not going to ruin his surprise."

Abbey heard motion above them. She looked up. There was a magnetic rig attached to beams that crossed the warehouse in a grid. The large, round magnet was lowering directly in front of them.

"He wouldn't have found it without me," Jequn said. "The smell. I knew I recognized it."

The magnet continued dropping until it hit the stone floor.

"Back up a few steps," Benhil shouted.

They did.

The magnet started to rise again. Abbey was surprised to see a large square of the floor rising with it. The awful smell nearly became unbearable as it did.

"What the frag?" Abbey said. "I'm not going to thank you for this."

She slowed her breathing, the stench making her nauseous.

"It isn't that bad," Benhil said, running back to them once the slab was over their heads. "Look."

Abbey did. There was a ramp leading down beneath the factory.

"Did you go down?" she asked.

"Yeah."

He started down the ramp. Ambient lighting appeared along the sides of it as he moved, revealing that it continued beyond the edge of the slab.

"Gant, wait here. Holler if anyone shows up."

"Aye, Queenie."

Abbey and Jequn followed Benhil down the ramp. The smell only got worse, and she had to cover her nose with her arm to adjust to it.

"What the frag is with the sewer?" she asked.

"You'll see," Benhil said.

The ramp sank another twenty meters underground, dropping them out into a second warehouse. A secret warehouse. Everything in it was covered in a layer of dust and soot, except where Benhil and Jequn had already been, their footprints visible in the dirt. They had walked the perimeter of the space, around the many boxes and crates, around the large shapes hidden by larger tarps. A couple of the boxes had been pulled open. One of them had a rifle resting on top, suggesting it was a sample of the contents.

"The smell is coming from back here, Queenie," Benhil said.

Abbey followed him, towards a darker corner of the room. Jequn produced a light from her suit and turned it on, shining it at the corner.

Abbey's heart began to pound. "What the frag is that?"

"We called it an Extinctor," Jequn said. "It's a Nephilim derivation from a seed of the One."

Abbey stared at the thing in front of them. It had been dead for a long time, but that didn't make it less frightening. Eight meters in height, humanoid in shape. Most of the flesh was decomposed, but she could see from the skeleton that its arms and legs were covered in bony spikes. The neck was thick, the skull thicker. Its teeth were long and vicious looking. A gun nearly as large as she was sat on the floor beside it.

"You can see how difficult it would be to kill with a Uin. The bones are dense, making them hard to get through to reach anything vital."

"What the hell is it doing here?" Abbey said softly, still trying to recover from the sight of it.

"I'm not sure," Jequn said. "If I had to guess, I would say a prospector found it somewhere in the mines, down where the climate would preserve it, and Sam brought it here to hide it."

"And killed the prospector for the trouble, I'm sure. You've fought these before?"

"Not personally, but they are part of our histories of the Nephilim. I told you, Queenie. There are other monsters under the Gloritant's control beyond the Goreshin. The seeds Lucifer took, he modified them to make weapons to kill the One and his followers."

Abbey stared at the massive humanoid. She could see the vague similarities between it and the Trover, both in size and the general shape.

The Devils Do

"And they have more of these things?"

"I'm certain they do, though I would doubt Thraven would use them against you. They're strong, but they also wouldn't fare well against a high powered railgun or a higher level explosive."

"Score one for our violent nature," Benhil said.

"That isn't the true prize," Jequn said. "These crates are."

"Weapons?" Abbey said.

Benhil nodded. "Lots of them. That shithead Sam was stockpiling them here, preparing for the war, I guess. There's even a squadron of Devils over there."

"How suitable and relatively useless," Abbey replied. Starfighters from three generations past. They couldn't outmaneuver Shrikes, and they would look stupid in a dogfight with an Apocalypse fighter.

"I showed them to Gant. He said he might be able to dress them up a little bit, make them a little more effective with some modification."

"Do they fly?"

"We'd need Lucif... Imp down here to make that call."

"What about the other boxes?"

"Take your pick of munitions, Queenie. There's enough here to outfit a few platoons."

"Suits?"

"Older models. This cache has been dormant here as long if not longer than Bunyon over there has been rotting the night away."

"Bunyon?"

"Old Earth legend. Paul Bunyon?"

"I don't know it."

"Doesn't matter. This is a serious haul, and just what we were looking for. And we get to keep our disterium." He smiled. "So, do you forgive me?"

Abbey smiled back. "Not yet, but you're off to a good start."

CHAPTER THIRTEEN

OLUS DIDN'T SLOW THE CAR until he had reached Bethesda fifteen minutes later. He had managed to somehow keep ahead of Thraven's forces after exiting the secret evacuation tunnel on the north side of D.C., lifting the vehicle skyward and hitting the same VIP lane he had been riding in before, using its light traffic to take a straight line to the smaller city. He had stopped the ride near a food center, quickly grabbing Omsala's communicator from the seat beside him and retrieving a multi-tool from a pocket. He turned the device over, using a laser to carefully burn through the joints before adjusting the tool to a small screwdriver, which he used to pull the two screws holding it together. From there, it took only an instant for him to pull the main battery and the smaller emergency battery that would disable the beacon.

When that was done, he exited the car, scanning the air for inbound units. He caught sight of a dark craft in the distance, headed his way. He shook his head, tucking the pieces of the communicator in his pocket and abandoning the car, walking briskly toward the food center.

He had barely made it to the front door when the craft arrived, dropping down beside his stolen car almost at the same time two more units showed up, taking a ground route into the area. Four soldiers emerged from each vehicle, wearing blacksuits and carrying rifles. They

The Devils Do

went to the car first, sweeping it before turning their attention to the building.

Olus ducked inside.

The center was a standard grocery distribution point, a fully automated system that took orders from the net and assembled them for pickup. A single human worked in the large facility, a greeter for the shoppers who came to retrieve their groceries.

"Can I help you?" she asked.

"Do you have a car?" he replied.

"Excuse me, sir?"

"Do you have a car," he repeated, looking back out of the building. The soldiers were coming their way.

"Yeah, why?"

"Do you see those assholes out there?"

She looked outside. Her expression turned fearful.

"They'll say they're with the FBI or something. They aren't. They're hunting me, and I'm not really in the mood to die today, so if you want to stay alive too, I recommend we go to your car and get the frag out of here."

"What? I don't even know you."

"Olus Mann," he said. "Director of the OSI. Or at least I was up until fifteen minutes ago. You're wasting time."

The soldiers were almost to the door. Damn it, he should have just threatened her. He was getting soft in his old age.

"Really, you ought to at least get behind something," he said, turning to face them. He found his pocket knife. It was all he had left.

They raised their weapons toward him. Their faces were barely visible behind their helmets, but he could almost sense their intentions. He shifted his balance, and then threw himself at the closed door.

It slid open as he approached it, and he dropped and rolled toward the soldiers, drawing fire that was off the mark. He came up between the first two, stabbing one in the hand with the knife, turning and grabbing the gun of the other, pushing it downward as the soldier fired again, the bullets striking the cement at their feet. He used his momentum to carry him into that soldier, rolling across his side with the knife still in hand. He wrapped an arm around his neck and his foot around his leg, dragging him back and down, letting the soldier land on top of him. He ran his arm sideways across his neck, using the knife to cut it, taking hold of the rifle and firing into the second soldier before he could recover.

He threw the soldier off him, bouncing to his feet and closing on the other soldiers, keeping them too close for them to risk shooting. He slammed one in the head with the rifle, a fist from another landing on his gut. He ignored it, stabbing the outstretched hand before bringing his weapon up and firing point-blank into his attacker's chest.

He kept moving, not letting himself lose the kinetic energy, floating toward another soldier. He waved the knife ahead of him, batting his opponent's hands aside when they reached out, leaning in and shoving their arm aside, pushing past their guard and shooting the man in the gut. He bounced sideways from that tango, feeling a bullet come way too close as he tossed the rifle at the soldier in front of him. The distraction worked, and he pushed his way into the soldier, shoving his head up and back and creating a space between lightsuit and helmet and stabbing the knife into it. The soldier fell back and he rolled over the top of him, picking up the rifle on his way back to his feet, diving to his right and coming up ahead of the next, shooting him in the helmet, grabbing him and turning him, putting a finger on the trigger of the soldier's gun and shooting the target approaching him from the rear. He skipped toward the remaining pair, slapping the gun away from one with his, letting it fall as he smacked at his opponent, quick, precise blows that put him off-balance despite his armor. Olus pulled a sidearm from the man's belt, shoving it in the side of his neck and firing. He turned back toward the remaining soldier, facing off as they both prepared to shoot.

The weapons fired at the same time.

The soldier missed.

Olus didn't.

He scanned the area. Twelve soldiers in black lay around him, bleeding from the various holes in their bodies. He doubled over, breathing hard, using his knees to balance while he sucked in extra air. He

The Devils Do

hadn't needed to work so intensely in a long time. Hell, even Hell had been a lighter workout. Bureaucracy had made him soft, but in a way, it was good to be back in action.

Once a killer, always a killer. That was what the Republic had trained him to be.

He didn't have time to waste. He leaned down over the nearest soldier, grabbing another sidearm and quickly rifling through tightpacks until he found some ID. He synced it to his card, and then ran back to the center, pushing through the doors.

The woman was still there, having ducked behind her desk when the shooting started. He leaned over it, looking down at her.

"Car?" he said.

She reached into her purse and pulled out the key card. "It's out back," she said, tears in her eyes.

"I'm sorry about this," he said, taking it. "If anyone comes to question you, tell them they should have taken care of me when they had the chance."

CHAPTER FOURTEEN

Olus didn't keep the woman's car for long, taking it north to Baltimore and dumping it there. It was further away from OSI HQ than he had wanted to go, but the response from Thraven's units had forced him to seek a more dense environment to hide in, and the city fit the bill.

He had read once that ancient Baltimore had been a nice but troubled place, the diversity of its populations both in racial and social standing causing tension across the board. That had started to change with the discovery of disterium and the invention of the first FTL drives, when settlers from the planet began making their way off-world to seek something else somewhere else. Thanks to its closeness to D.C., the city had become an extension of the nation's capital, and now it was a valuable right hand, built up and proud as a city of tall glass buildings and a number of businesses that operated locally and across the Republic. Its spaceport was one of the largest and busiest in the world, behind only Beijing and Mumbai, and it was a popular starting point for travelers from around the galaxy on their way to more famous destinations like New York City and Seattle, as well as points across the globe.

For Olus, it was a place to disappear, to finish killing the beacon on Omsala's comm and try to get what data he could from it. A place to settle in and begin the second phase of his primary mission to identify and

The Devils Do

protect the remaining Council members from Thraven's plot to unseat them.

He went on foot from the random garage where he left the car, using untraceable payment transfers to pay for a loop ride downtown, and then locating a cheap hotel to hole up in. He kept his head down, his face hidden, staying unimpressive and unnoticeable, a regular, ordinary individual all the way until he reached his room on the fourth floor. He slipped inside, maintaining his calm as the door closed and he removed Omsala's communicator. He placed it on a nearby desk, went to the bathroom to relieve himself, and then took off his jacket, noticing a scuff on the sleeve from a bullet that had grazed his elbow. That would have hurt.

He tossed the jacket aside, sitting at the desk and leaning over the communicator. He removed the toolkit from his inside pocket and laid the tools out on the table, working quickly to detach the circuit board, locate the emergency beacon, and leverage it off the device. He placed it aside before putting the whole thing back together, leaving the battery for last.

He was about to insert the battery when the communicator tucked beneath his shirt collar intoned an incoming ping. His eyebrow went up, and he tapped the collar to activate it.

"Ruby," he said. "This channel isn't secure. Be quick."

"Sir," Ruby said. "The Queen requires a Knight for a quest. The lost treasure is in your kingdom."

"Priority?"

"Critical."

"Timeline?"

"Immediate."

Olus cursed under his breath. He had other work to do.

"Transfer?"

"All contents."

"Affirmative. Twenty-four Earth Standard."

"Confirmed."

Olus dropped the link and then leaned back in his seat. Damn it. This was going to get ugly. He looked down at the communicator. Would he be able to get enough data from it to take care of both needs at one time?

There was only one way to find out.

He slipped the battery back in, turning the device over so he could see it power on. He flipped it face down again, putting his jacket back on and running the wire from it to the communicator. The size of the device made it more challenging to make the connection, but he managed to get it into place. The command line interface appeared in the lense over his eye.

The communicator was locked. That was no surprise. It didn't take long for Olus to determine that Omsala was an idiot. That wasn't much of a surprise either. The General hadn't bothered to harden his personal comm against Breaker tools, even though the opportunity was available to him. He had left the off-the-shelf device with off-the-shelf security, which to the OSI or HSOC was as good as no security. He could imagine what Thraven would think of the ineptitude and allowed himself a slight smile. Judging by Emily Eagan's fate, Omsala was lucky he was already dead.

"Let's see what you've got for me, General," he said, tapping his fingers on his jacket to enter commands into the system.

First things first, he needed to see if there was a link to Lieutenant Cage's 'treasure,' which he was guessing meant the mainframe she had been trying to crack when she had been taken into custody. He wished he could have gotten more information and found out how she and the Rejects were faring overall, but he knew his official Milnet account was likely already shut down, and his special secured channel would soon be discovered and tapped.

He wondered how the Committee was going to spin Omsala's death and his departure. Would they pin the murder on him? If so, what motive would they use? He supposed they could connect him to Feru and the death of Mars Eagan, but only loosely. It might be enough to satisfy Thraven's minions, and maybe some of the public. It would never convince his people, and that was dangerous. There was a reason Thraven had diverted him instead of removing him, though now he had no other choice.

Good.

The Devils Do

The fact that Abbey and the Rejects were still out there and on the loose, still moving the mission forward, was a good sign. He knew General Kett was connected to the mainframe, so if Abbey wanted it, then it meant she needed to know more about that. For what purpose? To what end? Was Kett on their side or Thraven's?

"Just figure out where it is and get it to her," he said to himself. "She can handle the rest."

Abbey reminded him so much of himself when he was younger. Damn, that felt like a long, long time ago. Except she had the Nephilim's Gift to take her to the next level. A part of him envied her for that. He could only imagine what he could have done with a power like hers. Then again, he knew what they said about power and corruption, and he wasn't fool enough to think he was incorruptible. At least she had a reason to stay on the right side of this fight. He had been betting it would be enough when he encouraged her to embrace the Gift. So far, so good.

He dove into the communicator's stored data. He wasn't looking for anything specific yet. He scanned the contacts to and from the device, taking note of the ones that repeated consistently. Omsala had a wife and children back on Fezzin, and he seemed to talk to them the most. Outside of that, he only had communications with a few individuals, and one name stood out above the rest:

Abraham Davis.

He remembered Abbey telling him about Mr. Davis, a man whose first name she had never learned. He was willing to risk his career that this was the same Davis. He quickly went through the General's messages to him. They were short and simple. They spoke about inconsequential things. Encoded. Maybe Omsala wasn't as stupid as he had originally thought.

Then again, he knew enough of the story to begin to guess at the meaning behind the innocent looking words, and he was also experienced enough to begin picking up the patterns in the messages not long after he began sifting through them. Omsala had met with Davis for 'dinner' in New York City on multiple occasions. The last was only two days earlier. There was no indication of what they were discussing, but he was sure it wasn't sports. The important thing was that if Davis was hanging out in New York, then the mainframe was likely there somewhere as well. Not that finding something as small as a Republic issue server in the densest city in the world was going to be easy, but he had a lead and most times that was all it took.

He considered his other mission. It was clear that Davis was the link between Omsala and Thraven, and that he was directing the General in person. If there was a plan to begin assassinating the members of the Council who had yet to be turned, it was likely Davis was orchestrating it. It made sense that he would try to catch them all in one shot, because picking them off one at a time might cause the others to take cover and secure themselves beyond approach. That was his second clue.

He needed more than clues, though. He needed more than he had time to gather on his own.

He disconnected the wire from the communicator, closing the device and shoving it back into his pocket. Then he picked up the beacon and examined it. It was barely a centimeter around, with a connector to both the main battery and the emergency backup. He smiled as he looked at it. He could already imagine a dozen uses for it.

He stood up, picking up all of his things, quickly grabbing a towel from the bathroom, wetting it, and wiping down everything he had touched. He had been hoping to grab an hour or two of sleep, but that wasn't going to happen. Not yet. He abandoned the room, heading back out to the streets.

He needed a little extra help.

He knew exactly who to contact.

The Devils Do

CHAPTER FIFTEEN

Olus ducked behind a shattered wall. Plasma bolts hissed over his head, striking the building behind him, while voices echoed over his communicator.

"Four One, advance to position Delta. Six One, flanking position Echo."

"Roger," a voice replied.

"Affirmative," another answered.

Olus leaned up, glancing over the wall. The defenses were laid out ahead of him. Three squads of mechs and an entire company of infantry. They were well-secured behind steel barriers, ahead of a tall iron fortress bristling with weapons of its own.

"Calling in air support," the first voice said. "Foxtrot One, do you copy? The target is painted."

"This is Foxtrot One, we copy. Target verified. Commencing run."

Olus kept his eyes on the scene ahead, watching as the Apocalypse fighters streaked in, releasing their payload of heavy ballistics as they neared the fortress. The mechs aimed their heavy gauss rifles skyward, sending projectiles up at the fighters. One of them was hit, and it exploded in a ball of flame, almost at the same time the missiles struck the defenses. Massive walls of smoke and fire exploded from the strikes, leaving the defenders blinded.

"All units, go, go, go," the voice shouted.

Olus hopped over the wall, bouncing along the terrain in his battlesuit, joined by the rest of his battalion. They charged the defensive position, guns blaring, as the fighters circled back for a support run.

Something big and heavy began chewing up the ground around him. He bounced sideways, evading a spout of chewed up dirt, rolling to his feet as the mech crashed down one hundred meters away, its arms out and munitions pouring away from it and into their attack. He shouldered his rifle, unhooking the portable launched on his other arm and planting it in the ground. He eyes his HUD, watching the soldier he had marked with the carat coming up behind him.

The mech began swiveling his way. He aimed the launcher, having to remain static to prep the mech-buster. The second soldier had nearly reached him.

The mech started firing, bullets chewing up the earth around him, one of them hitting the launcher and taking it offline. Olus was about to be shot himself when the soldier grabbed him by the waste, bouncing away, dragging him from the scene as the whole thing exploded behind them.

"Bad maneuver, Four Six," the soldier said. "Mech-busters are handicapped in this sim."

Olus looked back at the helmeted soldier. "Zoey," he said. "The shit is hitting the fan."

The soldier froze. "How do you-"

"Of course, your boss knows how to find you," Olus said. "This is the only secure channel. I need you to meet me in New York City. The Penn loop terminal. Three hours."

"You're on Earth, sir?"

"I've been shut down. Nobody told you?"

"I was off today. My boss should have known that, too."

Olus laughed. "Check your messages. I'll need a full debriefing when you get to New York."

"What's happening, sir?"

"There's a new, old asshole in the galaxy, and he's making his power play. He's got the Committee in his pocket, and he's working on the Council. We need to stop it."

"Roger."

"You might get dragged down with me. Get what you can and get to me. If you can reach any of the others securely, tell them to do the same."

"I've got Shaw here with me, sir. I'll wake him up and drag him along."

Olus made a face she couldn't see behind his helmet. Officially, the OSI didn't approve of operatives getting romantically involved. Not that they could stop it, either.

"Do it. Three hours, Lieutenant."

"Roger, sir. Die with honor."

She bounced away from him, heading toward the mech. He watched for a second, and then brought his rifle up, giving her cover fire while she moved in. Bullets from the machine tore into her, but she landed and managed one last bounce, pulling a grenade from her hip as she reached the mech and put the explosive against the neck joint. The resulting explosion left a gaping wound, and Olus drove toward it himself, preparing his grenade.

He managed to avoid getting hit, the first wave of damage taking out the mech's targeting sensors. He landed on top of the weapon's platform, shoving the grenade into the open hole. It would be more than enough to blow its head off. He remained crouched there, staring off at the battlefield as the seconds ticked away.

It was just as well. He could tell their team was going to lose this Construct match anyway.

The grenade exploded.

CHAPTER SIXTEEN

Getting to New York was easy. The fares for private hoppers were reasonable, and Olus had the unmarked credit to cover it. The flight took a little less than an hour, leaving him with more than enough time to navigate the urban center and find his way to Penn Station.

New York City had been around a long time. It had seen its share of misery and heartache, along with an equal measure of glory and success. It was the most densely populated place in the world, and still one of the ten major hubs of human civilization, a place that had been torn down, rebuilt, upgraded and renovated, and yet still maintained a classical charm that couldn't be duplicated anywhere else.

It was late evening. Cars littered all of the available travel lanes, moving slowly but smoothly at various heights, weaving between the skyscrapers, entering and abandoning landing corridors and keeping everything flowing. Though he couldn't see it, Olus knew the same thing would be happening below ground, where loops and tunnels carried millions of people under the earth like ants in a series of passages designed and organized by a renowned Plixian Queen.

"Here we are," the pilot said, slipping into the landing block and descending to street level. Another car rose up beside them, exiting the block and joining one of the lanes.

The Devils Do

Olus reached out with his card. The pilot scanned it, and the door beside Olus swung open. He slipped out onto the street, straightening his jacket and waving as the door closed and the shuttle lifted back into the air, likely to pick up a fare for the return trip to Baltimore. Olus watched it join the crowds above and then joined the rest of the individuals on foot.

He didn't see many off-worlders as he made his way to the opposite block and below ground into the station. A pair of Plixians, a Curlatin, and two Trovers. That was it. Foreign species struggled to deal with the experience of the city, and he couldn't blame them. A lot of native humans still felt overwhelmed, too.

He entered the large, open concourse, activating his cap as he did. He felt a bit of heat on his face as the material changed shape against it, adding subtle adjustments to his bone structure to alter his appearance. He didn't know if Thraven or Davis had put the word out about his presence on the planet, but he wasn't taking chances.

He entered the crowds, moving through them to wait at a Starbucks. The ancient corporation had been through a lot over the centuries, but it had managed to stay relevant and profitable even as alternate civilizations had opened up the galaxy to new beverages and ways of making them. He knew Zoey well enough to know she would wind up here when she arrived.

He watched the individuals pass through the station. It still amazed him that any single place could maintain its population when there were so many more worlds to live on. Nobody had to be part of a crowd. Nobody had to limit their personal space or force themselves to live a life they didn't want. It wasn't a utopia by any means, but the opportunities were there for anyone with the guts to grab them. He had seen it with other species as much as with humans. The majority of individuals liked what they knew, or at least were afraid to abandon it. Most of the ones who didn't usually ended up in the Republic or as merchant traders or otherwise employed in interstellar endeavors, traveling the stars because of their career. That's what he had done, and he had never regretted it. He never regretted the travel, at least. Sometimes the killing ate at him when he gave it the time to.

He couldn't give it that time right now. He spotted Sergeant Zoey Haeri headed toward the tables in front of the store, with Sergeant Gyo Shaw at her side. They were both dressed for business, in similar attire to his, though he doubted it was quite the same. They were both field operatives and well-trained, but they weren't assassins.

He watched them as they took one of the tables. Gyo sat. Zoey headed for the counter. Her eyes passed over him, but she didn't know who he was.

He remained seated, scanning the crowd. Zoey had finished picking up her order and returned to her seat by the time he had made the four marks who had circled back to the area a few times. He had been hoping they hadn't been followed, but he wasn't surprised. He wouldn't have waited otherwise.

He activated his TCU, tapping on his pants beneath the table. He sent a short range encrypted message using Zoey's alternate identifier, a personal code only the most trusted members of his team knew. If she was sporting a SOC anywhere on her outfit, she would catch the missive.

You brought friends. Four of them.

He waited a few seconds for the reply.

Lose them or disable them?

Olus considered. It would be tough in the crowd, but they could escape the crowd. He scanned the departure schedule.

Loop Seven, five minutes, he wrote.

Confirmed.

He waited another minute before standing and heading away, walking right past them as he did. He didn't know if they knew who he was yet, but it didn't matter. They would take care of this quietly.

He went down the steps to the platform below. It was clean and well-lit, modern and open. A few hundred people waited for the transport to arrive. He waited with them.

The transport came to a stop three minutes later. He entered after the others, remaining near the doors, and then stepping back out as they chimed to alert their closure. He saw Zoey and Gyo at the far end of the platform, stepping out as well.

The Devils Do

Thraven's four goons evacuated the transport between them.

They were further away than Olus would have liked, but it was one variable he couldn't control. He sprang forward, shouting and running toward the group as they took notice of him, reaching beneath their coats to find their sidearms.

They were all on the ground before Olus could reach them, each with a nerve dart planted at the base of their necks. Zoey and Gyo stood behind the downed group with guns in hand, smiling as Olus examined their work.

"Nice," he said. "I approve."

"Thank you, sir," Zoey said, holstering her weapon.

Gyo was making a face.

"What's wrong with you?" Olus asked.

"I bet Z two hundred that you were the old guy with the chai."

"I picked you out," Zoey said. "Who are these assholes?"

"It's a long story," Olus said.

He bent over them, going through their things. He took two of the sidearms and their holsters. He found their ID. They were NYPD.

"Cops?" Gyo said.

"He's got to be watching everybody in the OSI," Olus said.

"Who?"

"My guess is a guy named Abraham Davis. He's our target."

"What did he do?"

"Besides the fact that he's most likely one of the enemy's prime wizards? That's what we need to figure out."

"Wizard?" Zoey said. "I don't follow, sir."

"I'll explain as we move. The platform's going to start filling up again. Stay close, but not too close."

"Yes, sir."

They left the platform, ascending back to the station. Olus kept a good distance from them to minimize suspicion. He also kept his eyes out for more police. He was hard to identify with the mask, but Zoey and Gyo would be easy to spot.

He entered the auto-queue to hail a transport, waiting in line while his subordinates stayed back and out of sight. It arrived within a minute, and he kept his arm in the door, forcing it to remain open as Zoey and Gyo dashed across the distance and piled in.

"Where are you headed?" the pilot asked.

"Harlem," Olus said. "Riverbank Park."

"Yes, sir."

"The park?" Gyo said.

"For now. I need intel."

"They'll be tracing us," Zoey said.

"That's why we're going to the park. I don't want any civilians getting hurt."

"Yes, sir."

CHAPTER SEVENTEEN

"Gyo, I need to know who owns the Gilded Cafe," Olus said. "Zoey, see what you can pull up on Davis."

"Yes, sir," Zoey and Gyo replied.

They were sitting on a bench in the park, looking out at the Hudson River. A dinner cruise was floating down the waterway in front of them, the diners fully visible behind the transparent frame of the long, low boat.

"We should do that sometime," Gyo mentioned.

"Looks boring," Zoey replied.

"Focus," Olus said. He reached into his pocket, withdrawing the beacon.

"What's that?" Zoey asked.

"Tracking beacon. I lifted it from General Omsala."

"You really killed him, sir?" Gyo asked.

"Yes. He was a traitor. What do you have on the restaurant?"

Gyo looked away, putting on a pair of connected glasses and getting to the search. He looked back a few seconds later. "It's one of Pierre Gavron's."

"Interesting," Olus said. "Look deeper. See if he pulled a loan for it, or if there are any other stakeholders. The restaurant is a front."

"How do you know?"

"I've been around the universe. I know."

Gyo looked away again.

"Abraham Davis," Zoey said. "Harvard Law School. Graduated at the top of his class. He works for the Republic as a prosecuting attorney. There's a pretty long list of soldiers he's gotten court-martialed."

"What's my question?" Olus asked.

"How does a Harvard-trained lawyer wind up working as a military attorney?"

"Exactly."

"Searching."

"Do it faster. We have about three minutes before we need to move."

"That's pretty precise, sir," Gyo said.

"Better too early than too late."

"Yes, sir."

"Here you go, sir," Gyo said a minute later. "Tridium Corp has a forty percent stake in the Cafe."

"Tridium?" Zoey said. "The company that makes the Apocalypse fighter?"

"Yup. Well, not directly. I traced three shell accounts back to them."

"You traced three shells that fast?" Zoey said. "I'm impressed."

"How impressed?" Gyo asked, waggling an eyebrow.

"You know OSI regs, don't you?" Olus said.

"What are you going to do about it, sir?" Gyo said. "You aren't the Director anymore."

"I guess you're right. It isn't my problem anymore. This is. And if Tridium is involved with Thraven and the Nephilim, we're getting more screwed by the second."

"Nephilim?" Zoey said.

"Another long story, and not that important."

"I've got a business address for the cafe," Gyo said. "It's not the restaurant. Looks like an old sweatshop in Soho."

"Give it to me," Olus said.

The Devils Do

Gyo recited it. Olus committed it to memory.

"This probably won't surprise you, sir," Zoey said. "But Abraham Davis doesn't exist before he joined Harvard fifteen years ago. There are no prior education records, no voter registration, no juror selection. He has no public presence at all outside of his duties as a prosecutor for RAS."

"You're right; I'm not surprised. Anything else?"

"I checked a few of the names on the list of soldiers he sent away. Four out of four are listed as deceased."

He doubted that.

"Time to go," he said.

"Sir?" Zoey asked.

"Follow me."

They made their way across the grass toward a newer structure nearby.

"Shouldn't we be leaving, sir?" Gyo asked when they took a position in the shadows.

"I want to see who comes to check on us."

"What for? If they know what we were looking for and what we found, they're going to be waiting there for us. They don't need to-"

Olus held up his hand. A black car dropped from the sky, coming down over the lawn near the bench. Olus took one of the guns from under his jacket. "You were saying?"

"That was fast," Gyo said.

"They were probably already headed this way."

A squad of soldiers hopped out of the car, followed by another man in a dark suit.

"That's Davis," Zoey said.

Davis approached the bench, looking at it thoughtfully. Then he reached into the inside pocket of his coat, withdrawing a glove. It was metallic, with spikes on the ends. He circled the spot where they had been sitting.

"We need to get out of here," Olus said, not liking the maneuver. "That way."

Davis started reaching for the bench. Olus didn't see anything else.

He started running for the opposite side of the building, out of sight of the enemy.

He felt a cold breeze a moment later, as though something was giving chase behind them. A chill ran down his spine. He recognized the feeling of the Gift. Could it reach this far?

"Faster," he said, increasing his speed. He didn't use the added strength of his suit, not when his people couldn't do the same.

He heard movement behind them and turned to look. The soldiers were running after them, weapons drawn. Davis wasn't with them.

He pulled his sidearm, prepared to shoot back. They reached the street.

"This way," Zoey said, pointing.

They kept running, streaking across the lane ahead of oncoming traffic, the interruption giving the blacksuits momentary pause. They reached an alley and kept going, hurrying past garbage collection modules. There was an emergency door on the building to the left. Olus stopped in front of it, putting his hand on the control pad there. It didn't open.

"Frag," he said. It would only be locked from the outside.

He looked back. The soldiers were crossing the street. Zoey and Gyo had pulled their sidearms and taken defensive positions on either side of the alley.

"Cover fire," he said.

They responded dutifully, taking careful shots at the incoming soldiers, making sure not to let their fire reach the street.

He pulled an extender and stuck it to the panel, his fingers working rapidly. Where the hell was Davis? He reached the command line, entering the most common passwords. The third try opened the door.

"Form up," he shouted.

Zoey and Gyo followed behind him, bullets hitting the frame as they escaped inside.

"That wasn't normal, sir," Zoey said.

"No, it wasn't. Did you see where that bastard went?"

"Back in the car, I think," Gyo replied.

Probably to contact Thraven and see what the Gloritant wanted to

The Devils Do

do about him. They couldn't outrun someone with the Gift, not unless he could catch Davis off-guard the way he had caught Vee.

"I've got an idea," Olus said. "We need to make it back to the street."

They moved through the building, running through clean, well-lit corridors. Olus could hear the soldiers at their back, even if they managed to always stay a turn or two ahead of them. He could feel his heart pounding, his reflexes heightened by the adrenaline. He was too old for this, and at the same time, he had missed it. He drew the small knife from his pocket. Let Davis come. His aim was still good.

They made it to the front of the building at the same time a second squad of blacksuits were coming in.

"Down," Olus shouted, dropping onto his stomach as the soldiers reacted, bringing up their rifles and firing too high.

He squeezed off three quick rounds, sending them into the head of one blacksuit and the knees of another, who cried out as he fell to the ground.

At least these bad guys were human.

The other soldiers were hit in succession, Zoey and Gyo's shots almost as precise as his. Olus bounced to his feet, still running for the door.

"Go out ahead of me," he said.

They didn't question. They trusted him. They exited the building. A moment later, they froze.

Olus gripped the knife. He closed his eyes. He had told Lieutenant Cage that he wasn't a good man. His training had made him cold. Now he was going to have to prove it.

"Captain Mann," Davis shouted from outside. "Why don't you come out? Maybe I'll even let your people go."

Olus opened his eyes. He had tried to save them. Some things were too important. Some sacrifices had to be made.

He turned back the way they had come, sprinting across the floor. He reached the adjacent corridor, slamming into the other soldiers on their way to him.

He growled as he slammed the knife into the joint between the armor and the helmet of the first, wrenching it through and out, sending blood splattering everywhere. He shot the second point blank in the chest, kicked the third into the wall before shooting him in the neck, bouncing sideways off the side of the corridor and knocking the fourth with his shoulder, sending him sprawling backward. He landed in a crouch, rolling to the side and firing at the fifth, three rounds that tore into the man's gun hand and made him drop his rifle. He sprang up, leading with the knife, getting under the armor to the flesh and digging in deep. He turned back to the fourth soldier, picking up the dropped rifle and firing it into the man's helmet.

He ran past them, hearing motion at his back as he did. He turned to see all of the blacksuits moving again. Fragging Converts.

He kept going, finding a stairwell and going up. There had to be a back way out of the building. He went to the third floor, guessing at where the rear of the building was and breaking in the door of one of the apartments. A woman was sitting on a sofa, a pair of Construct goggles on her head. She turned her head and screamed at the noise, but he was already past and to her window. He looked out. He was over the street on the other side of the building. He took a few steps back, took off his jacket and held it in front of him. Then he charged forward, firing into the window, puncturing the material right before he went through it.

He fell twenty feet, locking the jacket so it spread out behind him, acting as a foil in the air. He still hit the ground hard, but it was enough to keep him from breaking anything. That didn't mean it didn't hurt. He clenched his teeth in pain at the impact before straightening, dropping the rifle, and running to the nearest pickup lane. He pulled the beacon from his pocket, along with the smallest of his tools. A car arrived, and he climbed in.

"Broadway," he said. "Move it."

The car began to lift back into the sky. Olus manipulated the beacon, reattaching the battery. The small LED on it began to blink once more.

He leaned back in his seat and told himself that Thraven wouldn't kill Zoey and Gyo for helping him escape. He was too calculating to callously cut them loose.

Not like he had just done.

He cursed and shook his head. He knew he was a bastard. But if he could get Cage what she needed and help the Council, it would be worth it.

Maybe.

CHAPTER EIGHTEEN

Olus left the beacon on the transport when he got out on Broadway. He was momentarily overwhelmed by the bright lights and massive projections, the crowds and all of the surrounding steel and glass. He had picked the most populated place in the city to disappear, knowing that Davis would follow the beacon but not expect to find him with it.

Did it even matter? If the Nephilim resorted to torture, he could make Zoey or Gyo tell him where Olus might be headed. Davis would probably be waiting for him there.

He had years of experience and plenty of skill, but none of it mattered when the enemy had a power you couldn't stand up to. He hadn't gotten the chance to look into Iti's death, but he could imagine it now. Davis somewhere nearby, pushing her transport out of control with the Gift and causing the accident.

He had been in deep before.

He was drowning now.

He made his way through the crowds. He couldn't fight Davis or any of his Converts with a pistol. He needed something more. Something bigger and better. He hurried toward Grand Central, picking the pocket of a civilian as he wandered past and syncing his identity. He put a hand over his face while the cap adjusted, changing his appearance within a few

The Devils Do

seconds as he descended into the loop.

He caught a ride back toward Soho, getting out at one of the subterranean stations that diverted into the Plixian underground, better known in the city as Little Plixar. Thousands of insectoid immigrants had found their way here over the years, their planet overpopulated and their love of digging in high demand to maintain the tunnels that helped ease the above ground congestion. Many of them were engineers. Not just diggers, but makers, inventors, and tinkerers.

There was one in particular he had come to see. One he had worked with multiple times across the years. The OSI was nothing without informants, especially in a place like New York.

He found Dilixix right where he expected her to be, at the counter of her pharmacy near the southern end of Little Plixar. The pharmacy sold Plixian meds above the table, enhancers and uppers below it, along with some other not-very-legal things. Olus had kept her from getting raided on more than one occasion in exchange for her cooperation. She was a fixture down here, and the workers had no problem telling her everything they heard on the daily. That intel went over to the OSI when it was juicy enough.

"Dilixix," he said, walking in.

She cocked her head to the side, confused. She didn't recognize him.

"Sorry," Olus said, clearing the disguise.

She clacked in response. "Captain Mann." Her face didn't carry much expression, but her antennae curled back, guarded. "Why are you here in person?"

"I need your help," he said. "More than usual."

"What is the benefit to me?"

"Payment. Whatever your price is, you'll get triple. Net thirty."

"A loan? That isn't good for business."

"Come on, Dil, we've known one another for how long? Almost twenty years?"

She clacked in acknowledgement. "For you, then. What do you need?"

"I'm going to war. I need a softsuit and heavy ordnance. I also need something sharp. Something that can get through a neck fairly easily."

Her antennae went straight up in surprise. "I can't get you a softsuit just like that, Captain. Why did you not bring your own?"

"This came up last minute. I lost two of my team tonight, Dil."

She lowered her head toward him, shaking it. "I understand." She moved to the counter, reaching into a cabinet and withdrawing a bottle. She opened it and dumped a handful of pills out. "Take two of these. Save the rest."

"What are they?"

"They will strengthen your defenses."

"Those are Plixian meds. Different chemistry."

Dilixix stared at him. "You may need them tonight. I believe I know what you are hunting."

Olus froze. "You do? How?"

"We've been watching."

"We?"

She didn't respond to the question. "I don't have a suit. Take the pills a few minutes before." She dropped them in his hand. "Come with me; we can get you weapons."

She scuttled toward the back of the shop. Olus followed her.

They passed through the rear of the pharmacy, past the shelves of inventory and out through a hidden exit in the rear. A dank, dark tunnel carried them a few hundred meters to a matching hole.

"Wait here," Dilixix said. She vanished into the hole, returning a few seconds later. "Come."

He climbed through. A second Plixian was there, a small male.

"Captain Mann," he said. "Dilixix tells me you need weapons." He waved one of his hands across the room. "Take what you need. She will cover the payment for you."

Olus felt a slight stab of guilt, knowing she would never get that payment. How many lives was he going to destroy tonight? He could only hope it would be worth it in the end. Thraven probably didn't have much use for Plixians. He would either kill them or enslave them. This had to be

The Devils Do

better.

He surveyed the room. He needed to stay fast. Anything too big would slow him down. "Where did you get all of this?" he asked. "And how did you get it through customs?"

"You're in intelligence," the male replied. "You should know."

Olus nodded. Anyone could be bought. "I need something armor-piercing. Something violent and messy." He looked back at the Plixian. "Something illegal."

"That will cost."

"The Republic can afford it."

"He lost two team members, Xalix," Dilixix said.

The male's antennae twitched. He moved over to a shelf and pushed it aside, revealing a second shelf behind it.

"The special inventory," he said, taking a case from it.

He brought it to the counter and placed it down, unlocking the case. Inside was a pistol design Olus had never seen, with three detached grips arranged on the side, sized for different species. Xalix lifted the pistol out with the Terran grip, snapping the parts together. He removed a shelf in the case. There were four magazines beneath, and he showed Olus how to reload the pistol, snapping the cartridge into the side of the weapon, perpendicular to the grip.

"There are three penetration settings," he said, showing it to Olus. "All of them are violent and messy. The first will expand near the surface and tear into muscle. The second will explode internally, and destroy the interior. The third will punch all the way through a battlesuit, and leave a hole the size of your fist behind."

"The RAS doesn't have anything like this," Olus said.

"You said you wanted something illegal. This is a miniaturized electromagnetic launcher with specially designed ammunition. It will calibrate the distance to the target, and sensors will detect the surface material and body composition and adjust velocity accordingly. It is the weapon of a killer. I am giving it to you because you lost soldiers, and I am a loyal servant of the Republic." He clacked in amusement. "And because you can pay for it."

Olus didn't want to know how many of these weapons might be out there. At least he was fairly confident it hadn't been designed for the Nephilim.

"Thanks," he said. "Do you have anything sharp?"

Xalix retrieved a sheath from the same shelf. "Standard issue combat knife. This one is made of rhodrinium."

He slid the blade out slightly, and then handed it to Olus.

"It'll do," Olus said. "I don't suppose you have a softsuit, by any chance?"

"No, Captain. Such armor is difficult to move, since it is fitted to the wearer and dependent on species."

"Fair enough." He turned to Dilixix. "Send the bill to my office, the usual method."

"Of course, Captain."

Olus removed the magazine from the pistol so that he could fit it into the holster beneath his jacket. The weapon was a marvel of engineering. A terrifying marvel. He took the rest of the magazines and shoved them in the other holster. Then he strapped the combat knife around his calf beneath his pants.

"You can head out this way," Xalix said, pointing him toward the front of his shop.

"Thank you," Olus said. "Both of you. The Republic owes you."

"Quite a bit," Dilixix said.

Olus left them there, passing out the front and through a small Plixian eatery.

He had a mission to complete.

The Devils Do

CHAPTER NINETEEN

THE TRANSPORT DROPPED HIM TWO blocks from the address Gyo had provided. It was in an older part of the city, a relative slum, where the trash wasn't picked up daily, and there wasn't an army of bots keeping everything clean and fresh. It was a depressed area. Quieter than most. Even the skies were mostly clear of traffic.

It was the kind of place where he could kill and nobody would notice.

He stayed in the shadows, finding a back route toward the older building and sticking to it, keeping his eyes out for any sign of sentries along the streets. There was nothing out of the ordinary. No guards. No cameras. No drones.

Then again, if the building was home to a Venerant, they didn't need to worry about shit like that.

He crossed the block, coming up to the side of the building and double-checking the address. This was supposed to be the place. A long, five-story cement block with opaque windows and a ramp leading down into an underground garage. The spaces around it looked vacant.

He drew the pistol from his holster and snapped a magazine into it. He scanned the building for a door, and briefly considered going in through the garage. He was done being subtle. He dug the pills Dilixix had given him out of his pocket. She said they would strengthen his defenses. She seemed to know about Davis. How? Why?

It didn't matter right now. He tossed the pills into his mouth, swallowing them dry. He remained hidden for a minute, a sudden feeling of nausea working its way up. He fought against it. This was supposed to help?

He crossed to the front of the building and tried the door. It was open. He went in, through a second door and into a small, empty lobby. There was a directory kiosk on the left. He walked over to it.

A door opened behind him.

"Captain Mann."

He turned slowly, clutching the gun. The man in the doorway was tall and muscular. Not Davis, though. A regular soldier.

"Nephilim?" Olus asked.

The man smiled. It continued to grow as it spread, his body changing. "Yes," he replied roughly.

Olus felt for the toggle on the gun. He flipped it to two.

"Bad night to be a Nephilim," he said, fighting back the sudden fear. What the frag was this?

The Goreshin threw itself at him. He raised the gun and pulled the trigger.

The bullet was nearly invisible, firing almost silently from the weapon and piercing the creature's skull. Olus fell to the side, sliding on the floor and coming up on a knee as the bullet detonated, causing the enemy to cry out and then flop to the ground.

Olus stood and stared at the creature. "Damned demon."

He knew the Converts needed to be decapitated. He would have done the same to this thing, but there was no time. He went back the way it had come. He could hear noises coming from inside now.

He had upset the monster's friends.

Good.

He paused for a moment to button his jacket. Then he reached down, grabbing the knife with his free hand and pulling it from its sheath. He had always been better in close quarters than the open field. He

The Devils Do

wondered if these things, whatever the frag they were, could say the same?

He was going to find out.

He moved down the hallway. He could hear the movement around him. It seemed like it was coming from everywhere at one time.

His eyes landed on a stairwell a few meters away, and he pointed the gun at it, switching the toggle to three as something appeared behind it. He fired, the bullet whipping from the weapon and through the door, into whatever was behind it. Another cry of pain and the creature fell inward toward him, wounded but still alive.

A second vaulted over the first. Olus crouched, bouncing sideways as it tried to grab him with sharp claws, trailing with the knife and cutting into its hand. He shifted his weight, rolling across the wall, ducking as it turned, flipping the toggle on the gun to one and shooting point-blank. The bullet still sunk in deep at that range, and when it detonated the Goreshin fell limp.

He brought the knife down on its neck, chopping hard, the ultra-sharp blade slipping right through. He looked back toward the stairwell. The first creature was up again, advancing toward him. He toggled to two and fired, hitting it in the head. Again, the shell exploded, sending fragments of metal throughout its brain. It fell and didn't move.

He ran past it, onto the stairs, ducking as bullets began pinging off the metal around him, a few of the rounds edging against his hardened suit. He went down a flight, getting out of the line of fire, feeling himself becoming angrier, his heart pumping, his adrenaline flowing. He clenched his teeth, steeling himself, checking the rounds he had left in the current magazine. Four. He didn't have enough to waste any of them.

He went ahead, turning the corner, finding the targets and shooting in rapid-fire, faster than he would have believed. Pop. Pop. Pop. The bullets tore into their chests and exploded, nearly ripping them apart. He bounced up the steps in one jump, landing beside the enemies and digging in with the knife, not taking chances that they weren't Converts.

He continued up, reaching the next flight. The stairwell door opened. Olus slammed his shoulder into the soldier there, pinning him to the wall and bringing the knife up and across his throat, turning and shooting the second soldier there, switching the toggle to one. He moved past them, onto the second floor, not sure exactly where he was going. If he had to clear the entire building, he would. He was furious, his whole body burning with energy. It had to be the pills Dilixix had given him. How long would it last?

He pulled the magazine from the gun, dropping it and replacing it with a fresh one. He moved down the hallway. He had to find Davis if he was here. He had to try to hit him while the pills were active.

He moved through the building, the muscle memory of his past career returning with a vengeance. He heard movement to his left around the corner, and he set the toggle on the gun to three, aiming it at the wall and firing. The round went right through, digging into whatever was on the other side and causing it to cry out. Olus reached it, kneeling over it and digging his blade through its neck before moving on.

He cleared the second floor. It was mostly small rooms that had once been offices but had been converted to sleeping spaces, with small mattresses and blankets and stand-alone clothes lockers. He could feel the effects of the meds beginning to wane by the time he did. He had to hurry.

He skipped the other floors, heading to the top. He could work his way down from there. He needed to find Davis, or at least find a terminal to break. He needed to finish this quickly.

He emerged onto the top floor, out into a more open penthouse, with a cathedral ceiling and full length glass. Desks were organized along the floor, each of them with a terminal resting on it. A large bank of servers sat against the wall. It reminded Olus of the main working floor of the OSI.

Was that what this was? Thraven's version of the intelligence agency?

There was nobody up here, but there was a desk at the front of the room projecting a pale blue light into the air above it. A small box sat beside the projection.

Olus approached it, the details of the box becoming clearer as he got closer. It was a computer mainframe, Republic issue.

He reached the desk, picking it up. He found the serial number on the side. It was the mainframe Cage had captured on Gradin and brought onto the Nova.

Davis had left it there for him to find.

The projection beside him changed. A smaller version of Davis was standing there, a satisfied smirk on his face.

"Captain Mann," he said. "My apologies that I couldn't be there in person. I had a party to attend at the museum. Some of the Council members are going to be there. Or had you not heard? Yes, Captain, that is General Kett's mainframe, and yes, I am giving it to you. I don't need it anymore. My team, or should I say, your team, has finished helping me break the algorithm used to hide the contents. No, not the two you so kindly abandoned to save your skin, but members of the OSI all the same. Don't worry about Haeri and Shaw. They didn't feel any pain. Of course, their deaths are on you in more ways than one. Thank you for making it so easy for us to turn the Republic, and now your office, against you."

The recording ended, returning the projection to a blue light. Olus shook beneath his anger. Damn Davis. Damn Thraven. Son of a bitch. He picked up the mainframe, pulling the wire from his jacket and connecting it, activating the command line. It was open, wide open. There was hardly anything on it. A guidance system for a starship, with numeric starmap coordinates. He took a snapshot of them to send them to Ruby. Thraven knew where Kett was hiding. For how long?

He detached the wire from the mainframe and reconnected it to the terminal. It had Galnet access, and he used it to search for Davis' reference to the museum. There was a party tonight at the Museum of Natural History. A new exhibit on prehistoric creatures from around the Republic's worlds. Eight members of the Council were going to be there to represent the Government. He cursed when he discovered which eight.

Davis hadn't mentioned it by accident. He was toying with him. Mocking him.

Checkmate.

Frag.

He stayed on the Galnet, entering Ruby's private identifier and sending her the shot of the coordinates. The public net was barely secure, but he was out of time. He had to get to the Museum.

He abandoned the area, his body shaking as it came down from the adrenaline and drug-induced high. He had to get to the Museum. He had to stop Davis, somehow.

The fate of the whole Republic might depend on it.

CHAPTER TWENTY

GLORITANT THRAVEN WATCHED AS NOVIANT Soto held out her hand, trying to use the Gift to lift a ten-kilogram weight from a nearby table. He could sense the Gift within her, churning under her skin and within her blood, the power of it bursting out from her hand and striking the weight.

It didn't lift from the table. Instead, it began to melt.

Interesting.

"I said to lift it," he said.

"I'm trying," she replied. "Frag."

She was naked, and still covered in the remaining blood of the Font, which he had allowed her to bathe in and drink from for nearly an entire minute. She was alive with the Gift. Thick with it. Her strength was decent. Not impressive like Trinity or Abigail Cage, but acceptable.

What she lacked was control.

"Not everything needs to be destroyed," he said. "Even when you are angry. Even when you hate. Sometimes, destruction is too much of a kindness."

She looked back at him over her shoulder. "When do I get the other half?" she asked.

"When you learn to control the Gift."

"What if I can't?"

"Then you will go mad, and either become a Convert or die. That is the way of things. The Father does not tolerate the weak."

"You're saying if I can't lift the thing instead of melting it, I'm weak?"

"Yes."

She turned back to it, trying again. This time, she knocked over the table the weight was resting on, sending it across the room and into the wall.

"Frag!" she shouted again. She lowered her hands and turned all the way around, walking over to him. "You keep referring to the Father. Who is he?"

"Lucifer," he replied. "The Morningstar. He uncovered the truth of the Seraphim's enslavement before the Blood of Life drove him mad."

"If the Gift made him crazy, does that mean he was weak?"

Thraven stared at her. She started to choke.

"Do not question the strength of the Father. He was the only one who had the courage to question the Shard and to recognize the truth. He was the one who developed the Serum that made his blood fully ours. Too late to save himself, but not to save all of his kind."

"I. I'm sorry."

He let go.

"Is he still alive?"

Thraven nodded. "In a sense."

"The Gift will make me immortal?"

"If you learn to control it. If you earn the Serum."

"You were going to give it to Lieutenant Cage, weren't you? The Serum?"

"She has control over the Gift. Control that few master on their own. Yes. Try again. Control your anger. Control your fury."

"When do I get some clothes?"

"What do you need them for? I told you, I have no interest in your flesh. Neither does the Immolent. Are you ashamed of what you are? It is the One who made you to feel ashamed."

"I thought he was dead?"

The Devils Do

"You are of his seed. You carry his guilt."

"You wear clothes."

"Cloth is not equivalent to shame. Consider its purpose. Consider your purpose. Stop talking." He pointed to the table and weight sitting on the floor.

She left him again, returning to her task. She tried to lift the table now, and it rocked on the ground before settling again.

"At least I didn't blow it up that time," she said.

He didn't reply. The door to the chamber opened, and Honorant Piselle entered. She glanced over at Airi, barely noticing the other woman's nude and bloody state.

"Gloritant," she said, her voice quivering as she saluted him. She was holding a communicator. "Evolent Ruche."

"Open the link," he said.

She did. The projector turned on, placing the Evolent in the room ahead of Thraven.

"Gloritant," Ruche said, kneeling in front of him.

"Evolent," Thraven replied. "Stand."

Ruche stood. His eyes drifted over to Airi. "A new recruit, Gloritant?" he said. "She's attractive."

The table shot forward, slamming into the wall again, hard enough that it crumpled against it.

"And angry," Ruche said. "Where did you find her, your Eminence?"

"She was one of Captain Mann's renovation projects, along with Lieutenant Cage."

"A traitor?"

"Do you have something to report?" Thraven asked, ignoring the comment. It was none of the Evolent's concern.

"Yes, Gloritant. The Breakers General Omsala provided have finally cracked the algorithm on the mainframe. We have the coordinates to what we believe to be General Kett's location in the Bain System."

"The Bain System?" Thraven replied. "Interesting."

The system was on the bleeding edge of the galaxy, so close to the

Extant he could hardly believe it. How did the Terran saying go? Keep your friends close, and your enemies closer. General Kett had taken the statement literally.

"Honorant Piselle," Thraven said.

"Yes, Gloritant."

"Contact Honorant Ward. If any more of the ships have been completed, I want them launched and on their way here immediately."

"Yes, Gloritant."

Piselle placed the communicator on the ground, turned on her heel, and left.

"You're going to attack, your Eminence?"

"Of course, I'm going to attack. Kett escaped from me twice already. He won't escape again. He and his army will be reduced to nothing but corpses by this time tomorrow."

"Do you think the Focus is with him?"

"No. Which is why we can't simply bombard whichever rock he is hiding under from orbit. I need them intact." He paused, considering. "What about the Council?"

"Everything is going according to plan, Gloritant," Ruche replied. "I'm on my way to the museum now. Our people report that all of the invited Council members have arrived." He smiled. "Oh, and Olus Mann is here on Earth."

"What?"

"He killed General Omsala and left a dagger in Venerant Elivee's eye. Then he used the data on his communicator to locate our local operation with the help of some of his team at the OSI. I give him credit for efficiency."

Thraven felt his anger flaring, along with a measure of respect. Taking the Venerant by surprise and disabling her would have been no easy feat, but also not beyond the Captain's skill. "Where is he now?"

"Likely on his way to the offices. I nearly had him earlier, but he sacrificed his people to escape." Ruche smirked. "I didn't expect the Captain to be so cold."

That was because he didn't know Killshot that well. Thraven did.

The Devils Do

He had been following him for years. How else could he use him so effectively? They were so alike in so many ways.

"Did you eliminate the data there?"

"It has been handled, your Eminence. I left three squads of Children and Converts there to greet him."

"They're going to die," Thraven said.

"I've anticipated that as well. I also left him the mainframe, with the coordinates to Kett's location. If he passes them to Cage, she may decide to try to help the General."

Thraven smiled, the hint of a laugh escaping before he stifled it. "You've done well, Evolent. Very well. It will be remembered."

"Thank you, Gloritant. All I do, I do for the glory of the Nephilim, in anticipation of the Great Return."

"Finish your work with the Council, and then -"

Thraven paused as Honorant Piselle returned.

"My apologies for the interruption, Gloritant," she said. "We've received a comm from Machina Four."

"This had better be important," Thraven said.

"I believe it is, your Eminence."

She placed another communicator on the floor beside Evolent Ruche. It turned on, and a fat Skink appeared in front of him.

"Thraven," Gilliam said.

"That's General Thraven," Ruche said. "Show some respect."

Gilliam glanced at the other projection. "Sorry. General Thraven. I just found out, Sam and his crew are dead."

"How?"

"An old contact showed up with some other individuals a few hours ago. I didn't think much of it at the time, but then I saw one of Sam's transports hop up the ravine and land next to their ship. I thought it was strange, so I sent Melchor down to check it out. He came back and told me they were all dead; their heads cut clean off their bodies. Sounds fragging sick to me." He shook his head. "I knew that woman was some kind of demon when I saw her."

"Woman?" Thraven said.

"About this high. She was wearing a softsuit, and she had a peach fuzz of silvery hair. It looks almost like it's made of metal. I think she's in charge. Like a damned Demon Queen."

"Cage," Ruche said.

"On Machina Four," Thraven said. "Why there, Abigail?"

"That's not all, Thr- General. He said they found the stash under the floor. You know, the one the Republic isn't supposed to know about? You paid me good money to keep quiet, and I haven't said a thing. They're loading everything onto their ship. Even those old shitbucket Devils that got dropped there. That had to be what? Fifteen years ago? They have a Gant fixing them, and a pair of pilots taking them into orbit. I guess they must have another ship up there?"

The Brimstone. Of course. It must have been damaged in their escape, and Machina Four was a good place to pause to repair and reload. If he had cared enough to consider it, he might have warned the Children that she could be coming their way.

It seemed they had found out, regardless. But what had brought Cage to them? What had caused Sam and the others to reveal themselves? He supposed he would never know.

It didn't matter. A few old starfighters and some guns weren't going to help her. Not when he was on the cusp of destroying General Kett and his rebels before they could mount an offensive against him. Even so, she was a variable he couldn't predict and couldn't control. He hadn't spent years in preparation for the harvest to have it disrupted by her again.

"Fifty million for each member of her entourage that is disposed of," he said. "One hundred million if anyone somehow manages to capture or kill her. Ten million to you for each kill, in payment for spreading the word."

Gilliam's small eyes seemed to glow in response, and he brought his hands up and rubbed them together. "It will be done, Gloritant."

"A word of caution, Gilliam. Make sure you remove her head."

"Yes, sir."

Gilliam closed the link, his projection vanishing.

"You should have left her in Hell, your Eminence," Ruche said.

The Devils Do

"The Gift burns fiercely within her," Thraven replied. "She will be dealt with one way or another. Either she will prostrate herself before me, she will go mad, or she will be killed. A suitable outcome whichever way it ends."

"You aren't concerned?"

"No."

"Then why?"

"Because there is no downside. And on the off-chance the individuals of Steel Town can kill her?" He paused. It was doubtful, but there was no risk in it. "Go now. Take care of the Council. Let me worry about Cage. When your business is done, we can begin preparing to mobilize our forces. We'll take Earth without a single ship. Without a single bullet."

"Yes, Gloritant," Ruche said, disconnecting his link, his projection fading away.

Thraven turned away from the communicators on the floor, to where Noviant Soto was standing. She was facing him, both the table and the weight floating in the air, orbiting around her.

"I think I'm starting to get the hang of this," she said.

CHAPTER TWENTY-ONE

"THIS ONE IS SHOT, QUEENIE," Gant said, poking his head up from the rear of the starfighter. "Dead on arrival."

"Then don't waste any more time on it," Abbey replied. "We got four of them out."

She scanned the underground warehouse where they had discovered the cache. Five hours and a number of trips later, the space was nearly empty, save for the single Devil, a few random crates, and the dead, smelly monster in the corner.

"Pik should be almost ready to go, too," she added.

"I'm eager to get the hell out of here," Gant said, hopping down from the fighter. "Nobody has said anything to us about taking the equipment out of here, and I don't like that."

"Jester said it's standard operating procedure for the locals to ignore pretty much everything. Curiosity gets you killed."

"Curiosity killed the Gant," Bastion said, coming down the ramp. "Get it? The purring. The Gant, instead of the cat?"

"There's no part of you that's funny," Gant said.

"Especially if you have to explain it," Abbey said.

"Really? Because I crack myself up."

"I wish you would."

The Devils Do

"Is she ready for me?" Bastion pointed at the Devil.

"That one isn't coming along," Abbey said. "Gant said it's too beat up to fly."

"Roger that," Bastion said. "I'll help Jester load the last of the crates into the hopper then. Where's home once the big guy is out of surgery?"

"The little guy now," Gant said. "Dak is much bigger."

"Anywhere but here. Ruby gave Olus twenty-four hours to see if he could find the mainframe."

"You haven't told Jequn what you're planning?"

"I don't intend to."

"She'll figure it out sooner or later. What if she has a fit?"

"Since when do I care?" Abbey asked. "We can lock her down somewhere if we have to."

"You're a meanie, Queenie." Bastion smiled.

"Gant's right, you aren't funny."

"You two just have no sense of humor. That's all."

Bastion headed over to one of the remaining crates, lifting it easily with the help of his lightsuit. Benhil was coming down the ramp with Jequn behind him.

"I'm going to check in on Pik," Abbey said. "Keep them in line for me, will you?"

"Aye, Queenie," Gant said. "We should have everything packed and ready by the time you get back."

Abbey nodded, turning and ascending the ramp out into the warehouse, threading back into the factory and out to the street. She ignored the dead Goreshin as she passed, crossing the open space, out through the gate and into the town. The area had been quiet the entire time they had been there. Were they afraid, or just actively trying to stay out of their business?

She passed a few of the residents on the way back to Phlenel. They kept their heads down as she went by, reminding her of the other inmates on Level Twenty and the way they had treated her. Fear then? She was okay with that.

She reached the storefront, eager to get off Machina Four, and at the same time nervous about meeting with the Hurshin again. Phlenel had said she was going to process Abbey's form, to estimate how she would change and match that visage. What would she find inside? What was she going to become? A part of her wanted to know. A much larger part didn't.

She stopped in front of the sealed door. She could hear the camera moving above her.

"You will enter," the voice said.

The door unlocked.

Abbey slipped inside. The door closed again behind her. She felt her heart start to pound as Phlenel's bot appeared in the doorway. It didn't speak, simply turning and walking back, suggesting she follow it.

She did, trailing it to where she had left Pik.

He smiled when he saw her. "Hey, Queenie," he said, waving with his new hand. "Check it out. It's fragging fantastic."

He wiggled the thick, metal fingers, and turned his wrist. Then he picked up a fragile looking glass beside him.

"I only broke four of these getting the hang of it," he said, putting it back down. "Watch this." He opened the hand, spreading the fingers wide. The tips hinged back, and three-inch blades popped out. "I'm like you now." He laughed. The blades retracted and the fingertips closed. "Fragging nice."

"Where's Phlenel?" Abbey said.

"I will be there in a minute," the bot said. "I'm cleaning up."

"She didn't change shape or anything, did she?" Abbey asked.

"I dunno. I only woke up a few minutes ago. She wasn't in here. Gerald was helping me with the hand."

"Gerald?" Abbey said.

"That's what I'm calling it. Phlenel said it doesn't have a name."

"Why Gerald?"

"Why not?"

Abbey shrugged. "I thought you might have a reason."

"I think I killed a guy named Gerald once," Pik said. "Maybe that's where I got it."

The Devils Do

"How many individuals have you killed?" Abbey asked.

She knew it had to be more than one. Other comments he had made led her to believe it was a lot more than one.

"You're asking me why I was in Hell?" Pik said. He smiled. "I'm innocent. I never hurt anybody."

Abbey rolled her eyes, and he laughed.

"Captain Mann didn't tell you?"

"He didn't get around to it."

"You heard of the New London massacre?"

Abbey raised her eyebrow.

"I can see you have," he said. "Yeah, that was me."

Over one hundred innocent civilians gunned down in a rampage. Abbey felt cold. Was that why Olus hadn't told her about Pik's history?

"Why did you do it?"

"The Republic had me on one of their Death Squads. You know, the ones they claim don't exist? They used to send us to Republic planets near the Fringe. We'd go in late at night and make some trouble, and then they would blame it on the Outworlds. I shit you not, Queenie. The Republic had us kill our own. Not just soldiers. Innocents, too. My commander used to say they had to keep the tension up, keep the media interested, keep the money flowing into the military. There was always a part of me that knew it was wrong, but you know how they treat grunts. Or maybe you don't. They broke us. They wiped our minds. They made us into heartless machines. We only heard one voice. The voice of our commander. Sergeant Bones. He was a Terran. Meanest frag I've ever met. I think they pulled him out of Hell to lead the Squad."

His eyes grew distant. He stopped talking.

"Anyway," he said, breaking out of it. "I was on Terra Two on leave, just hanging out, taking in the nightlife there. Something happened to my brain. I cracked. I lost it. I don't know. It's like there was a glitch in their programming. All I heard was Bones' voice screaming at me. 'Don't stand there like a fragging baby, Corporal Pik. These fraggers want to take away the security of the Republic. They want to put the life of everyone you care about in danger. You shoot them, and you do it now!'"

He looked over at her. He had tears in his eyes.

"So I did. I was in Hell for almost a year before I started to regret it. I don't know how Captain Mann knew about that. I don't think he would have let me out if he thought I would crash like that again."

Abbey stared at him in shock. She had heard rumors of the Death Squads, but they had never been more than that. Could the Republic do something like that?

"I'm sorry," she said. "It's possible Thraven was behind the Squads. Keeping tensions between the Outworlds and the Republic certainly benefitted him."

"Does it matter?" Pik asked. "I killed one hundred twenty six people in New London. I killed over a thousand in those raids. I'm a killer, Queenie. That's all I'm good for. That's all I am."

"Bullshit," Abbey said. "No, it doesn't matter whether Thraven's goons assembled the Squads or not. What does matter is that you have remorse. That you give a shit about what you did. You're here now. You're a Reject. You're one of mine. We protect innocents."

"You were going to let me kill Mars Eagan."

Abbey blanched. "I know. I've made a few mistakes, too. I should never have let you take the weight of that decision for me. If I had to do it again, I can't say I wouldn't make the same call, but I would do it myself. It would be my burden to bear."

"It's okay, Queenie. You're doing the best you can with a shitty situation."

"So are you."

"Affirmative."

There was movement at the back of the room. Pik glanced over, his expression changing. Abbey tried to read it, finding it difficult to translate. Was it fear? Disgust? Interest? She knew she would have to look for herself. She had to stop being such a baby. The Gift was already inside of her. It was already changing her. Seeing what she might become wasn't going to stop that. Nothing could, except perhaps getting her hands on the other half.

Maybe she could on Kell.

She turned slowly, ready to accept whatever she saw. It was only the Hurshin's guess, anyway. That didn't mean Phlenel was right.

She was bigger than before, nearly half a meter taller. Her head was larger, with ridges extending from her forehead in twin points like a pair of horns. There were other ridges all along her body, similar to the ones on the Nephilim in the warehouse. Her hands were both claws, her feet the same. Her breasts were modest to begin with, but on the Hurshin they were almost gone. A long tail with a spike at the end swished back and forth behind her.

"You have a tail," Pik said. "That's so fragging cool."

"It is not a convenient form," Phlenel said, moving the fingers. "There is no precision with these."

Her voice was muffled when she spoke. Abbey realized it was because she had fangs.

"That is not cool," Abbey said. "Not cool at all."

"Aww, come on, Queenie. You look like you could stomp me like that."

"That isn't human," she said. "I want to stay human."

She would find the other half of the Gift. She would stop the change. Somehow.

"The augmentation is complete," Phlenel said. "The Trover requested the blade mechanism. It is an extra five thousand."

Abbey was glad to have a reason to take her eyes off Phlenel. She didn't want to see herself like that. Ever. She glared at Pik. "Five thousand?"

Pik held up the hand, extending the blades again. "But it's so cool."

She pulled the payment card from her pocket and let the bot scan it.

"You're one thousand short," Phlenel said.

"Damn it, Pik," Abbey said. "I can barter. That's all the money I have."

Phlenel's body lit up like lightning in a bottle.

"What do you have?" she asked. Then she paused. "One moment."

A projection appeared in the room, provided by the bot's left eye.

Someone was at her door. Abbey recognized them as one of Gilliam's lackeys.

"What is it?" the bot said, the voice coming out of the speaker at the front.

"I wanted to let you know. There's a bounty on the newcomers. The bitch in the armor and her friends. Fifty million for them, one hundred for her. Dead or alive. We're splitting into shares if you help out."

Phlenel didn't have eyes, but Abbey could still sense the Hurshin observing her.

"What the frag?" Pik said.

"My sentiment exactly," Abbey replied.

"There's a group headed down to Sam's factory if you want in."

Abbey stared at Phlenel. Pik stood up, covering the bot.

"Go away," the bot said.

Gilliam's goon hurried away from the door.

"You're safe in here," Phlenel said. "You will remain."

"Thanks, but my team is out there," Abbey replied. "I can't stay."

"Then I will help you."

"Why would you do that?"

The bot began playing back part of her conversation with Pik. The part where she told him he wasn't just a killer.

"Most go to far places to escape their demons," Phlenel said. "Perhaps I was waiting for a demon to find me."

Abbey wasn't sure what that meant, but she wasn't about to argue. Not with a lynch mob headed for the rest of the Rejects.

"Can you fight?" she asked. She didn't know enough about Hursans to know what they were capable of.

"Watch me," Phlenel replied.

Two compartments opened up on the sides of the bot, and a pair of guns emerged. The bot took them in its hands.

"Follow me," she said.

The bot led them out. The door opened ahead of them, and they stepped out into the street. There were fifty or so residents of Steel Town nearby, funneling toward the larger group that was on its way to the warehouse.

"There she is," someone shouted, drawing the group's attention their way.

Abbey found the Uin, picking it out of a tightpack and snapping it open. She resisted the urge to call on the Gift, though she could feel it responding to the danger. She wasn't going to use it unless she had to.

"Gant," she said.

"What's wrong, Queenie?" Gant replied.

"We have a situation."

CHAPTER TWENTY-TWO

"Shit, shit, shit, shit, shit," Bastion said, looking out across Steel Town from the rooftop.

"You can say that again," Benhil said beside him.

"Shit."

He backed away from the roof, running toward the stairs. "Gant, there are at least five hundred assholes coming this way."

"Roger," Gant replied. "I'm closing the gates."

"That ought to hold them for at least two minutes."

"Every second counts."

"What the frag are we going to do?"

"Ruby," Gant said. He waited a few seconds. "Ruby? Come in."

"Sorry, but your little sex synth isn't going to help you," Gilliam said over the comm.

"Gilliam, you fat fragging toad, what the hell did you do?" Benhil said.

"It ain't personal. The General's offered me ten million for each of you that dies, and I don't even have to be the one to do it. Don't worry about the synth; I'm not going to hurt her. At least, not in any way she won't like."

"The General?" Bastion said.

The Devils Do

"Fragging Thraven," Gant replied.

"I'm ready for a few more shits," Benhil said.

Bastion heard gunfire in the distance. Queenie.

"Just so you know," Gant said to Gilliam. "Whether I die or not, I'm going to kill you first."

The way the Gant said it gave Bastion a chill. He needed to be more careful with his teasing.

"We. We'll see about that," Gilliam said, clearly frightened by the threat.

"Nerd," Gant said. "Take a look in that last round of crates and see if there's anything we can use."

"Aye, sir," Erlan replied.

Bastion reached the warehouse floor. Gant was running back in from the outside near the gate. The hopper was resting on the ground, the back hatch open. He could see Erlan inside, prying open the containers.

"Got some grenades, sir," Erlan shouted.

"Bring them out," Bastion said.

He heard shouting from the gates. Then he heard a motor. Then he heard something crash into them.

"They're trying to ram their way through," Jequn said, appearing on top of the shuttle, looking out.

"Are there any launchers for those grenades?" Bastion asked.

"No, sir," Erlan replied, dropping the container at the base of the shuttle.

Bastion leaned in, picking two of them up. Fragmentation grenades. Cheap shit, but volatile cheap shit. "Jester, grab a few and help me make some noise."

"Roger," Jester said, dipping into the crate.

Gant caught up to them. "That isn't going to be enough."

"It's a start," Bastion said. "It might scare them."

Another crash, this one was different.

"Gate's down," Jequn said.

"Take this," Benhil said, tossing his rifle up to her.

She caught it, vanishing over the edge of the hopper. A moment later a shot rang out. Then another. Then another.

Bastion looked past the transport. The vehicle that had smashed the gate was veering off to the side and slowing to a stop, its driver dead. Jequn was a good shot.

"Fire in the hole," Bastion yelled, tapping the top of one of the grenades to activate it and hurling it from his position. It landed a hundred meters away, exploding ahead of the incoming mob and slowing their approach. Bullets started pinging off the hopper, and he ducked back behind it.

"Not enough," Benhil said.

"Not nearly," Bastion agreed. "Thanks for bringing us here, by the way. It's a lovely city, except for the fact that it's filled with shitbags who want to kill us."

"How was I supposed to know Thraven owned Steel Town?"

"I'm getting the distinct impression Thraven owns everything."

"I found some rifles," Erlan said.

Bastion looked. The pilot was holding one of them up. It was an older model, but he would take what he could get. "Ammo?"

Erlan reached into the container, grabbed a magazine, and slapped it in. Then he threw it to Bastion.

"Fire in the hole," Benhil said, tossing another grenade out. Screams followed as it exploded ahead of the targets outside.

Erlan threw Benhil a rifle, and then assembled another and left it on top of the hopper for Jequn.

Bastion looked around. Where the frag was Gant?

"Abandoning ship, freak-monkey?" he asked, getting annoyed that the Gant was missing, and then immediately regretting his choice of words. Hadn't he just told himself to be more careful?

"I'll let it slide due to the heat of battle," Gant said. "I'm downstairs. Count to sixty and then join me there."

"What for?"

"Just do it, Imp."

Jequn's head appeared over the hopper. "There are more coming. It seems like half the damn city. They're moving mining vehicles ahead for cover."

Armored mining vehicles. Frag.

"Keep shooting," Bastion said, counting the seconds in his head. What was Gant doing?

He leaned out past the ship, getting a look at the enemy force. A lot of them were backing up, staying away while the second round moved into position with the armored craft. They were regular folk, not soldiers, even if most of them were armed. The things individuals would do for a little bit of money. What the hell were they even going to spend it on around here?

"Nerd," Gant said. "Get the hopper ready to go. I want everyone inside in fifteen."

"Aye, sir," Erlan said. He immediately pounded on the top of the ship. "Cherub, we're bugging out in fifteen."

"Imp, did you forget how to count?" Gant said. "I'm up to sixty-three."

He was only on fifty-eight. Damn it. He turned and sprinted down the ramp into the underground storage space. He didn't see Gant right away.

"Where are you?"

"The Devil."

Bastion looked over at the starfighter. Gant was on one of the wings, doing something to the mechanicals there.

"I thought you said that thing wouldn't fly?"

"I never said it wouldn't fly. I said it was shot."

"What the hell does shot mean, then?"

"It isn't combat ready."

"So what are we going to use it for?"

"Combat."

Bastion reached the fighter. "No offense, but what are you barking about?"

The canopy over the cockpit slid back. Gant closed the panel on the wing and climbed in. "I think I fixed one of the pulse cannons, and I believe we have half power to the main thrusters. It's going to be like trying to redirect a starship by bouncing off the interior walls, but you think you're a good pilot."

"I know I'm a good pilot," Bastion said, climbing in. "Move aside."

"It's a single-seater," Gant said. "And the hopper is already leaving."

"What?"

Gant leaned forward to let Bastion slide into the pilot's seat. Then he sat back on his lap.

"Try not to get too excited," Gant said.

"Frag you," Bastion replied. "Queenie never hears about this; you got me?"

Gant chittered in reply. "Let's go."

Bastion took the stick with his right hand, using his left hand to work the secondary controls. He tapped a few buttons, and the canopy closed, a HUD appearing against it. He tapped a few more and then slid his fingers forward, adjusting thrust. The fighter began to slide forward on its skids.

"I thought you said half power?" Bastion said. "We'll be lucky if we can get this bitch off the ground."

"I thought you were a good pilot?"

Bastion manipulated the controls, trying to find a balance between thrust and anti-gravity. Neither of the systems was working optimally, probably because the reactor behind them wasn't putting out max power.

"We might need to lose a few kilos," he said suggestively.

"You're free to stay behind. Nerd, what's your status?"

"We're up and away, sir. It's a fragging mess on the ground. There have to be two thousand tangos down there. Maybe more."

"Do you see Queenie and Okay?"

"Aye, sir. It looks like she's holding court in the center of town, but I think she could use some backup."

"We'll be on our way as soon as I can get this fragger going," Bastion said.

He fiddled with the controls a little more. The Devil jerked forward, the power suddenly making it to the thrusters that hadn't been there moments before. Gant was shoved back into him, and he was shoved back into his seat as the fighter slid up the ramp and out into the warehouse, the momentum putting them into the air. He held the stick, pointing it sharply at the ground and just barely getting them under the upper edge of the building and out.

"Hmm," Gant said. "Must have been a kink in one of the transmission conduits. I should have thought of that."

The Devil screamed out and into the sky, bypassing the reactive fire that came up from the ground as they passed.

"Queenie, this is Imp. Prepare to be impressed."

CHAPTER TWENTY-THREE

Abbey watched as Phlenel's body compacted, her gelatinous structure compressing like a spring, sending her launching forward when she released. She powered into a line of residents, the claws on her hands digging deep into them, their bullets passing through her, leaving holes that were quickly knit back together, her shape reforming.

Her bot trailed behind her, firing at the attackers nearby, accurately striking them in rapid succession, and quickly validating the Hurshin as an accomplished fighter.

"She's making you look bad," Pik said beside her.

Abbey glanced over at him, and then called on the Gift. She didn't want to, but they were out in the open, and half the residents who had redirected toward them were armed.

The bullets came in, striking the invisible wall she put up ahead of them, the Gift churning beneath her flesh. She felt her anger flaring, some of it intentional, some beyond logic. These people were reacting to the promise of a lot of money, a promise of a better life, maybe even a promise to get off this shitty rock. Even so, she was furious with them for the very idea that they would try to harm her or her team. She had heard what Gilliam said about Ruby. She was going to be sure to kill him before Gant got the chance.

The Devils Do

"This way," she said, bouncing toward a group of opponents, with Pik running beside her.

She let go of the Gift as she reached them, coming in hard with the Uin, slashing one of the attackers across the chest, ducking under a clumsy punch, spinning and kicking, letting the softsuit power the blow and resisting the temptation of the Blood. It was more than enough, anyway, sending the man tumbling back and into the second tango.

Pik roared beside her, using his new hand to stab one of the attackers, lifting him and throwing him back, turning and grabbing another with his bare hand and shoving him away. He ducked down as bullets started flying overhead, trying to hit him above the smaller individuals surrounding them. He fought from his knees, his reach long enough to keep most of the residents back.

Abbey reached out with the Gift, pulling a gun from the hands of one of the attackers before he could shoot Pik with it, turning it around and sending it back and into his head. She caught a punch in her free hand, turning the man's wrist until it cracked, and then elbowing him to shove him back. She looked out again, finding Phlenel coming their way, her bot still clearing a path, hitting only the armed attackers while she took care of the others. She saw the Hurshin's mock-tail curl and lash out, spearing one of the mob and throwing him to the ground. Another tango stabbed her with a large knife, the blade getting stuck as the cells around it condensed and held it. Phlenel punched him in the face, knocking him down. The blade fell out of her without leaving a mark.

They continued into the fray, the density of the attackers continuing to grow and adding to the chaos. The disorganization only made it easier for Abbey, Pik, and Phlenel. They stood in the center of the masses, knocking aside all comers, keeping them from landing any serious blows. Phlenel's bot ran out of ammunition, and it returned the guns to the compartments at its sides, switching to using its appendages to make quick, hard jabs.

"Queenie, this is Imp. Prepare to be impressed."

Abbey smiled. "I'm prepared."

She looked up, spotting the hopper a kilometer or two above them.

She scanned the sky, finding the Devil a moment later. Gant had said it wouldn't fly? Had he managed to fix it?

A heavy rumble interrupted the thought.

"Oh, shit," Pik said beside her.

She spun around. A large borer had rounded the corner and was heading toward them, surrounded by armed residents using it as cover.

She put up her hands as the crowd parted around them, giving the machine space to get through and the attackers a lane to shoot in. Their bullets hit a new invisible barrier, smacking against it and dropping to the ground.

"I said I'm prepared," Abbey repeated.

She clenched her jaw, angry that she had to use the Gift again. Angry that she was going to change faster. The thoughts only made her more angry. So was Bastion. What the hell was taking so long?

Then the lane ahead of them lit up in bright flashes of blue light, tracer light flowing with the laser pulses from the Devil's cannon. The blasts spread across the street, burning into the boring machine and the attackers around it. The fighter flashed overhead, making a long, slow turn to come back their way.

"She steers like she's in fragging glue," Bastion said.

"Not that impressive," Abbey replied.

"Queenie, I'm coming in for pickup," Erlan said.

Abbey looked behind them. The hopper was coming down recklessly fast at their backs.

"Fall back," she said, retreating toward it. Pik and Phlenel did the same.

The Devil appeared nearby again, coming at the boring machine from the side. It unleashed another round of laser pulses, the energy spearing into the armor and hitting something useful, causing it to smoke heavily and slow down. The residents of Steel Town were becoming more cautious, using the buildings as cover and taking pot shots at them. A round hit the ground beside her. Another grazed Pik's shoulder. He put his metal hand up over his face to protect it.

Abbey growled, spreading the Gift around them, protecting them

The Devils Do

inside a shielded bubble. The Devil came back a third time, Bastion spreading laser fire around them, keeping the residents back. The hopper hit the ground, shaking it with the impact, the rear hatch already open. Jequn and Benhil stood on either side, rifles up and ready.

Abbey dropped the shield. They started shooting, forcing their attackers to get behind cover or get hit. Pik charged onto the hopper, with Phlenel and her bot right behind. Abbey backed away, her entire body throbbing. She wanted to kill them. All of them. She wanted them to pay for challenging her. For trying to hurt her.

"Queenie," Jequn said. "Let it go. Remember whose side you're on."

She heard the words. She turned and ran into the ship. The ramp began to close as the hopper rose into the sky.

She sat on the side of it, closing her eyes, trying to calm the Gift. "I'm in control," she said, reminding it of the fact. "You do what I say."

The hopper bounced and lurched before smoothing out, rising above the range of the enemy fire.

"Rendezvous at the top of the ravine," Gant said.

"Roger," Erlan replied.

Abbey got to her feet. She looked over at Phlenel. The Hurshin was changing shape, losing the demonic look she had taken, replacing it with a smaller iteration of Pik, minus the genitals.

"Hey, nice," Pik said, noticing the change. "Too big to keep, right?"

"Not really," the bot said. "But it is unnecessary."

"Maybe for you. Where'd you learn to fight like that, anyway?"

"I've watched many streams. And taken lessons."

"But you've never been in a real fight before?"

"I didn't say that."

The hopper touched down at the top of the ravine. The ramp lowered, and Abbey ran out. The Devil was coming to a stop nearby, the canopy opening. She noticed Gant climbing off Bastion's lap and jumping down. She was going to give him shit for it; she just had to figure out how.

There was more important business to settle first.

"Cherub, Jester, secure the lift," she said, pointing to the small station. "We don't need them ferrying the assholes up here."

"Roger," Benhil said, heading for the lift.

Gant and Bastion joined up with them, and the remaining Rejects all moved toward the Faust.

"Gilliam," Abbey said, using Ruby's comm. "I suggest you surrender."

He didn't reply.

"Gilliam?"

The Skink appeared at the entrance to the Faust, holding a gun to Ruby's head.

"I'll shoot her," he said.

"Uh, yeah," Bastion said. "Are you really that stupid? She's a synth. Oh no. You shot her. We'll just buy another one. Idiot."

Abbey glanced over at Bastion. He wasn't completely wrong. Except Ruby had been re-programmed as a military synth and had linked access to Olus that couldn't be easily replaced.

"Yeah, go ahead," Gant said. "Shoot it. We'll wait." He folded his arms.

Gilliam looked unsure.

"If you do, I'm going to kill you myself," Abbey said, holding up her hand.

She let the Gift flow into it, just enough that a claw extended from her middle finger. Her control was getting better. Much better. Too bad it was going to make her insane.

Gilliam began shaking. The gun fell from his hand. Ruby elbowed him in the gut, and then turned and punched him in the face. He collapsed like a sack of shit.

"Asshole," she said. She turned back to Abbey. "He had his cronies with him when he grabbed me. I was distracted by a message I received from Captain Mann."

"What message?" Abbey said.

The Devils Do

CHAPTER TWENTY-FOUR

"Coordinates, Queenie," Ruby said, projecting the image Olus had sent. "To a system near the edge of the Outworlds."

They were in the Faust's CIC, on the way back to the Brimstone. Machina Four was a quickly fading memory, though Abbey was sure Gilliam was calling in to Thraven right now to tell him that they had gotten away.

Or maybe not. Was the Skink smart enough to know how the Gloritant would reward failure?

She looked at the image. She had asked him to recover the data from the mainframe, even if it was all ones and zeros, and he had returned this instead. It could only mean one thing. Thraven had set her up and gotten her sent to Hell to keep her in reserve, to hold her so she could crack the wipe on the box if none of his other people were able. He had sent Clyo to give her the Gift to make her easier to control and had sent her down a path that had led all the way to here.

And now?

It was all for nothing. Thraven had gotten what he wanted without her. He had sent Mr. Davis, Evolent Ruche, back to Earth with the evidence, and the asshole had managed to find someone to crack it. Who? Another Breaker? Someone from the OSI? A genius hacker from outside the system? As long as Thraven didn't know where Kett was, they had a chance to find the General first and make him help with the assault on Kell. They had a chance to take Thraven by surprise and make a mess of his plans.

Not anymore. Damn it.

Thraven was going to follow the coordinates to the Bain System. He was going to use the *Fire* and the other converted ships to destroy the General's base, to kill any last vestige of a potential uprising from the only organized force in the galaxy who wasn't compromised by the Nephilim in some way.

And it had come down to nothing more than time. Another few days, and maybe Olus would have gotten her the data and she would have cracked it first. Another few days, and maybe they would have arrived at Kett's base and led him and his forces on their first sortie in this new war. Another few days, and maybe they could have ended the threat before it got too far out of orbit, destroying the rising fleet and maybe even destroying the *Fire* and the *Brimstone* and freeing all of the poor souls being used to power them.

Instead? She wasn't sure what instead was going to look like yet.

She wasn't giving up. She wasn't giving in. She wasn't going to change sides. She knew that much. The big things didn't seem to be going their way, but what did she expect? They were a crew of criminals and outcasts and mercenaries. They were the scum of the galaxy, and it was the cream that was supposed to rise to the top.

"The Bain System," Benhil said. "Uninhabited. Why would he suggest we go there?"

"Are you sure it's uninhabited?" Abbey asked.

"As sure as I can be. You know the Outworlds. Could be someone terraformed a rock there and didn't tell anyone."

"Not someone," Abbey said. "General Sylvan Kett."

Jequn's head whipped in her direction. "What?"

"I'm sorry, Cherub. I had Ruby ask Captain Mann to find the mainframe I took from Gradin. I used the terminal back in Steel Town to trace it to the asshole who put me away, a guy named Davis. It turns out he's an Evolent, like the bitch who attacked me on Drune. He has the Gift. Anyway, he took the computer back to Earth, and I assume someone finally got it restored."

"You were trying to find the General," Jequn said. "Why?"

"You know why. I told you I do things on my terms. He's going to help us invade Kell, one way or another."

"You would have wasted time finding him instead of launching your attack?"

"What attack?" Gant said. "We have lots of guns now, but not nearly enough individuals to hold them."

"Excuse me," Phlenel said. "I will require a debriefing."

"You'll get it," Abbey promised. She glared at Jequn. "I'm not playing Kett's game. Like Gant said, I need soldiers. He has soldiers. According to you, he's been collecting quite a few."

"A small force could infiltrate the base on Kell and place charges on the ships," Jequn said.

"Bullshit," Benhil said. "An entire fleet? We found some heavy explosives in Sam's cache, sure, but who would carry it all? Pik's big, but he's not that big."

"And I'm not a fragging pack *grangig* either," he said.

"Queenie, I told you before, General Kett and his units are all we have. If we waste them in a futile attack, the whole galaxy might collapse."

"The whole galaxy is collapsing," Bastion said. "I didn't want to believe it either, but it's impossible to ignore. We go to Orunel; we get attacked. We go to Anvil; we get attacked. We go to fragging Machina Four, guess what? We get attacked."

"And there's at least one Evolent on Earth," Abbey said. "Along with a Republic Armed Services Committee under Thraven's control. He's been laying this foundation for longer than most of us have been alive, and now he's making his move. We can't screw around hoping to get to the final battle and keeping our forces in reserve until we do. We have to fight one fight at a time, use everything we've got, and hope for the best. And by the way, you might be a descendent of a Seraphim, but you aren't in charge of a fragging thing, and as far as I'm concerned, your kind have been pretty much useless for the last ten-thousand years. You don't get to decide."

Jequn's eyes narrowed, and she glowered at Abbey. She also didn't continue the argument.

"We do have to make a decision, Queenie," Gant said. "We know Gloritant Thraven will send a force to the Bain System to confront General Kett. The odds are pretty good that he'll spearhead that assault. If he does, there won't be much we can do to stop him. On the other hand, if Gloritant Thraven is in the Bain System, he won't be on Kell."

"Meaning their defenses will be weakened," Benhil said. "I don't know. That might be the way to go."

"Lose Kett to destroy Kell?" Pik said. "I thought you just said we couldn't carry that much explosives?"

"We might not have to. If Kell is clear of the *Fire* and any of the ships like her, we can bombard the fleet from space."

"Except Nerd said we only have two torpedoes left," Abbey said. "What are we going to bombard the surface with? And, if Kett and his people die, even if we win on Kell, then what? We'll be completely on our own."

"We're already on our own," Bastion said. "We've been that way since Mann pulled us off Hell. And speaking for myself, I think I've done pretty fragging well so far."

"I heard you're only alive because she saved you," Pik said, pointing at Jequn.

"Well, I mean, of course, I had a little help."

"Queenie, didn't you suggest we must fight each fight?" Phlenel said. "That statement would indicate that we should adjust for the approach that would offer the best chance of success with an individual goal. In the case of this decision, trying to help the allied force has a much lower potential for victory."

Bastion laughed. "I didn't understand half of what jello mold over there just said, but I agree with her. We need to go to Kell. Kett doesn't want to help? Frag him."

The Devils Do

"Jello mold?" Phlenel asked through the bot.

"What if we could get to Kett before Thraven?" Ruby said. "What if we could evacuate the forces there before he arrived?"

Abbey looked at Jequn again. "You really can't reach him via communicator? Not even to warn him about this?"

"No. I wish that I could. I know you don't want my opinion, Queenie, but there is something you should know."

Abbey wasn't sure she wanted to ask, but she did. "What?"

"Thraven won't bombard the base from orbit, even if he can. He'll want General Kett."

"Why?"

"General Kett knows the location of the Focus."

"Who cares?" Bastion said.

"If Thraven gets the Focus, he'll have the remaining Blood of the Shard, and all of the naniates within. He will be able to use it to power the Elysium Gate."

"And return to his universe," Bastion said. "Sounds delightful to me."

"Do you think he'll just leave this one alone?" Jequn asked. "You're a fool if you do."

"A fool?" Bastion said, indignant.

"She's right," Abbey said. "The only way we can stop Thraven is by keeping him from getting what he wants. If he doesn't destroy the site from space, we have a chance to get in and get Kett out."

"A slim chance," Bastion said, holding his fingers up, barely apart. "Like this much of a chance."

"We can split up," Pik said. "Some of us can go to Bain, and some of us can go to Kell."

"Try not to hurt yourself by thinking," Bastion replied. "Queenie just said we need more bodies. Splitting up is the opposite of that."

"But if we can use the *Brimstone* against the defenses around Kell while the *Fire* is gone, we can clear a path for the reinforcements," Pik insisted. "And if the ships on the ground are offline, maybe we can use the starfighters we just picked up to deliver the explosives and knock them out. At least some of them."

"Kell is nearly eighteen hours away from the Bain System," Ruby said. "It would be a long wait for reinforcements."

"Nah," Pik said. "We just need to get the timing right. We can do it. I know we can. Hell, I'll go down there and bust some heads myself. I want this whole fragging thing over so I can go back to Tro and find a wife."

"I thought you were afraid of Trover women?" Benhil said.

"Every Trover male is afraid of Trover females," Pik replied. "That doesn't mean we don't want one of our own. What do you say, Queenie?"

All eyes turned to Abbey. She met each of them in turn. This wasn't a decision she wanted to make, but it was her crew and her call.

"I don't want to split us up again," she said. "But want has nothing to do with it. The way I see it, it's us against the universe right now. And I mean the whole universe. The Outworlds are ignorant. The Republic is compromised. The Seraphim are out of touch, and the Nephilim want to kill us. We only have one another. And the galaxy, all of this galaxy, is depending on us."

She paused, looking down at the floor. If there was ever going to be a time for the truth, it was now.

"Jester, Bastion, Pik, Gant, I need to tell you something."

"Queenie," Ruby said.

"No," Abbey replied. "This bullshit has gone far enough. We can't go any further based on lies."

"What do you mean?" Benhil said.

"You know that Captain Mann gave me the codes to trigger the kill switches Ruby inserted in your brains back on Feru?"

"Yeah?" Bastion said.

"He didn't give me anything."

Bastion and Pik looked at one another, confused. Benhil made a face like he was just as lost.

Gant barked in laughter. "I was wondering when you were going to tell them."

"Tell us what?" Bastion said. "I don't get it."

The Devils Do

"There are no codes, you nitwit," Gant said. "There is no implant. No virus. There never was."

"You knew?" Abbey said. "The entire fragging time?"

Gant kept laughing. "Not the entire time. It took me a few days to build a scanner to look inside my head. My original intention was to find a way to remove it."

"You didn't say anything."

"No."

"Why?"

"Because I go where you go, Queenie. That's how I work. And even if you had known before Feru, you would have stayed. That's how you work."

"Frag me," Bastion said. "So, you're saying we're free to go?"

Abbey looked at him and nodded. "I can't stop you. Well, I could kill you, I suppose. But that wouldn't help anything."

"You lied to us," Benhil said, getting angry. "You let us keep thinking we were going to die if we stuck around. Frag, we went back to Feru to save his ass because we thought we were going to die otherwise."

"I did what I had to do," Abbey said, staying calm. "The same as Olus did what he had to do. Do you remember what he said after he got us out of Hell? Just because we're free doesn't mean we're innocent. We owe a debt to the innocent people of the Republic for not upholding the oath we made to protect them."

"Bullshit," Benhil said. "I don't owe anybody a damn thing." He looked at Bastion. "You're with me, right?"

Bastion still looked lost. "I don't know."

"You don't know?"

"I do," Pik said. He looked at Abbey. "I don't care. You've always had my back, Queenie. I've got yours."

Abbey smiled. "Thank you, Pik."

"Fragging traitor," Benhil said.

"Benhil, you asked Olus about contacting your family," Abbey said. "I assume that means you still have one?"

"Yeah."

137

"Where do you think they're going to be a month from now? Where do you think you're going to be?"

He sighed. "I know what you're saying, Queenie. I do. But if we're going to lose anyway, I want to see them one more time before we do."

"Or you can stay here and try to save them, and maybe we won't lose. You're an explosives expert. We could use that right now."

"Shit. It's not personal, Queenie. Not really. I mean, I'm pissed at you for lying, but I can sort of see why you did, and I know I owe you because of Sam."

"I'm with you, Queenie," Bastion said, interrupting. "On one condition."

"What's that?" Abbey asked.

"I'm taking you to Bain. I'm flying you in, and I'm flying you out."

Abbey shook her head. "I need you to fly one of the Devils. We don't have another pilot as good as you."

"That's the deal. I'm not making the same mistake a second time. I'm not losing another member of my team because I wasn't there."

"Fine," Abbey said. She couldn't argue with that. "Thank you, Bastion."

He nodded. He looked like he was going to cry. "Since I'm getting all blubbery already, I want you to know. I hated you all when Olus got us out. But that was then, and this is now. I don't have any family out there. All the family I've got is right here. That includes you, freak-monkey."

For once, Gant didn't get mad. "Any friend of Abbey's is a friend of mine, even if that friend is a loudmouthed moron."

"It looks like I get left out in the cold again," Benhil said. "Will I ever stop looking like King Asshole?"

"You're more like the royal fool," Bastion said.

"And every Queen needs a Jester," Abbey added. "Does that mean you're in?"

Benhil nodded. "I'm probably going to regret it when I'm dead, but yeah. I'm in. Once a Reject, always a Reject, I guess."

"Group hug?" Pik suggested.

"Uh, no," Gant said.

The Devils Do

"I don't think so," Benhil said.

"I'm going to go help Nerd dock us to the Brimstone," Bastion said.

"I need to oil my bot," Phlenel said.

"I'll help," Jequn volunteered.

"You all aren't funny," Pik said.

"Yes, we are," Bastion countered, disappearing into the cockpit.

Abbey walked over to Pik. "Just don't crush me," she said, putting her arms out.

He laughed as he wrapped his big arms around her, squeezing gently.

"We're going to die, aren't we, Queenie?" he asked.

"Not if I can help it," she replied.

"I know you'll do your best. But as long as I get to die doing something good, I can handle that."

Abbey wished she could say the same. She couldn't. Not when Hayley's future was at stake.

Winning was the only outcome she was willing to accept.

Whatever it took.

CHAPTER TWENTY-FIVE

OLUS COULD BARELY STAND BY the time his ride reached the closest access point to the Museum that was still open to the public. The meds Dilixix had given him had worn off and left him in a pretty bad state, his heart thumping and his head spinning, to go with his difficulties maintaining balance. He had no idea how he was going to stop whatever Davis was planning from taking place like this.

He was glad the Plixian had given him a few extra shots.

He dumped another pair of pills into his hand, looking at them hesitantly. He needed to be conservative with them. The first pair had lasted about twenty minutes, and he was still a ten minute walk away. And even once he reached the front of the Museum, he would need to find a way in. Security might have let him past yesterday, before he had become almost as much of a fugitive as Abbey and the other Rejects. There was no way that would happen now.

Not unless he did something underhanded.

He was okay with that.

He kept the pills in his hand and started walking, joining the individuals who were being shunted around the path near the Museum, making his way closer to the site one shaky step at a time. The event was supposed to begin at nine, and it was already eight-thirty. He knew from

The Devils Do

experience if something bad were going to go down it would happen right away, not at the tail end of the night. Violence had a tendency to be impatient. He could only hope that one of the Council members arrived late and delayed the proceedings for a few minutes, buying him time to figure out Davis' play.

He thought about Zoey and Gyo as he walked. Forty years ago, he wouldn't have registered his part in their deaths at all. He was nothing but a machine back then. A killing machine. An elite assassin. Time behind a desk had changed him. Time with a team. Time learning about them and caring about them. He had done what he thought he had to do, but he still hated himself for it. He still felt responsible for them. He couldn't bring them back to life, but he could make sure they hadn't died for nothing. It drove him to keep moving, to keep going even when his body was telling him it was done.

Dilixix should have warned him about the side effects of the pills. She should have told him they would exhaust him. Would it have changed anything? They had saved his life, but they were costing him now.

He put his arm out, catching himself on a wall and catching a look from a passerby. He probably looked drunk to them. He pushed himself back up and kept going, concentrating on each step. One at a time. It was the best he could do.

The minutes passed. So did the distance. He closed within a block of the Museum. He could see the lights and hear the murmur of an assembled crowd. He had seen on the Galnet that this was a charity event and there would be entertainment celebrities in attendance, along with plenty of other wealthy individuals who weren't part of the government. Of course, the crowds had come to see the rich and famous, not the legislature.

He rounded the corner, getting a look at the museum. Like most of the classical buildings around the world, the original footprint and facade had been maintained, an outer shell added to increase the floor space around it. In the case of the Museum of Natural History, that meant a transparent frame which encased the original building, with an additional thirty floors of exhibits above it, most of which covered life on other

Republic planets. Those floors had full, clear windows, through which he could see the outer edges of the exhibits, carefully designed to be attractive from both viewing angles.

The newest exhibit usually occupied the original floor of the building, a space that was over a thousand years old. It had been cleaned and restored a couple of times, but it was still the original stone, still the original tile. It had survived the wars of the past, the violent history of what had then been called the 'modern' world, and was now one of the largest museums in the galaxy, along with the Louvre in Paris, and the Dryythph on Ganemant.

The Gants' love of Terran history wasn't limited to Gant.

Olus scanned the area, eyeing both the crowd and the security around it. The building only had one access point from the front, another from the side, and a third on the roof. He wasn't getting in through the roof, so that left him the front or the side. He noticed that there were a few catering trucks in a line a block away, waiting for access to the facility. That was his ticket in.

He tried to walk toward it, stumbling in his weakness. He cursed under his breath, withdrawing the pills and downing them. He didn't know if they would restore his strength; Dilixix hadn't said. He was hopeful.

It took about a minute for him to start feeling the effects of the pills. His energy started to return, his body responding to the stimulants and adjusting. He was near the caterers now, approaching the truck at the rear. A Policeman was attending to the front truck, checking their credentials. He looked around and then dropped onto his back, pulling himself on the ground beneath the vehicle. It was hovering slightly off the ground, but wouldn't stay that way once it was ready to park. He would have to be quick to get out before he was crushed.

He gripped the coils, ignoring the coldness of them, letting himself hang until they started moving. They did a moment later, and he used his arms to pull himself up and hold it, a feat of strength he wouldn't have been able to duplicate two minutes earlier. He could see the feet of the Police and the security guards as the trucks slid past the open transparent gate and onto the grounds, and then from the grounds into the original

The Devils Do

building. As soon as it slowed, he let go, falling onto the floor and rolling to his feet, diving behind a parked vehicle before he could be spotted.

He was in.

He made his way along the side of the room, back toward the caterers, keeping low and out of sight. Security was much lighter inside, composed of cameras that were watching the unloading area. He hesitated nearby, waiting for the workers to clear the area and then ducking into the museum proper without being seen. He stood up and straightened his jacket, walking casually through the corridor. One of the caterers came out of a nearby restroom, walking past him without sparing him a second look.

He kept going, down the hallway and into another corridor, from that corridor to the kitchen. A man in a black tuxedo emerged from it.

"Excuse me, sir," he said. "Are you lost?"

"Yes," Olus said, offering an embarrassed laugh. "I managed to find a bathroom, but now I can't find my way back out to the party."

"I'm going that way myself. I'd be glad to show you out."

"Thank you."

Olus followed the waiter.

"Crazy party, huh?" Olus said as they walked.

"It's been some time since we've had so many celebrities here," he replied. "Personally, I'm more interested in the Council. They promised to make a statement about the missing starships."

Olus was caught by surprise. "What kind of statement?"

"Hopefully that they've been recovered. I have a friend whose sister is out near the Fringe. She's worried the Outworlders are going to use them to start expanding their borders."

"The Outworlds have an open galaxy on the other side of them," Olus said. "Why would they need to expand inward?"

"Why does the Republic keep fighting with them? We both know there's enough space to go around. It's politics, right? The machinations of the powerful and stupid." He laughed for a moment before lowering his head, realizing Olus might be one of them.

"Everybody wants what they don't have," Olus agreed. "Just like the Outworlds wanted the *Fire* and the *Brimstone*."

"Is that what they're called?" the man said. "I hadn't heard their names anywhere."

Olus could have kicked himself. That was an amateur slip. Was it the meds?

"That's what I've been calling them," Olus said. "I don't have an official name, either."

"As you say, sir," the waiter said. "Here we are."

A hidden door slid aside as they approached, revealing the main lobby of the museum ahead of them. It was packed with individuals in tuxedoes and long dresses, most of them too pretty and much older than they appeared.

"Thank you," Olus said.

"Of course, sir."

The waiter wandered off. Olus moved along the outskirts of the room, looking for Davis, or even Vee. They had to be here, somewhere. He scouted for the Council members as well, eager to find them and warn them.

"Captain Mann?" someone said nearby.

Olus turned, finding Councilman Granges an arm's length away from him. How the hell had he not seen the man?

"Councilman," Olus said.

"I didn't realize you were invited to this thing," Granges said. "How have you been?"

"I've been better, Councilman," Olus said. "But I wasn't invited. I came here to warn you. The Republic is being threatened, sir. Half of the Council has been compromised. You're one of the few that haven't."

"What? Captain, are you feeling well? You're very sweaty."

Olus hadn't noticed. He wiped his forehead, feeling the moisture. "Sir, I'm very serious. Consider some of the legislation that has been presented these past few months, and you'll notice a pattern of deconstruction, one that aims to weaken the government of the Republic in anticipation of a military takeover."

Grange's entire face turned to stone. He glanced over at the woman near him, and then came toward Olus, putting his face in close. "Where did you get this?"

"I'm the Director of the OSI. Or, I was. They're in the middle of setting me up to take a nice fall because of what I know."

"Who is they?"

"It's a long story, Councilman. You need to get out of here. Now. Go home, surround yourself with security, and stay there. I need to find the other Council members."

Grange seemed convinced. He turned back to the woman, reaching out to her. "Cynthia, we're leaving."

"What?" his wife said. "You're supposed to be making a speech in twenty minutes."

"Change of plans. I-"

Granges froze in place.

"I," he said again. His head turned. He looked at Olus in a panic. His skin was pale, face flushing. He raised his hand to his throat, trying to pull his tuxedo away from it. Trying to breathe again.

Olus reached under his coat, finding his gun there. He slapped one of the magazines into it as he drew it out, spinning around and searching for Davis or Vee.

"Where are you?" he said.

"I'm right here, Olus," Davis replied.

Olus spun again. Davis was standing beside Councilman Granges.

"I was hoping you would make it, Captain. It will make it easier to blame this whole thing on you. A rogue assassin is a terrible thing. A tragedy."

"How do you propose to do that?" Olus asked.

"Like this."

Davis raised his hands and closed his eyes. Almost immediately he was on fire, blue and orange flames spreading around him and bathing him. He was unharmed by it. In fact, he smiled as it licked across his face.

"When they run forensics, they'll find you right at ground zero, Captain," Davis said. "Not eight hours after you murdered General Omsala."

It took Olus a moment to realize what Davis meant. He lifted the gun, trying to get it pointed at the Evolent's head. Someone knocked it out of his hand.

Vee. She was on fire as well, burning with the same flame. The others in the room had noticed, and they began to clap, thinking the two Nephilim were some kind of entertainment.

"It's showtime," Vee said.

The flames along her body exploded outward, washing over him and everything in the room.

All he heard then were screams. Hundreds of screams. He looked at his hands, noticing that he was unscathed. The flames weren't burning him. The pills? How were they protecting him from this?

"What?" Davis said, noticing as well.

Olus threw a hard right hook into Davis' jaw, the force of the blow knocking him down and putting out his flames. He turned toward Vee, bringing a knife into his hand and swinging it at her face. She ducked under it, putting out her hands. The Gift slammed into him, knocking him back a dozen meters. He slid on the floor and got to his feet. He was surrounded by burning guests. The screams were nauseating, the destruction already exponential. Flames ate at everything around him, and Davis was back on his feet ahead, burning up once more.

He scanned the room in a near panic, searching for Councilman Grange. He found him beside Davis, recognizable only by the few unburned scraps of his coat and hair.

Olus did the only thing he could think to do.

He ran.

The Devils Do

CHAPTER TWENTY-SIX

Abbey found Phlenel in the Brimstone's medical ward. It was more luxurious and modern than the space on the Faust, with enough room for six examination tables and two medical bots, as well as the latest equipment for treating all types of wounds. The Hurshin wasn't alone in the ward when she arrived. One of Ursan Gall's subordinates was there, too. Ensign Ligit. The one Dak had told her Ursan had nearly killed in a fit of wild anger. He was pressed into the corner of the room when she arrived, watching Phlenel fearfully.

Not that Phlenel was doing anything threatening. She and her bot were rooting through the cabinets of the ward, examining each container and putting them back.

"What are you doing?" Abbey asked.

"Inventory," Phlenel's bot replied. "I will move on to the supply room and hangar later, to see what mechanical surplus the ship might have. Pik has asked me about replacing his other hand."

"We aren't replacing his other hand," Abbey said. "Not while it still works." She shook her head. He was enjoying his augmentation a little too much.

"I understand you are in charge. I will do as you say."

"Good. Can we talk for a minute?"

"I believe you are intending to address the crew?"

Abbey nodded. "In a few minutes. I wanted to talk to you alone, first."

Phlenel stopped what she was doing, turning to face Abbey. She had changed her form again, mimicking Ensign Ligit.

"We are not alone," she pointed out.

"Right." Abbey looked over at one of the medical bots. "What is the status of Ensign Ligit?"

"Concussion. One additional day of rest is recommended."

"Can he be discharged to his quarters?"

"Yes."

"Ensign," Abbey said.

Ligit looked over at her. "Uh. Aye, ma'am?"

"Why are you still here? The bot says you can rest in your quarters."

"I. I wasn't sure where to go, ma'am. Considering the status of the ship. Considering, you know, you're the enemy."

He shrank back as he said it. Abbey sighed under her breath. So far, with the exception of Dak, she was unimpressed with Gall's mercenaries.

"I'm not your enemy," she said. "Your enemy is out there. Have you spoken to Commander Dak?"

"No, ma'am."

"He's on the bridge. Go and speak with him. Medical bot, please provide Ensign Ligit with a discharge report."

"Please authorize," the bot said, projecting a keyboard into the air ahead of it.

Abbey approached it, typing in the main authentication code for the Brimstone.

"Thank you," the bot said. It produced a small chit a moment later and held it out for Ligit.

Ligit climbed off the bed, took the chit, and gave Abbey a weak Outworld salute before fleeing the room.

"Dak," Abbey said, activating her communicator.

The Devils Do

"Yeah, Boss?" he replied.

"Ensign Ligit is on his way to you. The medical bot recommended another day of bed rest, but I want you to talk to him and make sure he's not going to lose it. He was acting a little squirrely."

"I don't know what squirrely means, but I'll talk to him."

"Thank you."

She closed the link and returned her attention to Phlenel. "Now that we're alone, I want to know why you helped us, and why you came with us."

"I was hiding on Machina Four," Phlenel replied. "It was not safe to hide there any longer. It is safer with you."

"Don't be too sure about that. What were you hiding from?"

"Gloritant Salvig Thraven," Phlenel said, surprising her.

"You know him?"

Phlenel's bot nodded in unison with a spot near the Hurshin's head flaring internally like a red lightning bolt. "How much do you know about my kind?"

"Not much," Abbey admitted. "You're the first I've ever met."

"We didn't have spaceflight before the Terrans found our world. We didn't have much technology at all. But we are mimics. We learn immediately from what we see. Two hundred years ago, Hurse was almost a swamp, and we lived communally, like algae in a massive pond. Then your kind arrived. We rose to meet you and delivered an emissary to your world. When the emissary returned, everything changed. He spread his learning, and we adapted and altered. We became modern."

She paused. A blue flare translated to synthesized laughter from the bot.

"I am nine hundred Earth Standard years of age. I was there when the Terrans came. I evolved with my people. I was one of the first to volunteer to leave, to collect knowledge to bring back to my homeworld and share with the others. It was challenging at first, but eventually I found a position in the RAS Supply Branch, first as a crewmember on Republic supply haulers, and later I was promoted to Captain, once I had learned to build and made an interface to communicate through." She motioned to the bot. "The position was adequate for a time. There is only so much you can learn about the galaxy when you are confined to one part of it."

"So you quit the RAS and went to the Outworlds?" Abbey guessed.

"I did. Forty years ago, I purchased a trading vessel of my own and made it a point to visit as many Outworlds planets as I could. It took nearly ten years, but eventually I had seen most. I would wear clothing then, and synthetic flesh to cover myself and hide my true origins. Very few had ever seen a Hurshin, and were often nervous around me, as Ensign Ligit was. I became very accustomed to passing as human, even if I couldn't speak. I've even had Terran lovers." She laughed again.

"Where does Thraven fit in?"

"Fifteen years ago, he hired me to ferry a dozen individuals from Gordon in the Outworlds to Earth. It was an illegal transport, but I bore no qualms about legality. What were a dozen more on Earth when there are already so many? The payment was high, the experience fresh. I accepted." She paused again, a dark thread winding its way through her translucent body. "I knew they were wrong as soon as they boarded. I could sense it, the way I sensed the difference in you. They were like the Hurshin, but not."

"Children of the Covenant," Abbey said. "Goreshin?"

"Yes. I tried to take them. I tried to make the delivery. But inside I felt only cold. Only wrong. They were abominations. Twisted from what they were intended to be. I could not accept it. I killed them, sold my ship, and went into hiding on Machina Four."

"You killed them? A dozen Children? By yourself?"

"As I said, Hurshin learn by observance. Once we learn a skill, we do not forget it. I know how to fight. And my form is adaptable." She held up a hand. It quickly changed form and hardened, tuning into a long blade. "Terrans rule the galaxy, but only because the Hurshin have no desire for possessions or power. We are interested only in knowledge and new experiences to share."

"But you don't mind murder," Abbey said.

"It is a mercy to kill something that has been changed from what it

The Devils Do

was supposed to be."

"Does that mean you would kill me, too?"

"Yes."

She said it simply and without hesitation. It sent a chill through Abbey. Then again, when the time came she might want her to do it.

"Sam and his people were Children, Goreshin like the ones you were transporting. Why didn't you kill them?"

"I feared Gloritant Thraven from the moment I met him. There is nothing inside of him. He exists for one purpose and only one purpose, and it drives everything he is. There is no compassion, no empathy, no remorse. He sees only the future."

"The one where he returns to Elysium and kills the One," Abbey said. "Hurshin are so rare. Sam never suspected?"

"He did. He confronted me once. I killed three of his kind and told him that if Thraven came for me, he would die. He knew I would do it. He never told Thraven I was there. I always told myself I would end him before I ever left Machina. You did it for me."

"What about Gilliam? He was working with Thraven, too."

"All of the Outworlds are this way. I suspect the Republic is as well, except for Hurse. Gilliam benefitted from my services, and I don't believe he knew Thraven was looking for me. If he did, he never said. Anyway, when you killed Sam, I lost my safe haven. One way or another, my presence there would be revealed, and I would be hunted as you are. I decided it would be better to help you. You are a curiosity to me. You are also fighting against Gloritant Thraven. And, I believe there is much to learn in this experience."

"I don't know if any of what you'll experience will be pleasant."

"All knowledge is pleasant."

"It is?" Abbey said.

"If you were a Hurshin, you would understand."

"Well, it seems like Machina Four worked out in my favor. I expect you to be part of the team, to follow orders, and to give everything you have to help us."

"Of course."

"In that case, welcome to the Rejects."

The Devils Do

CHAPTER TWENTY-SEVEN

THE COMBINED CREWS WERE ASSEMBLED in the Brimstone's hangar, the Rejects aligned on the left side and the remainder of Ursan Gall's mercenaries on the right. Seeing the two groups segregated so deliberately annoyed Abbey, and she approached the front of the columns and froze, her eyes sweeping from one side to the other. Phlenel and her bot moved away from her, joining the ranks.

"Attention!" Dak shouted, his deep voice rumbling across the hangar.

The mercenaries slipped into attention. The Rejects did the same.

She hated even thinking about them as two separate groups. They were all on the same side. They were all fighting against the same thing. Their origins didn't matter. Their nations didn't matter.

"What is this?" she asked, moving forward into the aisle that split the two groups.

"What do you mean, Queenie?" Bastion asked.

"This," she said, pointing at her feet.

"Your feet?" Pik said.

"Why are we here?" she asked.

There was a moment of silence from both sides.

"Why are we here?" she repeated. "Why are we on the *Brimstone* together? Why hasn't one side killed the other yet?"

"Because you won't let us?" Pik guessed.

"No," Abbey snapped. She walked down the aisle, looking to both sides, making eye contact with the soldiers there.

"Because there are no sides," Gant said.

Abbey turned and walked back to the front where Gant was standing, still at attention.

"You could have fooled me, Gant," she said. "What is that?"

"A space," Iann said.

"Or a line," Abbey said. "A dividing line. Us and them." She paused, using the silence as a tool, eyeing them all a second time. "What do you think about that?" she said at last.

"Hmmm. It's bullshit?" Pik said.

Abbey smiled. "It's bullshit," she said loudly. "Fragging bullshit. You have ten seconds to fill in that line. If you're standing next to somebody you know, you're going to piss me off. Now fix it."

They broke attention, scrambling to reorganize while Abbey counted to ten.

"Time's up," Abbey said. Everyone stopped and came to attention. She scanned the group. "For those of you here that haven't met me yet, my name is Abigail Cage. Notice that there's no rank attached to that. While I used to be a part of the Republic Armed Services, I'm not a member of the Republic military anymore. Guess what? Neither are you. Any of you. If you were in the Outworld military, that's over, too."

"So what are we, ma'am?" Iann asked.

"I'm glad you asked. It's Olain, right?"

"Yes, ma'am."

"We're the Rejects," Abbey said. "We're the ones who don't fit inside the boundaries. Of governments, of expectations, of laws. We're the ones who don't let petty bullshit hold us back and keep us from doing what needs to be done. Petty bullshit like whose side we used to be on. Because the rules have changed. The sides have changed. There's only one threat, and that's Gloritant Thraven and the Nephilim. You saw what he did to Anvil. You helped destroy a Republic border patrol in his name. He lied to

The Devils Do

you. He used you. He tricked you. He used me, too. He used Phlenel over there. He used Pik. He's been manipulating us. Moving us around like pieces on a fragging chess board. I'm done with that. So are you.

Today, we're starting fresh. Today, you aren't mercenaries. You aren't fugitives from Hell. You aren't running. You aren't hiding. Today we're starting our own legion outside of the Republic and the Outworlds. Today, you answer only to one another and to me. If you have people you care about out there, if you want to protect them, if you want our side to win, today you give up your loyalty to anything that runs counter to that mission."

Abbey paused. She had gone through this little speech in her head a few times, but she had always stumbled at this part. Not only did it sound kind of hokey, but it also wasn't something she wanted. It was the way things had to be.

"If you're in, then today is the day you swear your allegiance to the Rejects, and to me."

"Our Queen?" Benhil asked.

"Yeah, something like that," Abbey replied.

There was a moment of tense silence as the words washed over the group. Abbey kept her eyes on Ursan's crew. If anyone was going to resist, it would be them.

"What. What do we do?" Iann asked. "To swear allegiance, I mean?"

"On your knee," Gant said, standing near her. He lowered himself onto a knee and bowed his head. "You already know it, but I'm with you, Queenie."

"Yeah, me, too," Bastion said, falling to a knee.

"And me," Pik said.

"And me," Dak said.

"I'm with you, Queenie," Iann said, copying Gant.

"I'm with you," Benhil said.

"I'm with you," Jequn said.

"I'm in," Phlenel said.

"I'm in, too, Queenie," Erlan said. "For Feru."

155

The other assembled soldiers bowed to her, one by one until they were all on the ground in front of her. She felt a cold chill at the sight. She had never wanted to be in charge of the original Rejects, and now their numbers were growing. It seemed it was her fate.

"Your word is your bond," she said. "If you break it, expect retribution not only from me but also from any other member of the Rejects, now and in the future. Thraven wants to beat us through division. It's essential that we don't let that happen. Is that understood?"

"Yes, ma'am," they shouted back at her, getting it tight and on point on the first try.

"Good. Now stand up. We have work to do."

The assembly came to its feet.

"Whatever role you're in is the role you'll be staying in, unless I change it. You'll address me as ma'am, or Queenie, or Queen, or DQ. I'm not that picky, just say it with respect. What we're about to do is going to be dangerous. There's a good chance none of us will live long enough for any of it to matter. We need to work together to make sure that doesn't happen."

"Yes, ma'am," the soldiers said.

"Here's how we're going to do this. Bastion, Jequn, and I are going to take the *Faust* to the Bain system. We have solid intel that General Sylvan Kett's base is there, and that he's been building a force to counter Thraven. Unfortunately, we think the enemy has the same information we do, which means we need to reach him before Thraven does.

"While I'm gone recruiting, the rest of you will be going to the planet Kell. Your mission is to disrupt Thraven's operations there. Leadership has already devised a plan for the assault, and it will be shared with you over the coming hours. Each of you has a vital role to play in our overall chance of success. You all have specific strengths and skills, and we need every one of them if we're going to throw a wrench into the Gloritant's plans and save our homeworlds. Are you with me?"

"Yes, ma'am!"

"Good. Do any of you have any questions?"

Nobody came forward. Abbey could see the resolve on each of

their faces. The motivation. Thraven had lied to them. He had used them. She was using them too, in her own way. She cared more about Hayley than she did any of the Outworld planets. So what? Each of them wanted to save their own worlds and the individuals they cared about. It was a common goal to build around. Hell, even Benhil had given up on the idea of taking off in exchange for the chance to stop the Gloritant's invasion. History was filled with stories of desperate defenders surmounting impossible odds to save the things that were most important to them.

She had every intention of adding theirs.

"You're all dismissed to your assigned duties. Bastion, Benhil, Jequn, Gant, Dak, Ruby, please stay behind."

The rest of the crew filed out of the hangar in silence. The others assembled around her.

"Well spoken," Ruby said.

"What's up, Boss?" Dak asked.

"Where are we with the plans?"

"Jester and I have started assembling the explosives," Gant said. "We're only going to have enough for ten ships, at most."

"Which means we're going to need spotters on the ground," Benhil said. "We can't waste ammo on ships that aren't ready to fly."

"Do we have any way of identifying converted warships?" Abbey asked.

"I've been looking at the data from the engines, as you requested," Gant said. "I think I can put something together to sense the difference in energy output. I don't know exactly how the naniates are producing power. It seems to be some kind of fusion, but it doesn't match a typical reactor. The output is an order of magnitude larger than the input."

"Ship sensors don't typically bother with trying to pick up those kinds of variations," Dak said. "There's no point when everyone is using the same tech."

"We might be able to read the signature of a cloaked vessel if we can adjust the equipment properly," Gant said.

"We don't need them to be that sensitive right now," Abbey said. "Just enough that we can tell which of the ground targets already have the reactors installed. We need to save the people there from that torture."

"It won't help if they aren't online," Gant said.

"If they aren't online we don't need to worry about them," Abbey replied. "At least not right away. We can hit the obvious targets first, and then circle back once the prisoners are out."

"Assuming we can get them out," Benhil said. "And assuming they're in any condition to fight."

"He went after Anvil for a reason," Abbey said. "He wanted soldiers. Even if they're beaten, once we let them out they'll be ready to fight."

"Especially when we bring the equipment to them," Ruby said.

"With any luck, by the time Kett's forces arrive they'll have nothing to do but mop up, and Thraven will be down to four ships."

"Four ships like the Brimstone," Bastion said. "Still enough to do a lot of damage."

"Only until they run out of torpedoes," Gant said.

"Now that they have the technology, they'll be careful not to lose it again," Jequn said. "If we destroy Kell, Thraven will set up somewhere else."

"Which will take time," Abbey said. "And give us more time. It's the best we can do."

"He won't give up," Jequn said. "He won't retreat. Not ever. None of the Nephilim will. Not if they believe the time of the Great Return has arrived."

"That's fine with me," Abbey replied. "We won't either. This is our galaxy. I'm not letting them have it. Ruby, is the *Faust* loaded and ready to go?"

"Yes, Queenie."

"Seventy-four hours," Abbey said, looking at Gant.

"Don't be late," he replied.

"We won't be."

"And be careful, will you? I don't want to have to think you're dead again."

"You too." She smiled. "Even if we aren't friends."

The Devils Do

"We aren't?" Gant said, confused.

"No. We're family. Take it to the bank and deposit it."

Gant laughed. "Aye, Queenie. Deposited. Be safe. We'll keep the fires burning for you."

"Literally," Benhil said. "Good luck, Queenie."

"You, too. All of you. You know how to reach me if anything changes. Imp, Cherub, let's go."

CHAPTER TWENTY-EIGHT

THE *FAUST* CAME OUT OF FTL in the Bain System ten hours later, a plume of disterium surrounding the ship as it blinked back into existence and traveled away from the gas.

"Scanning," Bastion said, reaching over and tapping a few controls on the ship's worn dashboard.

"Obviously, the coordinates weren't an exact path to the planet," Abbey said, looking out of the viewport. They were in the middle of open, empty space, with no obvious celestial bodies close by.

"I'm sure someone will be out to meet us," Jequn said. "We just have to wait."

"Not long," Bastion said, pointing at the HUD, where a distant glint of metal had been outlined. "That's a sniffer satellite. I'm sure it picked up the plume."

Abbey leaned in to get a closer look at the outline, putting her face close to Bastion's.

Bastion turned his head. "I think this is the closest you've ever been to me."

"Don't get used to it," Abbey replied.

Bastion laughed. "Come on, Queenie. I'm not that bad, am I?"

She shifted her face, putting it right in his. She looked into his

The Devils Do

eyes. In truth, he wasn't as bad as she had originally believed. There was an actual person under the loudmouthed exterior. A person who didn't have an evolutionary component of loyalty like Gant, but was still loyal enough that he had gone to Hell for trying to save his team, even if it had been a ridiculously stupid thing to do.

"No," she said, smiling. "But you're still an asshole."

"Thanks, I guess," he said shifting in his seat. "Maybe one day I'll get a straight complement out of you."

"You're getting closer," she admitted.

"Oh, yeah? You told Gant he was family. Does that go for me, too?"

"Do you want to be family? I'm not into incest."

"You're suggesting I have a shot?"

"You have more of a shot today than you did two weeks ago."

"In that case, we aren't family." He stared at the HUD and then pointed to two dots in the distance. "There. Computer says they're Daedalus heavy starfighters. It looks like our boy Kett has some pretty sweet assets." Something beeped behind them. "We're being hailed."

"Open the channel," Abbey said.

"Excuse my reach," Bastion said, turning and leaning back to the comm equipment. He flipped one of the analog toggles.

"Unidentified vessel," one of the starfighter pilots said. "This is protected space. Please identify."

"Abigail Cage of the starship Faust," Abbey said. "I'm here to speak with General Sylvan Kett."

The starfighters were closing in a hurry, taking a wide path around the ship.

"I don't like that move," Bastion said. "That's an attack maneuver."

"I've never heard of Sylvan Kett," the pilot replied. "This space is protected by the Sovereignty of Azure. You have twenty seconds to clear the area."

"Sovereignty of Azure?" Abbey said, looking at Jequn.

Jequn shrugged. "I've never heard of it. It could be General Kett trying to throw us off. We are uninvited, after all."

"Could be," Abbey agreed. "Imp, get us some velocity. Be prepared to take evasive maneuvers if they attack."

"Roger."

"I know Kett is out here," Abbey said through the comm. "And nobody believes your bullshit."

"Fifteen seconds," the pilot replied.

The two fighters were angling back from the rear. The HUD beeped.

"They've got a lock on us."

"Seriously?" Abbey said, annoyed. "Listen, shithead; I'm here to see Kett. He isn't expecting me. Do you get what that means, or do I need to spell it out?"

"Ten seconds," the pilot replied.

"Fine, I'll spell it out. Thraven knows Kett is out here. How many seconds do you think we have until he shows up?"

"Five seconds," the pilot said.

They were coming up on the *Faust* from behind. Bastion had added thrust and was sitting still and focused at the yoke, ready to try to evade the starfighters. She doubted the *Faust* could handle it, even if her pilot was capable.

"Fragging bastards," Bastion muttered. "I thought Kett was on our side?"

"Damn it," Abbey said. "You didn't use the Focus to save me off Drune just to kill me here, did you?"

The fighters slowed suddenly, their vectors changing as they peeled away.

"Yeah, that's right," Bastion said. "Move aside before I blow your asses up."

"Identity confirmed," the pilot said. "Welcome to Bain, Lieutenant Cage."

"I'm not the Lieutenant of anything," Abbey said. "You can call me Queenie."

"Roger. Welcome to Bain, Queenie."

"And you are?"

The Devils Do

"Captain Jonathan Ness, Republic Intergalactic Navy. Former. Sorry for the scare, but we can't be too careful. I'm patching you through to General Kett now."

"Roger," Abbey replied.

There was a small beep from the comm link, and then a new voice filtered into the cockpit.

"Lieutenant Cage," General Kett said. "I was planning on coming to you, not the other way around."

"Tough shit," Abbey replied. "I don't like playing by other people's rules."

He laughed. "I gathered. Well, if what you said about Thraven is true, then it's a good thing you're here. I'm sending you the updated coordinates to Azure. I'm looking forward to meeting you. Kett out."

The link dropped.

"A man of few words, isn't he?" Bastion asked.

"Compared to you, everyone is," Jequn said.

"I don't talk that much."

"Yes, you do. Ten hours, and your lips barely stopped moving the entire time."

"I was sleeping for two of those."

"You were talking in your sleep."

"How would you know?"

"The doors on the sleeping quarters aren't that thick. I believe you might have been dreaming about Queenie."

"I don't want to know," Abbey said.

"And then you were singing in the cleanser," Jequn added. "And then you were talking to yourself while you ate. And then you came back to the cockpit and started talking about your father the botanist for two hours."

"I had a good relationship with my father, and botany is more fascinating than you would think. Sorry, I'm not from a broken home." A new tone sounded from the comm system. Bastion leaned back and flipped a couple of switches. "We've got the coordinates."

"Set a course."

Bastion transferred the data to the FTL computer. "Ten seconds."

"See you on the other side, Queenie," Captain Ness said. The fighters vanished from beside them, shooting into FTL.

The faster-than-light ride was only a dozen seconds long, dumping them out some ten-thousand AU from their original drop point. It was close enough that they didn't have to go to FTL to get there, but it certainly sped things up. With any luck, even once Thraven did arrive in-system it would take him days to find the exact location.

The planet Azure appeared to be gray from space, owing to a massive amount of cloud cover that seemed to hover over ninety-percent of the mass. In the few clear spots, Abbey could see blue and green and brown, suggesting a comfortably habitable Earth-like planet beneath. If she had to guess, she would have said it was in the late stages of terraforming, but she didn't see any of the telltale signs of the activity in the cloud patterns below.

As it was, there was no way to guess at the size or formation of Kett's forces from orbit. There were no starships waiting above the planet, no assets too large to bring into the atmosphere and to the ground. No orbital stations, regardless of size. They didn't even possess any other tracking satellites. It was obvious Kett wanted passerby to think the planet was uninhabited and uninteresting, and not the home to a rebellion against a war that hadn't even truly started yet.

"*Faust*, this is Captain Ness. I'm going to paint the landing track for you on my descent. Follow me in."

"Roger," Bastion said.

The starfighter moved into position ahead of the Faust. It was about a tenth the size of the star hopper, bulky and angled, with a large ass to house an FTL engine in addition to normal thrusters, and a deep hull that could hold an assortment of munitions inside. It had wings for atmospheric flight, but they were thick and short, relying more on anti-gravity to help with lift, though they packed half a dozen pulse laser cannons in total.

"Have you ever flown a Daedalus?" Abbey asked.

"Me?" Bastion said. "Nah. I only flew dropships before Hell."

The Devils Do

"You were pretty impressive with the *Imp* and with the *Faust*," Abbey said.

"Instinct," Bastion replied. "I have a good feel for what these hunks of scrap metal can do, and how to push them to the limits. I don't know why. Maybe because it's just so damn fun."

The *Faust* entered the atmosphere, trailing the fighter as it sank into clouds and vanished, leaving only the painted sensor line behind. Bastion followed it smoothly, dropping into stormy clouds that knocked them around a bit with turbulence and filled the viewport with lightning.

"This storm is nearly ten kilometers thick," Bastion said. "That's no joke."

"The good news is that I don't think Thraven could bombard the planet through this even if he wanted to."

"The site wasn't selected by accident," Jequn said.

"You've never been here before?" Abbey asked.

"No. The Ophanim were on Drune for a long time, until we had to leave."

"Where are the rest of your group now?"

"Scattered. Waiting. One of them delivered me to you on Anvil."

"You have ships, then?"

"Four Seedships."

"From the Shardship?"

"Yes. You remember."

The storm finally broke away, leaving them only a kilometer from the surface. The rain was falling in torrents, a wide, raging river visible on the ground below. The Daedalus banked into a canyon, following the river toward a waterfall so high that it vanished into the clouds.

"Wow," Bastion said. "That's fragging impressive. I'm taking bets the base is behind the waterfall. That's the best place for a secret base."

"This isn't an action vid or the Construct," Abbey said. "It doesn't work that way in reality."

The fighter kept going, into and through the waterfall.

"Ha!" Bastion said. "I was right about something for once. And, can you believe it, you were wrong, Queenie." He laughed.

"It does happen sometimes," Abbey said. "Hopefully Thraven thinks more like I do."

Bastion guided the *Faust* into the flow and through. The cavern behind the waterfall was massive, easily large enough to allow the ship to enter. There was light on the other side, two kilometers distant. They kept going, exiting the rock and finding themselves in a large, open canyon surrounded by high rock formations to the sides, and clouds above. The surface of the canyon was littered with barracks, warehouses, starships, starfighters, including Shrikes, mechs, and troops, too many to easily count.

"That's pretty impressive, too," Bastion said.

Abbey stared down at the force. She had to agree.

But was it enough?

"*Faust*, this is Captain Ness. A beacon is lighting up at your landing pad. General Kett will meet you on the tarmac. Enjoy your stay."

"Thank you, Captain," Abbey said.

Bastion guided the *Faust* to the beacon that appeared on the HUD, landing her between two larger armed haulers. Abbey could see an entourage waiting beneath one of them, keeping out of the rain. She wasn't sure which one was Kett.

"Meet us outside," Abbey said, putting her hand on Bastion's shoulder. "Jequn, come on."

"Aye, Queenie," Bastion said, tapping controls to wind down the ship.

Abbey made her way down the ladder to the bottom level, and then over to the hatch. She descended the ramp ahead of Jequn, finding a smaller man waiting front and center at the bottom, his face already soaked by the rain.

"Lieutenant Cage," General Kett said, saluting her.

"Not anymore," Abbey replied, not returning the salute. She put out her hand. "General Kett, I assume?"

He smiled, taking her hand. He had a firm grip. "Welcome to Azure." He looked past her. "Jequn. It's good to see you again." He moved around Abbey, hugging the Ophanim.

The Devils Do

"Dad," Jequn said.

Dad? She had read Kett's file a million times. It had never mentioned a child.

"I can see you're confused," Kett said. "I'll try to answer all of your questions if you can answer all of mine."

"I'll do my best," Abbey said.

There were three other people with Kett. Jequn went to the woman with him, giving her the same hug she had given her father. Abbey's eyes got stuck when they landed on her. She was beautiful beyond description. Ethereal.

"My wife, Charmeine. Yes, she's a Seraph. One of the few full-bloods that remain. This is Colonel Brink and Lieutenant Siddrah."

Abbey froze again when her eyes landed on Siddrah.

"I know you," Abbey said.

"I know you, too," Siddrah said. "From Gradin."

The two men she had seen in the corridor. Siddrah was one of them. Which meant the base they attacked had been Kett's, not the home of some Outworld thieves. She turned toward Jequn. She had said the mainframe was stolen. That clearly wasn't the case.

"You lied to me about Gradin," she said. "You lied to me about having never been here, too. Didn't you?"

Jequn lowered her head. "I did. I'm sorry."

Abbey clenched her fists, feeling herself getting angry. "Why?"

"Abigail," Kett said. "It wasn't her fault. I told her to do it."

She rounded on Kett. "Why? For what purpose? I'm sick and tired of these fragging secrets, these damn games. People died on Gradin. Your people."

"I know," Kett agreed. "It couldn't be helped. The Republic knew I was operating there and was going to send a team regardless. This damn game is a dangerous game, as you well know. The wrong move could doom us all. Come inside, have something to eat. I'll explain everything."

CHAPTER TWENTY-NINE

"Gradin was a risk," Kett said.

He was sitting at a table across from Abbey, with Charmeine and Jequn on either side of him, and his commanders on the ends. Bastion was beside Abbey, digging into the variety of prepared foods that had been waiting for them when they arrived.

"This is so fragging good," he said, taking a bite. "It's been years since I had real food. If I dided right now, I would die a happy man."

"A calculated risk," Kett continued once Bastion stopped talking. "But a risk all the same."

"You set me up," Abbey said. She had given the facts a check while they had crossed the tarmac to the bunker dug into the side of one of the cliffs that surrounded them. "You knew what was going to happen to me."

"We've known for some time now that we can't stop Thraven," Charmeine said. "Not on our own. The Seraphim who arrived with the Shard are nearly gone. With Phanuel's passing, there are only a handful of us left. The Nephilim's Gift is too powerful. Their technology too great."

"I didn't set you up, specifically," Kett said. "Thraven learned about the mainframe on his own. He arranged the drop with his cronies in the Republic. The only thing I did was pull some strings to requisition a

Breaker for the mission. It could have been any Breaker."

"Bullshit," Abbey said. "Do you know how many Breakers go into the field? She raised a hand, and then lowered one of her fingers. "Four, including me."

"Then there was only a twenty-five percent chance you would be the one, Abigail," Kett said. "I'm sorry if you're bothered that it was you. We saw an opportunity to enlist someone with the Nephilim's Gift. Someone who could fight back against Thraven and his Evolents."

"I was in Hell, General," Abbey said. "How the frag did you know Captain Mann was going to get me out?"

"We didn't," Charmeine said. "We expected you to go with Thraven. To train under him. To become stronger than him, and then hopefully betray him."

"That's not a risk, that's a fragging miracle."

"It may be" Kett said. "But we're at the point where it may be the only thing that will save us. We knew our best chance to gain a Nephilim to our cause would be to have Thraven give the Gift to someone whose loyalty to their people was stronger than their personal desire for power. I know from experience that Breakers tend to fit that mold quite well. If that were the case, it isn't unthinkable that such a person might betray their master."

"Did you just call me a Nephilim?" Abbey said.

"That's what you are, isn't it? You have their blood in your veins. Their version of the naniates. Their Gift and power."

"I'm not like them," Abbey said. "I'm human."

Charmeine shook her head. "You were human. Now you're becoming a Nephilim. A demon."

"Demon Queen," Bastion said.

"Thraven said I can't stop it without the other half of the Gift. But I can't get the other half without joining him."

"The Blood of the Font," Charmeine said. "And the Serum."

"What is that?"

"The other half of the Gift."

"How do you know?"

"I'm over ten-thousand years old, Abbey. I know many things."

"How can that be possible? How are you immortal?"

"I'm not immortal."

She reached up and moved her hair aside, turning to show Abbey the back of her neck. There was a small disc there, similar in look to the teleporters that Jequn had used on Anvil.

"It's a regenerative device. It requires power of its own. The power of the Shard."

"Naniates?"

"Yes. We have a few tricks of our own. But our naniates are in limited supply. They won't reproduce without the Blood of the Shard, and every time we collect them from the Focus we lose more of it. There isn't much remaining."

"So you know where the Focus is?"

"On the Shardship."

"And you know where the Shardship is?"

"I do."

"So why don't you use it against Thraven?"

"As I'm sure Jequn told you, the Focus doesn't have enough power remaining."

"That's why we needed someone like you," Kett said.

Abbey stared at him, her mind working.

"You think I can fight Thraven. You think I can kill him."

"That was the original goal," Kett said. "Captain Mann fragged it up when he rescued you from Hell. You're strong, Abigail. Stronger than most. But without the rest of the Gift you'll never be strong enough to fight Thraven."

"Then why lead me to Drune? Why save me at all, if you're so sure I can't stop him?"

"Because we aren't the One," Charmeine said. "The possibility remains that we might be wrong."

"Tell me more about the Font."

"The Font is a source of the Nephilim's Gift, as the Focus is to ours. It is a breeding ground for the naniates, where the ancient blood of

The Devils Do

the Seraphim is mixed with drops of blood from the Shard. When you receive the second part of the Gift, you are permitted to drink from it. To gorge on the naniates within. Some drink too heavily and are killed by the influx. Others drink too lightly and don't gain the power needed to earn the Serum. Thraven either allows them to change or kills them outright."

Abbey licked her lips absently. How much power could she gain by drinking from the Font? Not that she wanted to drink blood ever again, but if it would mean the difference between victory and defeat? She would never say never.

"I know what you're thinking," Charmeine said. "You can't drink from it. Not because it would harm you, but because the naniates in the Font are his."

"His?"

"Thraven can control them from anywhere in the universe. They're linked. Networked."

"Frag," Bastion said.

"Where is the Font?" Abbey asked.

"Wherever Thraven is, the Font will go with him. He bathes in it to keep his strength up. He too is thousands of years old, and requires it to stay alive."

"Then the Font must be on the Fire. If we capture or destroy the Fire, the Font will be destroyed with it, and Thraven will die."

"There is one large difference between the Focus and the Font," Charmeine said. "There is only one Focus."

"So there are multiple Fonts?"

"But not here. Thraven would need to go back to the Extant to get another, and he would need to petition one of the other Gloritants to give it to him. Or he would have to win it from them."

"Other Gloritants? The Extant?" Abbey didn't like the sound of either of those things.

"Did you think Thraven was the only one?" Kett asked. "He's the spearhead. Maybe the most intelligent. He isn't alone."

"The Extant is the galaxy where the Nephilim reside. It is beyond the reach of your ships, but not of his."

"Can the *Brimstone* reach it?"

"Most likely."

"You know what powers the Brimstone, don't you?"

"Yes. All of the Nephilim's technology was once this way, until we destroyed most of the life in this galaxy. It's the only thing that has held them back this long."

"It's fragged up, is what it is," Bastion said. "Queenie, tell them about the gate."

"Gate?" Kett said.

"Eagan Heavyworks wasn't just working on the *Fire* and Brimstone," Abbey said. "I found evidence that they were also researching how to build an Elysium Gate."

"They can't," Charmeine said. "Only the Focus." She paused. "We can't allow Thraven to get his hands on the Focus."

"Well, thanks to your amazing plan, Thraven got those hands on your mainframe, and now he knows where you're hiding." Abbey didn't try to mask her anger with the whole shitty deal. "There's a really good chance he's on his way here right now."

"Even if he comes to Bain, it will take him weeks to find Azure," Kett said.

"You're not going to be here for weeks," Abbey said. "In fact, you have about forty-seven hours to mobilize."

"Forty-seven hours?" Kett said. "Impossible."

"You'd better make it possible, General. I've got a team prepping to assault Thraven's base on Kell, and you're damned well going to be part of that assault."

"I don't think so," Kett said. "You should have stayed with your team, Abigail. You wasted your time and your resources coming here if you think I'm going to help you with that. Show me we have a chance to win this war, win the opening battle, and then I'll get involved. We've worked too hard for too many years to throw it all away on day one."

Abbey felt the Gift surging within her. She raised her hand, and Kett was thrown back, pinned to the wall by it. Siddrah and Brinks both stood, reaching for their sidearms. Bastion was quicker, drawing a pair of

The Devils Do

guns and pointing them at both the soldier.

"Nope," he said.

"You listen to me, General," Abbey said, getting to her feet and climbing to the top of the table. She kept her eyes on Charmeine. The Seraph wasn't making any effort to stop her. In fact, Abbey got the impression that she was on her side. "You pulled me into this fight. You made me into this so that I could go against Thraven. The whole things sucks, but unfortunately for you, you lucked into the right woman for the job. Win the opening battle? Frag you, I already did. I killed Thraven's Evolent. I took one of his best ships. I found out he was coming here in time to warn you. And I've got a spearhead of my own. Now, either you can agree to pack up your shit and follow me to Kell, or I can kill you and as many of your people as I have to until I find someone who will."

She smiled and let go of him. He dropped to the floor, remaining there, staring at her.

"Is that understood?" she asked.

He kept staring while tense seconds passed. Then he returned her smile. "You're more than we could have hoped for, Abigail."

"I'm just getting started," she replied.

CHAPTER THIRTY

GENERAL KETT VANISHED FROM THE room almost immediately after regaining his breath, excusing himself so he could start getting his soldiers mobilized. There seemed to be a new fire in him after Abbey roughed him up. A flaring sense of hope or purpose. It was more than Abbey would have expected, but then, for as much as she had thought she knew Kett from his exploits and his record before, she realized she didn't really know a damn thing about him. He had used her. He had lied to her. He had gotten his daughter to lie to her, too. She was a product of his design as much as Thraven's. A pawn.

Not anymore.

They finished eating, and then Charmeine brought them outside for a tour of the camp. It was still raining.

"It's always raining in here," Charmaine said. "If we want to see the sky, we take a ship up over the clouds. It can be a real strain on some of the recruits, but it keeps us hidden."

They were riding in a small car, a transparent canopy keeping them dry. There was an increasing volume of activity in the camp, with soldiers moving back and forth in the damp, most of them in full suits with helmets and TCUs to keep their movements coordinated and keep themselves dry and warm. They had already started loading items into transport crates from within the lines of barracks, looking up at them as they made their way past, and in many cases raising a palm to the Seraph. She repeated the gesture to them, smiling at them as she did.

"They respect you quite a bit," Abbey said.

"They respect Sylvan, and they know I'm his wife." She looked at Abbey. "And some of them just think I'm hot."

Abbey smiled. "You are."

"I don't want to sound conceited, but I know. It certainly doesn't hurt that I'm being genetically held at twenty-six Earth years by the regenerator."

"Ten-thousand," Abbey said. "I can't even imagine what that must be like. How did you manage to survive so long?"

"We were never intended to. Naturally, we live and die similar to humans. The regenerators became a necessity after the Shard was murdered and the war started. He knew some would have to survive, to carry the word of what happened forward. Without it, Thraven and the Nephilim would have already won."

"Why didn't you just write it down?" Bastion asked.

"Can you read Seraphim?" Charmeine asked. "Can it be translated to Terran by someone who isn't a Seraph? Written histories are valuable, but the stories we tell can be more valuable. That is why the Shard gave us the regeneration technology."

"What about the teleporters?" Abbey asked. "He gave you those, too?"

She nodded. "None of it is without a price. They're charged with naniates, which means they either must use the Blood of the Shard directly, which will further drain the Focus, or they must be powered by a Gifted Seraph. You know what happens when we take the Gift."

"I do," Abbey said, glancing back at Jequn.

"Don't feel sorry for me, Queenie," Jequn said. "It was my choice to make."

"All of the descendants have a choice," Charmeine said. "Free will is the most valuable gift we are given. Even our oral histories have lost their impact over time. There are millions of humans with Seraphim heritage, but so few know where they came from, or what their parents or their parent's parents were. So many have turned away from the truth and decided the Nephilim are nothing more than myth."

"You mean like the Bible?" Bastion said.

"Stories retold from our history, yes. There is some ring of truth to all of them if you know the context in which they occur."

"What do you mean?" Abbey asked.

"We used the Focus to destroy much of the life in this galaxy. We too were decimated. Torn apart by the use of the Focus. It stopped the war and drove the Nephilim away, but we always knew they would come back. And they did. In small numbers at first. They passed themselves off as gods and took people away in their ships, back to the Extant to use them for their blood, or recruit them to their cause."

"Wait a second," Bastion said. "You're talking about what? Like the Egyptians? The Pyramids?"

"How do you know about that?" Abbey asked.

"I read a book once," he replied. "And I went to elementary school. I'm not a total frag-up you know. I used to love that shit. The Egyptians, the Aztecs, the Incas. They had so much in common, even though they lived so far apart. I guess now I know why."

"Yes. That's one example," Charmeine said. "Do you remember the icons of Anubis?"

Bastion nodded. "Yeah." He paused. "Oh. Shit."

"What?" Abbey asked. Her education hadn't included ancient Egypt.

"Queenie, those things we've been fighting. The Goreshins. If you look at them a certain way, they could pass as Anubis."

"Seriously?" Abbey said.

"Yeah, for once." He looked at Charmeine, suddenly much more interested in the conversation. "I read that the Pyramids were aligned astrologically. So were some of the temples in South America. Related?"

"Yes."

"Why didn't you stop them?" Abbey asked. "If you knew they were on Earth, why didn't you do something about it?"

The Devils Do

"We couldn't fight them when we were at full strength. How were we supposed to fight them when we were so few? We did what we could. We fought when we could. In many ways, this war never ended." She took a deep breath and sighed it out. "I've killed enough Nephilim for ten times my lifespan. I've watched friends, husbands, lovers, children all die at their hands. I'm numb to it. No intelligent being should ever become numb to killing or to loss."

She froze, staring straight ahead. Abbey could sense the pain, the hurt, the tiredness. She had no idea how anything could live as long as Charmaine claimed without losing their sanity. She couldn't put her mind around the loneliness.

"It doesn't matter now," Chermeine said. "The past can help inform the future, but neither can directly change the other. For my part, I'm sorry that we weren't able to do more, and that we've left all of the Children of the Shard so unprepared for this fight. I'm sorry too that we had to drag you into this the way we did."

"I'm sorry for lying to you, Queenie," Jequn said. "I know I said it already, but it bears repeating. I couldn't betray my loyalties." She smiled. "I'm glad you found your way here, though. I think you're right about this fight, about focusing on winning one battle before worrying about the next."

"I understand," Abbey replied. "I honestly do, now. I'm not angry at you. I'm not angry at General Kett either. In a way, I'm glad it was me. When Olus first got us out of Hell, I took command reluctantly. I-"

"That's not how I remember it," Bastion interrupted.

"I didn't want to be in charge," Abbey said. "But I did want to be in control. I have a daughter. I can't imagine what it would be like to lose her. I can't imagine what it has been like for you to lose so many. I know I'm not the only one with a child or someone important to protect. I don't want to count on someone else to be that protection. I'll do whatever it takes."

"I'm glad it was you, too," Charmeine said. "Your passion is obvious, and it rubs off on those around you. It makes you a strong leader."

"You'd have to be, to put up with this one's mouth," Jequn said, elbowing Bastion.

"What?" he replied. "I haven't even been saying that much."

"Only because you were shoving too much food into your face too quickly to form any words."

"That was the first time I sat down for a meal that wasn't a food bar in years. So yeah, I was whole hogging it all the way."

"Whole hogging it?" Abbey said.

"All the way. Hey, since we're on a new topic, I have a question."

"What is it?" Abbey said.

"I don't see how all of this shit is going to fit on the handful of ships parked with the Faust?" He pointed in the distance, where a Gunner was making its way across the open space. "Like that mech over there. How are you going to get it out of here? You can fit maybe three of them on one of those ships."

"A reasonable question," Charmeine said. "These ships are for emergency evacuation. We have others nearby. We rescued them from the Republic scrapyards, paying the junkers for them instead of allowing them to be broken down. They're old, but they're functional."

"That's not a promising review," Abbey said. "Ships like the *Fire* will cut right through a fleet like that."

"I know. Which is why we need to remove those ships from the equation."

"Shrikes will eat ships like that alive, too," Bastion said.

"We have Shrikes of our own to counter them. We've been collecting across the entire galaxy. And we have the Focus."

"You said the Focus' power is waning," Abbey said.

"It is. We can't cause another mass extinction. But we can use it judiciously to help with the fight. I've already relayed a message to the Seedships to return here."

"I know the Seedships have teleporters," Abbey said. "Do they have anything else we can use?"

"Like weapons? No. They carry links to the Focus, and we can use the power of the Focus through them. That is the closest thing we possess."

The Devils Do

"So the Shardship won't be coming to the party?" Bastion asked.

"Even if it weren't too dangerous, the Shardship was badly damaged by the Nephilim and crashed thousands of years ago. We're fortunate that the enemy doesn't know it's location."

"But you and General Kett do," Abbey said.

"We are the only two here that know where it is. There are others who know, of course, or we wouldn't be able to draw Blood from the Tomb, but their identities are secret, for obvious reasons."

"Understood," Abbey said.

"Let me show you the rest of the compound. When we're done, I'll drop you at the War Room so you can plan your strategy with Sylvan. Make sure you come and see me when you're done. I have something for you."

"You do?" Abbey said. "What is it?"

"Do you like surprises, Queenie?"

"That depends."

"I think you'll like this one."

CHAPTER THIRTY-ONE

"I've been following you," Abbey said. "Tracking you since I first heard the Republic brand you a traitor. I never believed it."

General Sylvan Kett looked up from the projection ahead of him. It was messy with reports from his senior officers, all of them doing their best to get the rebellion mobilized.

"Why not?" Sylvan asked. "Thraven did an impressive job of setting me up for that fall, and getting enough plants on the Committee and the Council to support it."

"Intuition?" Abbey said. "Instinct? Or maybe I could see the truth through the reports. A war hero. A man who dedicated his entire life to protecting the Republic suddenly turning mercenary? It didn't add up."

"It's happened before."

"Maybe it didn't add up then, either. How long have the Nephilim been manipulating things? If they were around in ancient Egypt, how do we know they don't own the corporations that run the Outworlds?"

"They would have had the *Fire* and *Brimstone* a long time ago if they had access to those kinds of resources."

"Maybe," Abbey said.

"I assume Charlie gave you a little bit of a Seraphim history lesson while she was showing you around."

"She did."

"Do you believe it?"

"Do you?"

He smiled. "It sneaks up on you, doesn't it? The truth of human civilization. That we were made by some higher order intelligence."

"People have believed God made us for a long time. What is God, if not a higher order intelligence?"

"You can argue that I suppose."

"You don't agree?"

"I was a religious man when I met Charlie. It's tough to reconcile sometimes. I prefer to think that God created the One and the One created man. The Bible was never meant to be taken literally, so all of the meanings are the same. Even if the source material is based on an interstellar war."

"What does this have to do with current events?" Abbey asked.

"Not much, but I don't get to talk it out too often. What did you think of the resistance?"

"I'm impressed with how much you've been able to accomplish. You've managed to get your hands on a lot of equipment."

"Most of it is outdated."

"Not the Daedalus fighters. Not the Gunners."

"I bought them directly from StarDyne."

"It's illegal for them to sell to you directly."

Sylvan smiled. "Very. But I have a few connections there."

"It should be enough to destroy Thraven's base on Kell."

"Assuming we can catch them while Thraven's out to lunch. And assuming he took all of his new shiny warships with him."

"He arrives here, we arrive there," Abbey said. "It sounds good to me. Once we've diminished his forces, we can worry about picking off the rest. Does the Focus have enough left to destroy a few ships?"

"It should, but it might not be enough."

Sylvan manipulated the projection, hiding the reports and bringing up a news feed.

"I picked this up an hour ago. It looks like Thraven's goal of gaining full control of the Republic Council has been successful."

Abbey looked at the feed. "A terrorist attack on a charity dinner?" she said, scanning it. "Eight Council members dead, along with four hundred others. The entire original structure of the Natural History Museum destroyed. A suspect at large." She froze. "Captain Mann? That's bullshit."

"That's Thraven," Sylvan said. "He's going to gain control of the Council. Do you know what he's going to do with that control?"

Abbey felt cold. They had framed Olus for the attack. They had found a way to tear down his years of loyal service in the course of a few weeks. At least he was at large, as in still alive.

"I can guess."

"He's already captured Anvil," Sylvan said. "And destroyed a Republic battlegroup near it. He'll gather the Republic's resources and pool them there, ostensibly to retaliate for the attacks on the Republic the Outworlds have been carrying out, and the theft of the *Fire* and Brimstone. He'll push both nations to war with one another, directing one with his left hand, and the other with his right. And then he'll declare martial law in both and start conscripting citizens."

"Except those citizens will never make it to the front lines," Abbey said.

"That's right. They'll vanish without a trace. Their families will be told they're dead."

"Like Hell, but on a much larger scale."

"Exactly."

"What about the others? The Gants and the Atmo and the Rudin?"

"He'll control them or kill them. It won't matter at that point. If he controls humans, he has more than enough."

"He'll be able to power the Elysium Gate."

"If he's building one, yeah. But that was always the plan, wasn't it?"

"Frag. How do we stop this?"

Sylvan put out his hands. "I'm not sure yet. The good news is, wars don't start that quickly, and it'll take months for him to make those moves so that they don't look orchestrated. Step one, take out his fleet on Kell. Step two, kill the fragger. I'm glad you found me, Abigail. I was wrong to sit back and wait on this. I've done the best I can, but I'm not perfect."

"None of us are," Abbey replied. "Do you have estimates on when you'll be finished packing?"

"Early estimates. It's going to be close. I'm at forty-nine hours right now."

"That's two too many."

"I know. We have a lot of equipment, and we weren't planning on having to bug out of here just yet. I expected it to take months for Thraven to crack that encryption, not weeks. Even with you looking into it. I don't know how they broke it so fast."

"He sent it back to Earth. To the HSOC. They probably borrowed time on the Worldbrain."

"We accounted for that. Charlie wrote the algorithm. It was based on Seraphim encryption protocols written in Rudin tertiary."

"Rudin tertiary? Damn. I should have guessed that. I don't understand why you didn't just leave a decoy?"

"You would have figured out it was a dud in seconds. Like I said before, it was a risk. I guess we're splitting the difference on this one."

"Best laid plans," Abbey said. "We still have a fighting chance. Are you familiar with Kell?"

"It used to belong to a drug cartel. It's a terraformed planet. I assume that's all the intel we've got?"

"Pretty much. We're going in with the Brimstone, a handful of Devil starfighters, and a shuttle that can carry a small team to the ground. We know Thraven's got prisoners there, and we intend to free them and drop them a bunch of weapons to join the fight while the starfighters hit the active warships with heavy ordnance that will hopefully be enough to disable them. It'll go a lot more smoothly with your forces backing them up."

"I imagine. That isn't much of an assault."

"You were going to leave it that way two hours ago."

"It would be much more of an assault with an Evolent on their side."

"Please don't call me that," Abbey said. "Gift or not, I'll never be one of them."

"My apologies, Abigail. I was wrong about Kell."

"Apology accepted. It's all behind us, and we need to keep moving forward. We aren't going to have much data before we reach Kell. I'm counting on your experience to assess the situation and adjust your individuals appropriately. That's what you're known for, after all."

Sylvan nodded. "It is, and I will."

"Good. For now, you have two extra bodies to help you cut that estimate down. What can Bastion and I do?"

CHAPTER THIRTY-TWO

THE *FIRE* EXITED FTL ALONG with six other ships, each of them a Nephilim warship upgraded with the recently recovered technologies of the Covenant, the plans, and designs given by the Father in his Promise of the Great Return.

The disterium spread around them like a fog, the density much less than with a normal starship, the efficiency nearly doubled by their Gift-enhanced reactors.

"The Bain System, Gloritant," Honorant Piselle announced.

Gloritant Thraven looked out into the nothingness. Of course, Kett hadn't provided direct access to whichever planet he was hiding on. They would have to locate it in the system, a process that could take them weeks.

He didn't have the patience to wait for weeks.

"I want them found, Honorant," he said. "Immediately."

"Yes, Your Eminence," Piselle replied. "How?"

"Check your scanners," he said. "If arriving ships don't have exact coordinates, there has to be a satellite or active sentry nearby."

"Gloritant, we've detected a sniffer satellite," Agitant Malt said.

"Where?"

It appeared on the projection at the front of the bridge, highlighted in red. Thraven's eyes narrowed at the sight of it, and he raised both of his hands, feeling the Gift pour out of them. A moment later, a piece of the satellite sparked and went dark. He lowered his hands, reaching back and steadying himself. Projecting the Gift in such a way used a lot of energy, but he couldn't risk having Kett knowing he was close.

He only hoped that Cage would be with him.

He considered the possibility. Evolent Ruche had intentionally given Captain Mann the coordinates so that he would pass them to her, and he had no doubt she would use the information to try to warn the General. But what choice would she make? She couldn't be in the Bain System and preparing to attack Kell at the same time. True, she could split her forces, but what kind of force would that be? The *Brimstone* and a dozen soldiers against his entire compound? No. That wasn't going to work out well for her. He had seen to that.

And if by some miracle it did? Ruche and Elivee had succeeded in their mission to finish removing the independents on the Council. Ruche had even managed to frame Olus for the entire thing. It was brilliant, simply brilliant. He had seen potential in the Evolent from the day he had dragged him from Hell, but it had been far surpassed.

He rarely second-guessed himself, but he wondered if he should have put Ruche in Trin's place beforehand. Would he have succeeded where Trinity failed? It didn't matter. He had everything positioned perfectly. Even better? He was certain neither General Kett or Abigail Cage had any idea how futile their efforts were.

"Send a ship out to retrieve the satellite," Thraven said. "We'll trace the transmission log to see where it was sending its data."

"As you command, Gloritant," Piselle said, activating her communicator and relaying the orders.

Thraven lingered on the bridge long enough to watch the retrieval shuttle move away from the *Fire* toward the satellite. Then he left the area, trailed by his Immolent as he made his way to his quarters.

"Gloritant Thraven," Airi said, catching up to him in the hallway, approaching from in front of him. She saluted him stiffly as she came to a stop. "I've completed the task, Your Eminence," she said.

The Devils Do

"Already?" Thraven said, slightly impressed.

It had taken Noviant Soto hours to complete the most simple test, and only hours more to move up nearly five ranks. She wasn't on par with what Cage had done naturally, not yet, but he was growing more confident with each passing hour that she could get there. He would never have believed it when he had brought her off Anvil.

"Yes, Gloritant," Airi replied.

"Come with me."

"Yes, Gloritant."

Thraven reached his suite with Airi following dutifully behind. He entered, and then turned and beckoned the Immolent to wait outside.

"Why are you standing there, Noviant?" he asked. "I told you to come with me."

Airi had frozen outside of his door.

"How many times do I have to tell you I don't want to have sex with you?" Thraven asked, angry. He reached out with the Gift, grabbing her and pulling her into the room. "I have a new lesson for you."

She submitted to him, lowering her head. "I'm sorry, Gloritant. I'm-"

"I don't care," Thraven replied. "Whatever happened to you before happened when you were nothing but another Lesser who believed they were more than the resource they are. That is a thing that no longer exists. The sooner you understand that the more powerful you will become. Follow."

He led her to the bedroom. The bed had been removed, replaced with the Font. She had been here once already to drink from it, but his Immolent had been with him then. They were alone now.

"Am I permitted to drink again?" Airi asked.

"No," Thraven replied. "All I want you to do is stand there. Remain silent, or you fail the lesson."

She nodded, staying in place while he began to undress.

He stripped off the uniform jacket, the pants, the shirt, the tightly bound cloth beneath it all. He faced her while he did, watching her expression. He could see she was uncomfortable. Afraid. He didn't care about that, either. Her fear would hold her back if she let it. His job was to set her free.

He finished stripping. It was only then that Airi's expression began to calm.

"I couldn't if I wanted to," Thraven said, looking down at himself.

It had been thousands of years since he had been castrated, and he had stopped caring about it long ago. He turned around, showing her his back. He heard her gasp at the shape of it. At the sight of the scars.

"I know pain, Noviant," he said. "Better than most. I know mistreatment. I know fear. These things were once part of me. I was born a Lesser, you see. Like you. I was captured during a battle and made the slave of an Egyptian noble. He took my manhood after his wife used it for her pleasure. He whipped me nearly every night only because he enjoyed it."

Thraven felt his pulse thumping as he spoke the words. He had accepted the pain, but he had never completely lost it. Thousands of years and he could remember it as though it were fresh.

"I'm sorry," Airi said.

"Don't be sorry for me," Thraven snapped, spinning around. "For what? That was thousands of years ago. That was a different existence. I was brought to the Extant. I was saved from my life of servitude and given a chance to earn a life of glory, just like I have done for you. I would never have been anything if I had let the hurt destroy me. Instead, I am a Gloritant of the Nephilim, at the forefront of the Great Return. I am Blessed by the Father, called to be His Servant and to lead His Children to glory."

He paused, taking a step toward her. She didn't flinch.

"What do you want to be, Noviant Soto? I have many Evolents. They fall over themselves to please me because of the power that I hold. It is power that any of them can hold if they are strong enough. If they want it enough. But there is no margin for fear. There is no margin for doubt. You must decide who you are, and what you want. To be another of the flock, or to be at the front of it? Let go of your past. Let go of who you were."

The Devils Do

    He turned and walked away from her, stepping into the Font until the Blood was up to his waist. He turned his head back then.
    "That is your lesson. Go and practice your Gift."
    "Thank you, Gloritant," she said.
    He dipped his head into the pool, drawing in the Blood, his energy beginning to return immediately. When he raised his head again, she was gone.

CHAPTER THIRTY-THREE

"DID I THANK YOU FOR volunteering us yet?" Bastion asked, lifting another crate and carrying it over to the smaller transport.

"About a thousand times already," Abbey replied. She lifted her own crate, placing it onto the flatbed behind them.

They had four hours remaining to finish packing. Nearly two days had passed, two days that had seen Abbey work harder than she ever had in her life, assisting General Kett and his soldiers in tearing down a camp that had been in place for hundreds of years. Abbey had been surprised to learn Azure had served as an Ophanim refuge long before Kett had arrived with his armies. Once upon a time, a Seedship had sat in the center of the crater, hidden by the storms, providing food and shelter to the Seraphim and the families who lived here. It was a base of operations from which they carried out a number of smaller incursions against the Nephilim, trying to root out the Children of the Covenant, disrupt their financial interests, and otherwise continue the secret war in a guerilla fashion.

She hadn't slept at all in those two days. At the same time, she wasn't tired. The Gift was fueling her, keeping her going. As long as she ate, she was strong, and even though she wasn't actively calling on its power to help her help the group, she could feel how it was working for her, and at the same time continuing to alter her. Her base strength was increasing. Her stamina was increasing. And Bastion was certain she had grown at least two or three centimeters.

Her hair was growing, too. It had filled in, returning with a vengeance, beginning to pour down the side of her head in smooth, silvery locks. Bastion told her it looked good, but it only served to remind her of what the Gift was doing to her body. She shaved it off during one of her breaks, and could already feel it returning again. Her thoughts turned to the Serum more and more often. She needed to get her hands on it, one way or another. She had to stop herself from changing and from losing her mind.

She had said as much to Charmeine. She had asked her for her advice. She liked the Seraph a lot. She was strong but kind, a good listener. She reminded Abbey of her mother, who had passed away while she was away in HSOC training, out of communication with the rest of the universe. Charmeine had promised to speak to Kett about the situation. After all, it wouldn't do the cause any good to have a Nephilim monster instead of a Gifted warrior. But getting to the Serum meant getting to Thraven, and Abbey wasn't strong enough to do it.

She paused for a short break, looking out over the camp. So much of it was empty now. The barracks were gone, most of the starfighters were gone, half of the soldiers were gone. The ships around the *Faust* were gone as well, making runs back and forth to the larger battlecruisers waiting above, along with two of the Ophanim's four Seedships. Abbey was eager to get a look at them and to see what the Seraphim had used to impregnate the Earth with life. The ships were millions of years old and still functional, their power supplies seemingly endless. What kind of lasers could they power with that kind of tech? Damn it, why weren't the Seraphim better at making weapons?

"Queenie," Jequn said, coming up to them from behind.

Abbey turned around. The Ophanim looked tired, her face pale. She had been tasked with donating her blood, and with it her Gift, so that they could charge a number of the teleportation devices to be distributed among the units. She was one of only three Gifted on Azure. The rest remained either on the Seedships where they could control the Focus, or in hiding among the other settled planets in the galaxy, held in reserve to continue the fight for as long as they could.

"Hey, J," Bastion said. "You look like shit."

"I'll recover," she said. "Queenie, Mother asked me to find you. She has something for you."

"Now?" Abbey said.

"You've been at this for hours," Bastion said. "I didn't see you take a single break, not even to piss or sleep. I've got these last few."

"Are you sure?" she asked.

"Yeah. But thanks for caring now that I'm ready to drop dead."

"Who says I care? I'll be right back."

She left Bastion to finish loading the supplies, heading across to the bunker with Jequn.

They went inside. She led Abbey deep into the tunnels, to where Kett and his wife had made their home. It was a small, unimpressive space. Sparse and functional. Charmeine was waiting there, and she smiled and embraced Abbey when she saw her.

"Thank you for working so hard," she said.

Abbey returned the embrace. "I would never ask anyone to do more than I'm willing to do myself."

"That's why your team respects you. Wait here."

She vanished into a secondary room. Abbey glanced over at Jequn. "Do you know what this is?"

Jequn smiled. "Yes. I helped her prepare it."

The Seraph returned a moment later, carrying a softsuit. No, it wasn't a softsuit. It was shimmering and red, similar to the suit Jequn wore. A seraphsuit.

"That one doesn't fit you all that well," Charmeine said. "And this one will increase your speed and agility while offering you greater protection from puncturing, thanks to the weave of the material. Jequn told me I should dye it red for the Demon Queen. Sylvan had one of his techs integrate a SoC, TCU, and keypad." She held up the arm of the suit, showing her how it ended in an open-fingered glove. "This is a little different than what you're used to. When you move your fingers, it will select letters and numbers based on the movement. It may take you a few weeks to get used to it, but once you do it will be faster than typing on your hip."

She held up a cowl attached to the back. "This isn't going to stop a hit like an armored helmet, but it does provide HUD and TCU access. It's my own design. It will probably feel a little funny on your head, but it beats having to carry a second piece of gear around."

"I don't know what to say," Abbey said.

Gant had given her a softsuit, too. It had taken her about thirty seconds to destroy it. She missed him as she looked at it. They would be starting their assault soon. She hoped he would be okay. She hoped all of them would be okay.

"Thank you will suffice," Charmeine said.

"Thank you," Abbey replied.

"You're welcome."

Abbey stripped out of her softsuit in front of them. "Tell me if you see anything weird going on with my body," she said. "I can feel it changing."

"I don't see anything, other than your hair," Jequn said.

"Turn around," Charmeine said.

Abbey did.

The Seraph stepped up to her, putting a hand on the small of her back, right above her rear. "Do you feel this?" she asked.

Abbey closed her eyes, remembering Phlenel's depiction of her monster form. "I'm growing a tail. Frag."

"It's small right now. Barely noticeable."

"You noticed it."

"I'm literally older than dirt, and I helped the Shard create humankind."

"Do you know how long I have?"

"If you don't use the Gift? Years. If you do? Months."

"Not using it isn't an option."

"I know."

Abbey took the suit from Charmeine. "Maybe you should put a

hole in the back, for my tail."

Charmeine laughed. "Try not to think about that right now. It will stretch some to accommodate growth."

"That makes me feel better." Abbey sighed. What was complaining going to do about it? "I'm going to call it a hellsuit, to differentiate it. Even if it was given to me by an angel."

She slipped it on, pulling it tight across her body. It felt lighter but also warmer. She slid the ends over her fingers.

"We'll need to transfer the data from your current SoC over to this one," Jequn said. "Oh, and you have four teleporters in the packs here." She put her hand on Abbey's hip. "Just in case."

"Thank you," Abbey said.

She found the transfer cable on both suits and attached them. She pulled the cowl up and over her head. Charmeine was right, it did feel odd, like a second skin over her face, but it was also somehow transparent to her eyes. The HUD came up in front of her, only slightly distorting the view beyond the cowl.

"Visibility is a lot better than a helmet," she said, moving her fingers.

She watched the letters move on the screen, and it took her a minute to get the motions right to start selecting menus and get to the transfer view. It was fairly intuitive, and she had it mostly down by the time she had entered the credentials for her old suit, set them for this new one, and started the data transfer.

"Charmeine, I had something I wanted to ask you," she said. "You may not know the answer, but you're the best resource I have."

"Of course," the Seraph replied.

"I used the Gift to move some junk, searching for data left over from the station on Feru. Afterward, the Gift, I don't know, attacked me? It tried to challenge me for control, as though it wanted to take my body. When Thraven confronted me, he said I had asserted myself, and I've had more control over the Gift since, even when I'm not totally pissed off."

"And you want to know what I think that means?"

"There's more. Right before the Gift submitted, I saw a flash of

The Devils Do

blinding white light. Thraven seemed to think there was something to it, but-"

She stopped talking. Charmeine's entire face had changed.

"What?" she said.

"The Shard had the ability to communicate with us directly in our minds. It was always preceded by a flash of blinding light." A tear ran from her eye. "I haven't experienced that in so long. I wish I could have it one more time." She looked away. "I'm not sure what it means for you, Abigail. The Shard is dead. He can't talk to any of us. But this is the first time I've heard of it again in many, many years."

"I don't think it's that," Abbey said. "If it was, he didn't say anything."

"What if he was reaching out?" Jequn asked. "What if some part of him is out there?"

Charmeine shook her head. "And he's been hiding from his servants all of this time when he could have been trying to speak to us?"

"I'm sorry," Abbey said. "It was probably just my brain getting zapped by the naniates. Little fraggers."

Charmeine looked at her again. "Yes, that's probably what it was."

Abbey could tell she wasn't convinced.

A small message on the HUD told Abbey the transfer was complete. She disconnected the wires.

"It looks like the suit is all done. Thank you again. I need to get back out there and help finish up."

"Of course," Charmeine said. "I'll join you. I haven't done nearly enough to help us move out. Jequn, you should-"

She was interrupted by a loud, piercing siren. It echoed across the complex, momentarily deafening them all.

"What the frag?" Abbey said.

"Red alert," Charmeine replied. "Sent from the orbiting ships. We're too late. Thraven is here."

CHAPTER THIRTY-FOUR

"Shit," Abbey said.

The alarms were still blaring, hurting her head. Something hit the side of the crater, causing the inside of the complex to vibrate.

"Let's go," Charmeine said.

Abbey grabbed her Uin from the old softsuit and shoved it into a pack on the new one. Then she picked up her holsters, slipping them on over the demonsuit, joining the other two women as they raced out of the room and into the main corridors of the complex. There weren't many soldiers left inside, but the few that remained were joining them in the halls, dressed in lightsuits and weapons in hand.

"We didn't get any warning from the satellite," Jequn said. "And how did he find us so quickly? Father said it would take weeks."

"I don't know," Charmeine replied.

"It doesn't matter," Abbey said. "He's here, now, and we need to get the remaining units out."

She heard gunfire as she neared the entrance to the bunker. Bastion was out there, unarmed. Frag. She moved past Charmeine and Jequn, calling on the Gift to give her speed. She burst out into the open, into a fragging disaster.

A transport was on the ground, enemy soldiers pouring out of it,

The Devils Do

attacking the friendlies nearby. Their forces were caught by surprise and were slowly getting organized, finding cover and getting their hands on weapons to counter the offensive.

Abbey quickly scanned the field, finding bastion on the ground behind the transport. He wasn't moving.

She pushed off, leaping away, the Gift carrying her three hundred meters across the distance in one bounce. She landed beside Bastion, leaning over him. "Bastion," she said. "Bastion?"

He looked up at her, throwing a punch. It hit her on the side of the head, but the suit absorbed most of the blow.

"Damn it, Bastion, it's me," Abbey said.

He stared up at her in the suit. "Another upgrade?" he said. "Queenie, you look like one of those superheroes from the vids."

"Shut up and start shooting," she said, handing him her guns.

He slid to his knees, taking them. "I take it Thraven is here?"

"You think? We need to get the *Faust* ready to go. We have to take as many as we can."

"Roger. I'm on it. Cover me."

Abbey stood, looking over the battlefield. Both sides had taken what cover they could find and were exchanging fire. She found Jequn in the midst of the field, a Uin in each hand, dancing across the lines. Charmeine was nearby, having gotten a rifle from somewhere and shooting into the enemy with expert precision.

She felt the Gift pulsing beneath her skin, eager to be part of the violence. She would give it what it wanted. She came out from behind the transport, jumping to a group of enemy soldiers fifty meters away. She landed in front of one, grabbing him by the arm and throwing him into the others with enough force to knock them all off-balance. She drove into them, picking up the Uin and slicing her way through the line. She didn't know if they were Converts or not, but she wasn't going to take any chances.

The sky rumbled above them, the clouds keeping the action above invisible from the ground. She found a second group of enemy soldiers and moved toward them, joined by Jequn as she started her attack.

"Imp, status?" she said, thankful she had completed the data transfer before the attack. The demonsuit not only had the Reject's comm identifiers on it, but it had added Kett's as well.

"Almost there, Queenie," Bastion replied. "I think I was spotted, though."

"Cherub," Abbey said, hoping Jequn had her link open.

"Queenie?" Jequn replied.

"Imp needs backup at the Faust. Tell Charmeine to head that way. We're getting out of here. General Kett."

There was no answer.

"General Kett," she repeated.

"Abigail," he replied a moment later.

"Where the hell are you?"

"In the complex. I'm trying to direct the orbital evacuation."

"What?" Abbey said. "The ships are leaving?"

"Trying to. We don't have a choice. The Nephilim's ships are going to tear us apart."

"What about the Focus?"

"It's charging."

"Charging?"

"It takes time to build the energy and transport it from the Shardship. Time that Thraven isn't giving us."

"Damn it," Abbey said. The rumbling was louder, and a dropship appeared through the clouds at the same time a pair of Shrikes passed in from the waterfall. "We need to get out of here, now."

The Shrikes turned, angling toward the Faust. They had seen it sitting there. They knew it was their only way out. Thraven wanted Kett. Did he know he wasn't on any of the ships? How?

Her eyes shifted to Jequn. No, she wouldn't be a traitor. Neither was Charmeine. Bastion? She felt a lump in her throat. It couldn't be. She refused to believe that. Was the Gift betraying them? Did he know she was here?

The Shrikes were closing on the Faust. The dropship was opening up. More soldiers jumped from it as it touched down and a ramp began to

The Devils Do

extend.

A mech appeared to her left, one of the few still on the ground. It started firing at the Shrikes, its shots going wide. Damn it. They started firing on the Faust, the first rounds striking shields.

Abbey watched the exchange. The Ophanim had used the Focus to alter the course of a torpedo. Could she do the same to projectiles?

She held up her hands, pushing the Gift toward the sky, thinking about the mech's rounds adjusting course and hitting the target. Her skin began to burn beneath the demonsuit, the Gift flaring in response.

The Shrike began to smoke as the mech's heavy slugs started slamming into the lightly armored rear of it. It spun out of control and exploded against the crater.

"Frag you," Abbey shouted in victory. "General, let's go."

"I'm on my way," Kett replied.

CHAPTER THIRTY-FIVE

Gloritant Thraven's eyes swept the area ahead of them as they cleared the disterium cloud. He smiled immediately, the presence of the ships in orbit betraying the presence of General Kett's forces on the ground.

"We've found them, Gloritant," Honorant Piselle said.

"Yes, we have."

He paused a moment when his eyes landed on one of the ships. It was long and slender, itself almost the shape of a seed, with rows of energized tendrils running from bow to stern and spaced equidistantly along the outer frame.

A Seedship? He noticed another one further in the distance. Two? It was obvious he had caught the enemy in the middle of their evacuation. Cage had warned Kett, as he had guessed she would.

They were too slow to escape.

"Noviant Soto," he said.

"Yes, Gloritant?" Airi replied.

She was in her quarters, practicing with the Gift. His lesson had been as effective as he had hoped, helping to unchain her from her past wounds.

"Meet me in the hangar. We're going to the surface."

"Yes, Gloritant."

The Devils Do

"Honorant Piselle, release the transports. Send two dropships as well. I want Kett and his companion alive. If any harm comes to them, the soldier responsible and their platoon will be destroyed."

"Yes, Gloritant," Piselle replied, relaying the orders.

"Gloritant," Agitant Malt said. "We've been spotted."

"And? Look at those ships, Agitant. They're nothing. Dust. Target that one and fire."

He pointed to one of the battlecruisers on the fringe.

"Firing," Agitant Sol said.

A torpedo streaked away from the Fire, flashing in the black, crossing the distance in seconds. It struck the battlecruiser, shields flaring around it.

"It didn't penetrate," Sol said.

Thraven laughed, a sound the crew of the bridge was unaccustomed with. "They've improved their shields. Order all ships to open fire. Do not target the Seedships. I want them intact."

"Your Eminence, they might get away," Piselle said.

"They might, but those ships are irreplaceable. Warship Four is to launch two boarding transports to Target One. Warship Six will launch two transports to Target Two. Three squadrons of Shrikes each to penetrate their defenses."

"As you command, Gloritant."

Ahead of him, the other warships were releasing their torpedoes, sending them into the cruisers. Normal Republic ships couldn't stand up to this kind of attack, but while the Seraphim's offensive capabilities were pathetic, their defensive stance was challenging.

He preferred a challenge.

"Honorant Piselle, you have the command," Thraven said.

"Gloritant?" Piselle questioned, looking back at him. He could see that she was afraid to take the responsibility.

"Your fear will cause you to fail, Honorant. Bury it, or if the Seraphim don't bury you, I will."

She nodded. "Yes, Gloritant." She turned back. "Gloritant, Target Three is destroyed."

"Excellent," he said. Then he swept off the bridge. He had no intention of leaving Kett and Charmeine to his Converts. He didn't trust them not to fail.

Besides, he was hoping he might see Cage again.

"Target Seven is destroyed," Piselle said, her voice clear through his comm.

"Honorant, incoming starfighters," Agitant Malt said. "Daedalus."

"Launch a squadron of Shrikes."

"Yes, Honorant."

Thraven reached the hangar as the squadron was launching from it. He looked out into space through the force shield, noting the debris of the destroyed cruisers and the activity of the starfighters around the ships. Did Kett have the Focus with him? If he did, why hadn't he used it yet?

"Gloritant," Airi said, bowing to him as he approached.

"Noviant. With me."

He led her to one of the Shrikes. It was identical to the others.

"Get in."

"We're leaving, Your Eminence?"

"We're going to the surface. I'm bringing you instead of my Immolent. Do not make me regret it."

"Yes, Gloritant."

They climbed into the Shrike. The canopy closed over them. Thraven tapped the controls, bringing the craft online.

His whole body suddenly turned cold, every inch of him tingling. "The Focus," he said, closing his eyes to absorb the sudden rush of power.

The *Fire* went dead. The lights went out. The gravity turned off. The force field keeping the vacuum of space from the hangar vanished.

Thraven opened his eyes, releasing the Shrike's clamps and allowing the vacuum to pull them out and into the black.

"What just happened?" Airi said, turning her head to look at the Fire. It was completely dark.

"The Focus," he said again. "They used it to kill the naniates that power the reactor." And all of the humans they had collected to fuel it.

"It's more than that," Airi said. "Look."

The Devils Do

He looked. The *Fire* was dead, but it wasn't stationary. It was being pulled toward the planet.

"What are you up to, Kett?" Thraven said.

He engaged the thrusters, pushing the Shrike forward, turning it to get a better view of the battle. All of the enemy battlecruisers were gone. Only one Seedship remained. A frantic battle was occurring around it, Shrikes from both sides locked in a deadly dogfight while the boarding transports waited to make a move on the ship. The telltale signs of disterium gas suggested at least some of the force had gotten away.

"If we were on it when it went dead," Airi said. "We would be dead, too."

"You would," Thraven replied. He could survive without oxygen for a limited amount of time. Long enough to have escaped regardless.

He looked back to the Fire. It was still offline and accelerating toward the planet. Even if the Focus released it, there was no way for it to stop its descent. It was going to crash on the surface.

The Font was with it.

His body tensed. It was a smart move by the General. His Immolent would secure and protect the Font, but it would take time for him to recover it and Kett knew he wouldn't leave until he did. If Kell was going to come under attack, it would keep him away until it was too late.

Damn him for the inconvenience.

He would find the Font later.

First, he would deal with the Ophanim.

CHAPTER THIRTY-SIX

ABBEY CHARGED TOWARD THE ENEMY mech. She couldn't believe she was doing it. Running toward a fifty-ton hulk of humanoid metal that was doing its best to tear her to shreds. The ground was exploding around her, its aim off the slightest of hairs, its servos adjusting just a little too slowly. Her foot hit the ground one last time and she jumped, going in toward it, climbing until she got to the head and grabbed on. She activated the magnetic attachments on the pads of the demonsuit, keeping herself anchored while she put her hands to the side of the cockpit. A moment later, the base of it began to spark and smoke, the electrical connections between the pilot and behemoth severed by the Gift.

Within seconds, it was dead.

"Kett, where the frag are you, damn it," Abbey shouted into the comm.

He had said he was coming three minutes ago. Three minutes during which the enemy had continued to gather, their volume increasing along with their firepower. Three minutes in which it had taken all of the remaining forces and way too much of the Gift to keep them from overrunning the complex and catching up to the General.

Part of her felt like she should have left him there. The only problem? He knew where the Shardship and the Focus could be found, and if Thraven caught him it was going to put them at an even worse disadvantage than they already were. Another part of her wanted to kill him herself. With the Gift flowing so freely, she was almost angry and unstable enough to do it, barely holding onto her last thread of sanity and keeping the naniates under control.

"I'm exiting the compound now," Kett replied. "I'm sorry, Abigail. I was coordinating our defense. We used the Focus to bring down the *Fire*, and hopefully Gloritant Thraven with it."

"You killed him?" Abbey said, hopeful.

"I don't know. Probably not. Delayed him, at least. With any luck, I bought us enough time to finish destroying his base on Kell before he can stop it. Some of our ships are already on their way."

"Without you?"

"Colonel Brink is with them. I gave him orders."

Abbey jumped from the mech, landing in front of it. It didn't move. Without the cockpit controls it was just a big hunk of useless metal and munitions. She sprinted toward the exit to the bunker, where General Kett had just appeared, flanked by Siddrah on his left.

"Queenie," Bastion said. "We're hot and ready to go, but we need to go now. It isn't getting any softer out here."

"I know," Abbey replied. "We're on our way."

She reached Kett and Siddrah as a fresh round of fire started hitting the side of the crater around them, the bullets intentionally aimed wide to keep from hitting Kett.

"They want me alive," he said. "Where's Charmeine?"

Abbey didn't know. She had lost track of the Seraph during the fighting.

"She's not responding to the comm?"

"No. She might have lost it. Or it may have been damaged."

"Imp, is Charmeine with you?"

"Negative, Queenie," Bastion replied. "I thought she was with you."

Abbey spun around. The field was a mess. Bodies, broken mechs, crashed Shrikes, a pair of dropships and a number of grounded transports.

They had done well to hold the Nephilim back as long as they had, and even now there were soldiers under cover behind some of the wreckage, trading fire with the enemy. How many had she killed? She had lost count. She had a feeling as soon as she gave herself half a second to relax, she would lose the Gift completely, pass out, and wake to find herself hungry enough to eat one of the dead, or at least drink their blood.

The fact that she even had the thought disgusted her.

"I can't leave without her," Kett said.

"Get to the Faust," Abbey replied. "I'll find her. We're out of time. Go."

Kett nodded, and he and Siddrah moved toward the ship. She could hear him barking orders to the remaining soldiers as he did, ordering the retreat. She hoped they would all fit into the small star hopper.

She flexed her legs and jumped, almost straight up, gaining height to look down on the battlefield. She felt rounds striking her as she reached the apex, hitting the demonsuit, trying to puncture it and failing. Even so, every hit felt like a hard jab, and it hurt.

It also made her more angry.

She spotted Charmeine further back, still on her feet and fighting, her Uin a blur around her. How deadly could someone become with anything if they had all those years to practice?

She returned to the ground, rushing forward, holding up her hand and using the Gift to catch the rounds headed her way. She bent down as she reached a fallen soldier, picking up his rifle and cradling it in one arm. She rolled to the side, lowering the shield, coming up shooting. She hit one of the blacksuits in the head, another in the shoulder. They both fell. They were humans, not Converts.

She had figured out that it was one of Thraven's strategies, to mix the undying with the regular soldiers. You could never be sure which was which until they got back up or refused to fall, and by then it might be too late. She had seen the Converts kill a few of Kett's soldiers that way, when the soldiers thought they had scored a kill.

"Charmeine," Abbey shouted, finally reaching her, joining her in the midst of the enemy. "We need to go."

The Devils Do

She didn't slow. She didn't pause. It was as though she couldn't hear her. Abbey wasn't going to try to reach out. She would risk getting her head removed by those deadly blades. She helped her fight instead, slamming a blacksuit in the head with her fist, turning and impaling another on a set of claws, lifting him and throwing him away. She let out a snarl, rushing toward another soldier getting in position to shoot, knocking the rounds aside with the Gift and slashing the claws along his chest, the naniate composite cutting right through the armor of the suit.

Something high above them echoed, a growing rumble in the sky they couldn't see past the clouds and rain. Was it the *Fire* passing through the atmosphere on its way down?

She felt something hit her back and turned, grabbing the soldier and twisting his neck in her hands, feeling the bones shatter beneath her grip. She growled again, pouncing at still another enemy and jabbing her claws into his back.

She came up ready to fight, arms wide, claws extended. Charmeine was ahead of her, dropping the last of the nearby targets.

A Shrike dropped through the clouds and rounded overhead.

Charmeine killed the last of the blacksuits, standing frozen for a moment before realizing her area was clear.

Abbey grabbed the cowl and lifted it off her head. It was obvious the Seraph was confused, as though she had gone into some sort of fighting trance.

"Charmeine," she said. The sound of gunfire was still constant behind them, but for the moment it was headed away.

Toward the *Faust*.

"Charmeine, we have to go. There's no time left."

Charmeine turned around, looking at her. Her expression changed immediately.

"Queenie," she said.

Abbey noticed the dark blur tumbling toward the Seraph from the sky.

"Charmeine, move," she shouted.

Charmeine looked up, raising her Uin to defend herself. The blur unfolded, a wave of energy passing through it toward the Seraph, a burst of blue fire that engulfed her. She screamed in sudden agony, clawing at herself as she fell to the ground. She stopped moving a moment later.

The blur slowed as it continued the descent. Abbey felt her own fire beginning to sputter.

"Abigail Cage," Gloritant Thraven said, sinking from the air as though he was a feather. "We really should stop meeting like this."

"You son of a bitch. You killed her." All of those years. Millenia. Gone, just like that. She started shaking in her fury.

"Where is he?" Thraven said. "General Kett. I'd like to speak to him."

"Frag off," Abbey replied.

"Come, come, Abigail. We can make things easy. You don't have to die here. I'm still willing to take you on." His eyes danced around the battlefield. "I can see the signs of your work. Your Gift is incredible. It could be so much more."

"Charmeine told me the price," Abbey said. "You left that little detail out on Anvil."

He smiled. "What does it matter, if we're already on the same side?"

"I'm not a fragging puppet." Her anger was continuing to build. The Gift was pure fire within her, so hot it began to feel cold. "Imp," she said softly. "Go. Now."

"What? Queenie, I'm not leaving without you."

"You have to get Kett away. Charmeine is dead. Don't tell him until you're gone."

"Queenie, I'm not doing it."

"Thraven is here, asshole. He's going to kill us all if you let him."

"I can hear you," Thraven said. His eyes scanned the smoke and haze, looking for the *Faust*. "There we are."

"I'm not letting you near that ship," Abbey said.

Thraven laughed. "Not letting me?" His brow lowered, his anger obvious. "Like you even have a choice?"

He flicked his finger. She felt his power buffet against her, and her

The Devils Do

own fighting to defend. She was pushed back, managing to stay on her feet.

His face changed again. "Oh. You've grown stronger since Anvil."

"Imp, go," Abbey said. "We can't all die here."

"Damn it, Queenie," Bastion replied, his voice breaking. "Frag it all."

Thraven started walking toward the *Faust*. He held his hands up, pushing out at it.

"What the frag?" Bastion said. "We're stuck."

Abbey couldn't believe it. Was he holding an entire starship with his Gift?

"It's Thraven. I'll distract him, but you have to go."

She took a deep breath. Then she charged.

He turned as she approached, so fast she barely saw it. His hand reached out, slapping into her and sending her tumbling away. She landed near a downed soldier, and she picked up his rifle, getting back to her feet and firing on the Gloritant. He put his hand up, blocking the slugs.

"We're on the move," Bastion said. "Whatever you're doing, keep doing it."

"Easy for you to say," Abbey muttered as the rifle went dry.

She shouted, pushing herself toward Thraven. He pushed back with the Gift, trying to overcome her. She fought against it, using all of her anger, all of her hate, all of her fury and will just to keep herself from being torn away. She could see the *Faust* out of the corner of her eye, beginning to rise from the crater.

Thraven noticed it, too. He turned back to it, reaching up, catching it in the air with the Gift.

Something echoed in the distance, the ground shuddering beneath their feet.

The *Fire* coming to rest.

Abbey was free. She leaped toward the Gloritant, gaining velocity and heading in at his back. Why had he turned his back on her?

Something hit her from the side, slamming into her and knocking her off course. She rolled in the mud, coming up facing her attacker.

Her eyes narrowed. She thought she had been angry before.

"You," she hissed, teeth clenching, claws spreading. "You fragging backstabbing bitch."

Airi stood calmly ahead of her, katana in hand. Behind her, Thraven was pulling the *Faust* back toward the ground.

"I have people I care about, too, Queenie," Airi said. "I've seen things from the other side. We can't win this fight. My parents will be safe, now. Your daughter can be, too. Gloritant Thraven isn't evil. He was hurt like I was. He understands."

Abbey didn't feel like talking. Not to her.

She rushed toward her in silence, not using the Gift. Airi shifted position into a practiced stance, raising the sword as Abbey approached.

Abbey turned slightly as the sword came down, cutting the air a hair's breadth from her body. She could feel Airi's Gift as the other woman tried to hold her in line with the cut, to pull her back to the blade. She wasn't strong enough. Not nearly strong enough. Had Thraven believed she was? Or had he thought she would a least last a few seconds in this fight?

"I'm sorry," Abbey said as she brought her claws up and into Airi's chest, lifting her and holding her, looking up at her as she writhed on the end of them.

Then she drove her back down, pulling her to the ground and shoving, dropping onto her. Their eyes met. Abbey only saw more anger behind them. She brought her other hand down on Airi's neck. She looked away as she raked them across and through, removing her head.

The *Faust* was back on the ground, even though the main thrusters were still spewing energy. She couldn't imagine how much power it took to keep the ship static. He couldn't hold it and fight her at the same time.

She had an idea. She grabbed one of the teleporters Jequn had given her, dropping it to the ground.

The light turned green, indicating there was another one somewhere else, already active. She didn't know how to change that, but maybe she could use it. She took out a second one, tossing it a few dozen meters away. It activated, ready to be paired.

The Devils Do

Then she gathered the Gift, using it to throw herself at Thraven.

He was so focused on the *Faust*; he never saw her coming. She hit him from behind, knocking into him, his grip on the ship immediately lost as they were tangled together. Abbey held a third teleporter, throwing it ahead of them as they rolled along the ground and the *Faust* began to rise once more. It landed in front of them, the light turning green just before they went into it.

They came out on the other side, at the edge of the device's range. Thraven struggled beneath her, his power pinning her to the ground as he rolled off and stood, turning back to the ship.

Just in time to watch it vanish into the clouds.

"We're out, Queenie," Bastion said. "I'm sorry. I'm so sorry."

Abbey tried to move. Thraven's Gift was so strong. He turned back to her, looking down on her.

"You've stopped nothing," he said, lifting his hand. It began to burn with the same fire that had burned Charmeine. "He can't hide from me forever. But that isn't your concern anymore. I respect your courage, Abigail Cage. I respect the strength in you." He held out his wrist. "Bite it. Take in my blood. Be part of the Great Return."

"Will. You. Just. Stop. Asking?" Abbey said, struggling to breathe.

Thraven smiled. "Very well."

His head jerked. The fire went out. The pressure vanished from Abbey's body. Thraven turned around. A Uin was sticking out of his back.

"You forgot to take my head," Charmeine said. Her clothes had been burned away, but the regeneration device remained wrapped around her neck. She approached Thraven cautiously, still holding her other blade.

"You should be dead," Thraven replied, reaching back and removing the weapon. "You don't have the Gift. You can't hurt me."

"But I can," Abbey said, springing up and onto his back.

She slammed her hand into the back of his neck, her claws going through it. Thraven fell forward, onto his hands and knees. The Gift lashed out at her, throwing her aside before she could finish the decapitation. She caught herself in the air, landing on her feet. She had seconds, at best.

She threw herself forward with all of the strength of her Gift. Not at Thraven but at Charmeine, copying her earlier tactic. The two women collided, thrown across the field toward the waiting teleporter. Abbey didn't know where it would take her, but if it put distance between them and Thraven then it didn't matter.

They landed a few meters away from it. Abbey scrambled to her feet, pulling Charmeine with her. Thraven was back up, walking toward them, his face twisted in fury.

"Enough," he said, his body engulfed in blue flame. He waved his hands out and a wave of fire extended from him, rushing toward them too quickly to escape.

"No," Abbey said, raising her hands to try to defend against the attack.

"Live to fight another day, Queen of Demons," Charmeine said as she shoved her sideways, throwing her into the teleporter.

Abbey's voice faded as she crossed over to the receiving device. She dropped to her knees ahead of it. "Charmeine, no. Damn it."

She blinked away tears as she turned it off.

The Devils Do

CHAPTER THIRTY-SEVEN

"Time's almost up, Gant," Pik said from the back of the transport.

"I'm aware," Gant replied. "Thank you, Okay."

"Sure thing.'

Gant activated the transport's comm. "Dak, can you open a channel ship-wide?"

"Roger, Boss," Dak said. "Channel open."

Gant barked once to clear his throat. He looked over at Erlan, sitting in the pilot seat of the Crescent Hauler's shuttle. Then he began to speak.

"This is it, Rejects," he said. "We're almost to Kell. I know I haven't known a lot of you for very long. If I had, I probably wouldn't like most of you. But that doesn't matter. What does matter is that we have a job to do, and we've gone through it and practiced it a few times over the last couple of days. Do what you're supposed to, and maybe a few of us won't die. I believe in Queenie, and she believes in you. So don't let her down, and don't frag everything up."

"That was very inspiring, Gant," Benhil said over the channel.

"I think you need to work on your speeches," Pik said.

"I hate being in charge," Gant said. "I want Queenie back."

"You and me both," Pik said. "No offense, but you don't have the same I don't know what."

"How can I not have something you can't identify?" Gant asked.

"I don't know. That's the whole point, isn't it?"

"I suppose. Dak, you're sure this is going to work?"

"I told you," Dak replied. "It worked the last time, and that was with Thraven nearby. We take it nice and easy, and we'll slide right past their orbital defenses, no problem."

"The only reason I'm asking is because we didn't have a lot of luck with being cloaked the last time."

"That was a pretty big debris field. We'll be fine."

"Phlenel," Gant said, contacting the Hurshin. "Are the Devils ready?"

"Loaded and ready, Gant," her bot replied.

"Which one of you is going to be doing the flying, anyway?"

"Funny," Phlenel said.

"I'm ready, too," Ruby said. She was piloting one of the other Devils, and she announced her preparedness in a sultry, suggestive tone.

"I'm going to wipe you," Gant said. "As soon as we're done here."

"As you command."

"Locked and loaded," Erlan said. "I'm ready."

"Roger, Nerd," Gant said. "Try not to wet yourself."

"I've never wet myself," Erlan protested.

"Not ever?" Gant said, looking over at him. "Be honest. I can tell when you're lying."

Erlan's face flushed. "Well, there was that one time in space camp."

"See."

"I was eight years old."

"Doesn't matter."

"It does too. They had us in zero-g and wouldn't stop the anti-gravity to let me go to the head."

"I've heard that before."

Erlan's face was beet red. He looked away, staring out the forward viewport. "Fragging Gants," he muttered.

"I heard that," Gant said.

The Devils Do

"Disengaging FTL in thirty," Dak announced across the comm link.

"Time to suit up," Gant said, getting to his feet and putting his hand on Erlan's shoulder. "You know I'm just fragging with you to keep you loose, right?"

"Yes, sir," Erlan replied.

"Good. I believe in you."

"Thank you, sir."

Gant retreated to the rear of the shuttle, opening the locker there. He found his gear inside - the second iteration of the shoulder-mounted weapon system he had created to seize the Brimstone. He had improved on the design, adding a second rifle, an automatic reloading mechanism, a mag-clamp that would lock it to his lightsuit, and a recoil dampener that would make it much more comfortable to use. He ducked under it now, standing up with his head in the center of it and activating the clamps.

"I should call you mini-mech," Pik said, watching him add the mount.

"I should rip your fragging face off," Gant replied calmly.

"Heh. Okay."

"Devils, this is Jester. Remember, you have three missiles each. They need to strike precisely if they're going to disable the engines, which means you have to paint the spot before you release them. Otherwise, they may go off-course."

"Roger," they replied.

"Dak will relay targets based on the sensor refinements I made," Gant said. "Hit the ships that are active and able to launch first. Watch out for Shrikes."

"Roger," they replied.

"Castor," Gant said to Gall's lone remaining mercenary pilot, "if you take out all three of your targets, I'll give you an hour with Ruby before I wipe and restore her."

"Really?" Castor said.

"Really," Ruby replied. "I'm looking forward to it."

"Hey," Benhil said. "Queenie would never go for that."

Gant chittered. "Queenie isn't here. Does the word 'incentive' mean anything to you?"

"Jester, if your missles are effective, you can have an hour with me, too," Ruby said.

"No shit?"

"Just kidding."

"Fragging synth."

Ruby laughed. So did the others.

"Why am I always the punchline?" Benhil asked.

"You just make it so easy," Nerd replied.

"And you don't?"

Dak's voice interrupted them. "Disengaging FTL in five. Four. Three. Two. One."

Gant could sense the change as the *Brimstone* slowed, dropping out of FTL in a burst of disterium behind one of Kell's three moons. It was the same approach Dak said he had taken with Ursan earlier, one that had allowed them to almost land on the planet without being detected.

"Scanning," Iann said. "Standby."

Gant held his breath, waiting for the results. If their plan worked, it would take nearly thirty minutes for them to slip past the orbital defense. He had suited up in case the plan didn't work.

"Engaging cloaking systems," Dak said.

"No activity from the planet," Iann said a few seconds later. "Sensors are picking up four signatures matching the Nephilim reactors."

"Great," Benhil said. "Four ships, nine missiles. We can even afford to miss a few times."

"Two of them are in orbit around the planet," Iann said, finishing her sentence.

"Oh, frag," Benhil said. "Well, hopefully the *Brimstone* can handle two?"

"We have to make those torpedoes count," Erlan said.

"Sir, we've identified the slave camp. Sending coordinates to the shuttle now."

"Roger," Gant said.

The Devils Do

"Cloaking system active," Dak said.

"Lieutenant Iann," Gant said. "Run the secondary sensor protocol."

"Gant?" Dak said. "You said you weren't sure if it would work?"

"Worst case, we still pick up nothing," he replied.

Abbey had told him not to spend too much time on fine-tuning the updated sensor algorithms to try to pick out cloaked ships, and he hadn't. Well, he hadn't taken any time from his other duties. He didn't need that much sleep, anyway.

"Scanning," Iann said.

Gant waited. The only problem with his update was that he had no way of knowing if it worked unless the sensors registered something, and he didn't want there to be any other ships out there.

"Sir, we've got four more ships on sensors," Iann announced.

"We just rounded the moon, and I'm eyeballing the positions," Dak said. "There's nothing there."

"Cloaked," Gant said.

"That's so awesome," Nerd said, excited. "It worked."

"Not awesome," he replied. "There are six Nephilim warships in orbit around Kell, and two on the ground."

"Eight ships," Benhil said.

"Thanks, math genius," Gant said. "The point is, if we go in there, we're going to get torn apart. Thraven knew we were coming, and he left a seriously unfriendly welcoming party."

CHAPTER THIRTY-EIGHT

"What do you want to do about it?" Dak said.

"We can't just turn tail," Gant replied. "Queenie's going to be sending Kett here to back us up."

"So maybe we should wait for Kett," Benhil said.

"We can't. We planned this assault with the idea that Thraven would bring his best ships with him, not leave six of them behind. We didn't even think he would have six of them to leave behind."

"Well, whose stupid plan was that?"

"You were there, Jester. You didn't say it was stupid at the time."

"Because I didn't think we were going to be wrong at the time."

Gant growled softly. "Shut up and let me think. Iann, can you relay the Brimstone's feed to the shuttle's HUD so I can see the formation?"

"Aye, sir."

The HUD ahead of him changed, showing him the pings of the ships in orbit around Kell. It was a formidable force, one that the Rejects had no chance of standing against in a straight-on fight. But why would they even attempt a straight-on fight?

"Okay, Plan B," Gant said.

"You already have a Plan B?" Benhil said.

"Captain Mann didn't bring me along for my charming

The Devils Do

personality."

"That's for sure."

"Dak, you said you got the *Brimstone* past the orbital defenses cloaked, and managed to bring her in close enough that you practically landed?"

"Yeah. Why?"

"That's exactly what we're going to do. Slide in past the outer defenses and take her into the atmosphere."

"The thermospheric burn is going to give us away," Dak said.

"Maybe, but if we stay positioned over the top of the ships on the ground, the enemy may be a little more cautious about firing down on us. They don't want to send a torpedo into the midst of the fleet."

"Or crash us on top of it," Dak said. "Okay, I can get behind that."

"This isn't a good idea," Benhil said.

"Why not?" Gant asked.

"You're putting us in the middle of a fragging Nephilim sandwich. Above and below?"

"We have two advantages right now," Gant said. "One, we're cloaked, and they can't see us. Two, some of them are cloaked, but we know they're there. We need to use that."

"Both of those are going to fizzle out as soon as we hit the atmosphere."

"The first. Maybe not the second. Why give yourself away before you have to? We can use that, too."

"How?"

"Here's how we do it. Dak, get the *Brimstone* lined up to fire the last two torpedoes at the ass end of the first Nephilim ship. I'm marking it now." Gant reached over and tapped the spot on the HUD. "That should take care of one of them."

"And we'll be out of torpedoes."

"We'll still have the lasers, but we won't need them. The other ships won't fire and risk hitting the ground, especially after what happened off Drune. They'll send Shrikes in to harass and try to overwhelm the shields. When they do, the Devils will launch. Instead of going to the surface, they're going to go up."

"Up?" Phlenel said.

"The Shrikes will give chase. Take evasive action, make sure you get close to the cloaked ships."

"I see what you're thinking," Benhil said. "It isn't going to work. No offense to our pilots, but Shrikes versus Devils? Maybe if Bastion was behind the stick of one of them."

"I have a full dataset of offensive and defensive techniques," Ruby said.

"Great," Benhil replied. "There's a reason we still use living, breathing individuals to fly starfighters."

"Because synths make you feel inferior."

"No, because synths have no instinct."

"It has been proven time and again that data is more valuable than instinct. The only reason humans pilot starfighters or participate in armed conflict is because of the amended Geneva Conventions."

"That isn't why," Benhil insisted.

"I can prove this very easily."

"Can we save this argument for later?" Gant said. "That's the play. The cloaking system borrows power from the shields, meaning they can't stay invisible and absorb the impact from the missiles we made. If we're lucky, we can take out three of the cloaked ships before they know that we know they're there."

"If we're not lucky?" Erlan asked.

"We die. We knew this was a shit mission before we got here, and the truth is shittier than we were expecting. We have to deal. Nothing changes on the ground. We free and arm the prisoners, and lead them in an assault on the surface. Worst case, we still take some of the ships offline. Every one we destroy is one less that Thraven can use."

"Works for me," Dak said. "I wasn't planning on living very much longer, anyway."

"I approve of this plan," Phlenel said.

"Me, too," Pik said. "I'm fragging excited about it."

"Then let's do this, Rejects," Erlan said.

The Devils Do

"Did you have to be the one to say that?" Benhil said.

"What do you mean?" Erlan asked.

"I don't know; you just sound so meek when you say it."

"I do?"

"Let's do this, Rejects," Benhil repeated, mimicking Erlan. "What do you think?"

"I'll have to practice," Erlan agreed.

"Focus," Gant said.

"I'm bringing us in," Dak said. "Standby."

CHAPTER THIRTY-NINE

Phlenel checked the status readings of the Devil one more time. Everything was nominal, the old starfighter running optimally. The Gant was an impressive individual. Not only had he done well in the confrontation with Sam, but he had also fixed the ships in such a short time, and now was leading them to what she hoped would be a victory.

'She.' Phlenel considered the word. Hurshin were not limited in their gender. They could be male or female or neither or both. The capability had been useful when exploring the experiences of pleasure that many of the other intelligent races shared, experiences that were unknown on Hurse and as a result vital to learn and share.

But what would her kind become once she spread that knowledge to them?

Sometimes she was concerned that they would wind up as obsessed with it as the Terrans seemed to be. She had seen how it drove them and controlled them, and she feared the same happening to her kind. Then again, she had no choice. The Code was clear. All knowledge was to be shared with the whole.

She dropped the thought. It was distracting her, too. She needed to focus. She had found she preferred being female when around Terrans. She wasn't sure why. It simply was.

The Devils Do

Distracted.

She checked the readings for the tenth time. Her thoughts were wandering while they waited. Was it because she was afraid she might die? She decided it was. She hadn't been to Hurse in sixty years. She had so much to share with the others. To lose it would be sadness.

"This is Gant," Gant said over the wide channel. "We've moved inside the defensive perimeter, and we're entering the thermosphere now. Devils, be ready to launch on my mark."

Phlenel increased the thrust on her Devil, letting the magnetic clamps hold it to the floor of the hangar. She knew Ruby and Castor would be doing the same.

She was fortunate. She had flown Devils when the now aging starships were new. They were more capable than many gave them credit for, though their maneuvering thrusters were a bit more sensitive and took more finesse than newer generations. She didn't fear her ability to fly. She was more afraid of her team's ability. She couldn't survive out here on her own. If Thraven ever got his hands on her? Her form began to spread at the thought, and she had to pull herself back together.

"Roger," her bot said.

She had removed the head from the rest of the machine so that she could use it to communicate with the others. It was mounted in the rear of the cockpit, directly behind her.

"Roger," Castor said.

"Roger," Ruby said.

She tightened her grip on the Devil's controls. Her fingers had joined into a single tentacle that wrapped around it, offering her a much greater degree of control than a human hand.

"Mark," Gant said.

She released the clamps. The Devil rocketed forward, skids sliding along the floor until she retracted them. Then she was out of the hangar and into space, angling the fighter back out towards orbit.

"This is Devil One," she said. "Target Beta acquired. Vectoring into position."

She could see the visible starships above them, suddenly active as the *Brimstone* became visible to them, uncloaking to fire its torpedoes and power its shields. The two missiles were streaks of light that converged on the rear of one of the warships, striking it and causing a massive flash as the energy defeated the shields and washed along the hull of the ship. It began to crumble a moment later.

"This is Devil Three," Ruby said. "Target Delta acquired."

"Devil Two," Castor said. "Target Charlie acquired."

"Target Alfa is destroyed," Dak said. "Taking incoming laser fire. Shields are at one hundred percent and holding."

"Launching the shuttle," Erlan said. "Surface One is en route."

"Remember," Gant said. "Don't make it obvious you're going for a cloaked ship, or they may reveal themselves early. Wait for the Shrikes to chase you out."

"Roger," Ruby said.

"Roger," she said.

She altered her vector, adjusting her path. A tone sounded in the cockpit.

"Here they come," Castor said.

"Shrikes active," Dak said. "Iann, target the battleships. Full plasma."

"Aye, Commander," Iann said.

A blast of energy launched from the Brimstone, spiking upward and into one of the battleships. It speared the un-augmented ship right in the center, the volume of energy packed in the superheated stream cutting it in half.

"Target destroyed," Iann said.

"Don't kill them too fast," Gant said. "We can't look like we're winning until the Devils have done their dirty work."

"Roger," Dak said. "My apologies."

Laser fire began to pour from ground installations, heading up and into the Brimstone, joining the assault from above. Phlenel jerked the Devil to the side as the first wave of Shrikes reached her, firing on her with projectiles that mostly went wide. The rest were deflected by the starfighter's shields.

The Devils Do

"I've been engaged," she said. "Breaking for the target."

She rolled the Devil over and hit the thrusters, keeping her movements chaotic as she jetted upward and away from the Shrikes. They stayed close on her aft, continuing to fire as she climbed toward the invisible warship.

"Shields at ninety-eight percent," Dak said.

"Breaking for the target," Ruby said.

"Break-"

Castor's voice vanished. His positioning beacon went with it.

"Frag. It looks like Ruby wasn't enough of an incentive," Benhil said, noticing the loss.

"Devil One, Devil Three, it's on you," Gant said.

"Roger," Phlenel replied. "I'm nearly Target Beta. Preparing to fire."

"Once they know we can see one, the rest will uncloak," Ruby said. "We need to fire at the same time."

"Roger, altering course. Tell me when you are ready."

Phlenel shifted the stick, winding up and back, slowing with the help of the forward vectoring thrusters. One of the Shrikes went past and she opened fire on it, shredding it with dense flechettes.

"Don't keep me waiting forever, Devil Three," she said.

"Standby," Ruby replied.

"This is Surface One," Gant said. "We're ready to drop. Good luck up there."

"Devil Three, I'm in position," Ruby said a moment later. "Ready to fire on your mark."

Phlenel readjusted course, the Devil's frame struggling to handle her sudden inertial shift as her form softened to handle the force to it. She came about, splitting between two of the Shrikes and centering her targeting reticule on the area of the cloaked ship that Gant had singled out.

"Mark," she said, an appendage growing from the tentacle and resting lightly on the trigger.

"Fire," Ruby said.

Phlenel hit the trigger. The heavy ordnance launched from one of the wings, its rocket motor engaging and sending it streaking ahead. From her perspective, it appeared as though it was going to head out into deep space, as it crossed a dozen kilometers in a matter of seconds.

It disappeared for an instant as it entered the cloaking field. Then it detonated.

The warship became visible immediately, even as every suggestion that it had power vanished. The lights along it blinked out at once, a trail of debris pouring from the impact site. Phlenel turned the stick, adjusting course with another human-impossible maneuver, avoiding a streak of fire from one of the Shrikes.

"Target Beta disabled," she announced.

"Target Delta disabled," Ruby said.

"Echo and Foxtrot are decloaking," Dak said. "Now the real fun begins."

The Devils Do

CHAPTER FORTY

Gant could hear every round that pinged off the shuttle as it made its descent into the center of the Nephilim compound. They followed one after another in rapid succession, sounding more like a heavy rain than gunfire, leaving him impressed that the ship was able to handle the abuse.

Then again, it was a Crescent Hauler vessel, meant to be able to stand up to brutal punishment, even though it was extremely unlikely that it would ever have to.

In this case, it had to.

"We're one thousand meters up," Erlan said. "Passing target data."

Gant put his helmet on. It wasn't a standard issue, but a quickly hacked resize of a human-scale model, one that sat over the weapons mount and left him with a big bubble over his smaller skull.

"You look like you're in a fishbowl," Benhil said, laughing.

"Shut up," Gant replied.

He knew he did. Whatever. The targets on the ground were displayed on the HUD ahead of him as the linked TCUs synced the battlefield composition.

"Five hundred meters," Erlan said.

Gant moved to the back of the shuttle with Pik, Benhil, and three grunts from Gall's mercenaries: Rishu, Plax, and Qa. The last was a

Curlatin, the sole remaining member of the ground team that had shot up Queenie on Drune, found hiding in one of the Brimstone's crew quarters while they were on Machina Four. Gant hated him for both of those reasons.

"Weapons hot," Gant said, shifting his mount and bringing the triggers into his hands.

He didn't know why he had never thought to create something like this before. If he managed to survive all of this bullshit, he would have to patent the mount and get it out for sale. If the laser pistol he bought on Orunel was worth two-fifty, something like this should fetch close to five.

"One hundred meters," Erlan said.

The hatch opened, revealing the ground below. They were only a few hundred meters away from an open compound, where prisoners were being held behind laser cordons that would cut them apart if they tried to walk out. There had to be close to a thousand of them in this pen, and the Brimstone's data had indicated there were nine more just like it.

Ten-thousand soldiers, if they could get them out. They had loaded the shuttle with equipment, but that wasn't even enough for this single enclosure.

"This is Surface One," he said. "We're ready to drop. Good luck up there." He dropped from the wide channel to the platoon link. "Let's go, Rejects!"

Then he jumped, knowing the others had gone out behind him.

The TCU was showing a dozen tangos nearby, with more coming from the main compound a couple of klicks away. The cloaking maneuver had gotten them pretty close to the surface unseen and had bought them time they needed to have a chance. Even so, he could hear the whine of Shrikes coming down toward them, and he could almost feel the slugs whipping past as he dropped from the shuttle.

He rolled on the ground, clenching his jaw and hoping the mount held up to the abuse. He had tested it on the Brimstone, but that wasn't the real thing. He got to his feet, finding the first target and squeezing the triggers. He felt the pressure against his shoulders as the twin rifles began spewing flechettes, satisfied to see them hit one of the soldiers near the

The Devils Do

cordon.

"Watch our for friendlies," he said, almost in retrospect. He had been lucky the bullets hadn't missed and gone into the midst of the prisoners. Woops.

"You say that now," Benhil said. He was standing beside Gant, running away from him to duck behind the edge of a smaller building.

The shuttle was rotating, turning in the direction of the reinforcements from the main compound. A Shrike passed overhead, firing down on the top of it. The shields caught some of the attack. The armor caught some more. A few rounds made it into something important, and the shuttle began to whine louder.

"Damn," Erlan said. "I'm losing thrust pressure. Looks like a one-way ride. The good news is, I found an extra switch here. Check this shit out."

"Is it just me, or does Nerd cursing just not work?" Pik said.

A half-dozen plates on the shuttle slid aside, a half-dozen electromagnetic guns dropping into position.

"I wouldn't tell him that right now," Benhil said.

"No," Pik agreed. "Maybe later."

The EMGs opened fire, the soft sonic booms echoing as the slugs crossed the distance and tore into the oncoming soldiers, reducing the line to nothing in seconds.

"Hell, yeah," Benhil said.

"Guards," Gant reminded him, using the shuttle's offensive distraction to take down another one. "Okay, I've got you covered."

"Roger. It's fragging time!"

"It's fragging time?" Benhil said. "I don't think you mean that the way it sounds."

Pik reached the first guard, punching him so hard with the augmented fist that he flew back and into the cordon, shredded by the lasers as he passed through. The prisoners cheered at the sight, shifting position, spreading out to give the Rejects space. Pik turned on another guard, crushing his rifle in his new hand before the guard could shoot him, and then punching him in the helmet and knocking him down.

"They're opening up a field of fire," Qa said, shooting at the guards. The other mercenaries joined him, laying down a line of covering fire.

Pik ran from the downed enemy soldiers toward the guardhouse, a few rounds striking his battlesuit and sparking off. He barrelled into it, grabbing the guard inside and throwing him out into the open, where Richu picked him off.

"Incoming," Erlan shouted. The two EMGs on top of the shuttle began rotating and firing at the Shrikes as they dove toward the group. They evaded the potential attack, breaking the strafing run and circling back.

"Gant, I don't know how to work this thing," Pik said.

Gant began bouncing across the field toward the guardhouse. The Rejects were keeping the remaining guards pinned down, and the shuttle was holding back the reinforcements. So far, so good. He made it into the guardhouse, to the active terminal.

"Okay, there's a button right here to shut down the power to the cordon." He pointed at it.

"Oh," Pik replied. "I didn't see it."

"Nerd, get your ass to the rear and prepare to unload the goods," Gant said.

"Roger."

Gant hit the control to turn off power to the cordon. "Go direct traffic outside. Get the prisoners armed. Jester, see if we have anybody here who knows how to fly a starship or fifty."

"Roger," Benhil replied.

"Incoming," Erlan warned again.

The Shrikes made it over this time, firing into the midst of the prisoners. Painful cries went up as nearly one hundred of them dropped.

"Frag," Gant said. "Come on."

They emerged from the guardhouse with Pik bellowing. "Weapons this way. Come and get it."

A mass of prisoners rushed to the shuttle. Erlan was there, shoving the crates out of the rear and onto the ground. The prisoners tore at them,

The Devils Do

ripping them open and grabbing what they needed.

"Starship crews," Benhil shouted, making his way to them. "I need starship crews."

"I'm a navigator," one of the prisoners said.

"I'm an engineer," another said.

"Get your guns and free the others," Pik shouted. "Watch out for Shrikes. Welcome to the Rejects. Hoo-raahhhh!"

"Send starship crew back this way," Benhil added. "The only way we all survive is to get some of these ships into orbit."

"Jester, keep this group organized," Gant said. "Okay, you're with me."

"Where are we going?" Pik asked.

Gant pointed to the main compound. "There. We need to identify the space-worthy ships and paint the rest for the Brimstone."

They both looked up at the same time. The *Brimstone* was floating high above them, visible against the backdrop of the purplish atmosphere. The shields were active all around it, deflecting carefully aimed lasers from the batteries on the ground and the Nephilim ships above.

"We need to take out those positions, too," Gant said. He opened the wide channel again. "Dak, we've started freeing prisoners. What's your status?"

"Shields at forty percent. Taking heavy fire. Hitting as many of the weaker targets as we can."

"Give me three minutes and I'll have some ground targets for you, but you need to start attacking the fixed positions."

"Roger. We're going to die, you know?"

"Yes," Gant agreed. "But we're going to have a damn good time doing it."

CHAPTER FORTY-ONE

GANT AND PIK RACED FOR the main compound, bouncing across the landscape toward the main facility, a hardened structure partially hidden by the growth of trees surrounding the massive, open field of starships.

"Shield generators," Pik said, pointing out a pair of bulbs on either side of the building and a third in front of it. There was bound to be a matching one in the back, as well as another on top of the structure, able to create a web of energy to protect it in the case of bombardment.

The shields were down. The EMGs on the shuttle had turned the forward generator into a twisted mess of metal and wiring, just as it had turned the incoming soldiers into twisted flesh. The Nephilim had tried to get reinforcements out to the slave pens. They never had a chance to turn the defensive system on.

They bounced over the dead, moving at full speed, desperate to reach the building. The prisoners were working on freeing themselves, and while the enemy was being careful with their attacks on the Brimstone, the ship wouldn't survive forever, not once Thraven's forces saw how they were using it as a shield of their own.

They were a dozen meters from the front of the facility when a squad of soldiers emerged from the entrance, dressed in black battlesuits and heavily armed with a pair of portable rail cannons.

The Devils Do

"We can't let them get those running," Gant said, seeing the weapons.

"On it," Pik replied. "Watch this. It's fragging time!"

He laughed as he bent his knees and bounced, the musculature in his suit sending him hurtling toward the enemy. They scrambled to defend against him, two of them knocked back as he crashed against them, slamming his edged fingers into one and getting a massive hand around the helmet of the other, holding him back against the wall. He dislodged the blades, turning and swinging the soldier like a club, hitting another with the first.

Gant began shooting, the mount digging into his shoulders while the bullets pinged against the soldiers' body armor. They ignored him, setting the cannon down on a tripod that extended from the bottom of it, quickly leaning down and bolting it in.

"Uh, Okay?" Gant said, bouncing high into the air as the cannon began to scream, the bullets moving past where he had been at such high velocity he never saw them. Further back near the transport, prisoners began to fall, hit by the wayward slugs.

"Got it," Pik said, moving in behind the soldiers. His metal fist punished one of them, blasting right through the helmet and smashing their face. A grab and a twist crushed the weaker neck protection of the other, along with his neck and spine. "Clear."

Gant landed smoothly. "Help me with this thing," he said, motioning to his shoulder mount.

"You don't want it anymore?"

"Ammo's getting low, and it's bulky."

Pik lifted it from his shoulders as he released the magnetic clamps.

"That feels so much better," Gant said, stretching his arms.

"How are you going to fight?" Pik asked.

Gant retrieved a combat knife from his thigh. "Not that I'll need it. I've got you. Your skill is killing things, right?"

Pik grumbled in laughter.

They moved to the entrance, heading inside. The corridor was clear, and they ran through it.

"We're looking for a control room," Gant said. "Some place with a terminal or three. It's probably up higher, where they can see the work on the ships."

"Top floor looked like it had a big window," Pik said.

"Let's find-" Gant threw himself down as a pair of soldiers came around the corner and started shooting. His lightsuit was no match for their rounds.

Pik roared and charged grabbing them and smashing them against the walls, dismayed when they got back up. Their movements changed, becoming jerky and stiff. Converts. Gant stood and rushed forward, leaping to the shoulders of one and digging his knife into its throat. It took a bit of force, but he managed to slip around behind it and pull it through. The big Trover didn't have the same problem, grabbing the other one tight and ripping its head off with his hands.

"Gross," Gant said at the scene. "I'm going to have nightmares about that."

"It's us or them," Pik replied.

"Jester, how are we doing out there?" Gant asked.

"Three groups are free. We're out of guns, but they have overwhelming numbers. If we could get rid of the fragging Shrikes, we'd be holding out a lot better."

"What about starship crews?"

"I've got four with me taking cover on the shuttle. We're waiting for directions."

"I'm going as fast as I can. Brimstone, what's the status on the orbital defenses?"

"Most of the standard ships are taken care of," Dak said. "The augmented ships are a problem. We have nothing left to take them out."

"Devils, are you still out there?" Gant asked.

"Affirmative," Phlenel replied. "My ammunition is running low, but I do have two missiles remaining."

"So do I," Ruby said.

"Dak, can you coordinate an attack and try to take out one of the ships?"

The Devils Do

"Aye, Boss," Dak said. "I'll do my best."

Gant checked his HUD, doing a quick calculation in his head. "Kett should be here within the next few minutes. Be ready to give him directions. We need to consolidate our firepower on those upgraded ships, in the weak spot on their ass."

"Roger," Dak said.

"Are we winning?" Erlan asked.

"We're faking it pretty well," Gant replied. "Standby."

CHAPTER FORTY-TWO

Gant turned to Pik and pointed to a tube. "There."

They entered the tube together. Pik was so large and bulky in the battlesuit that Gant was left standing beneath him, between his legs, his head nearly up to the Trover's groin.

"Queenie never hears about this," he said.

"I can't wait to tell her," Pik replied.

They took the tube to the top floor, spilling out into it ready for a fight. They had found the control room like they were hoping. All of the technicians operating it were dead on the floor or slumped over in their seats. There was no sign of damage to any of them. A floor to ceiling transparency gave them a clear view of the starships arranged in the field ahead, so many that they vanished into the hazy distance.

Gant could also see the slave pens from here, and the fighting still raging around them. There must have been units already deployed to a few of the ships, both soldiers and mechs, and they had left them to join the battle. He changed his mind about his comment to Erlan. It was hard to pretend they were winning when it was such a mess out there.

"What the frag happened here?" Pik said.

Gant didn't have a chance to reply. Pik was thrown backward beside him, slammed into the wall. He bounced away by instinct,

The Devils Do

vanishing behind one of the terminals. One of them. Damn it.

"Ouch," Pik said. "You assholes think this is funny, don't you?" He was pinned against the wall again, just like on Feru.

"Necessary," the Evolent replied, appearing from the shadows in the corner of the room. "You're a little stronger than me, otherwise." He was short and stocky and too young to be as powerful as he was. "I like the hand," he said, motioning at Pik's replacement appendage.

"Thanks. Come a little closer; I'll show it to you."

"I saw you have a Gant. Where is it?"

"Have? It?" Gant grumbled under his breath. Then he started moving along the side of the room, slipping silently around the terminals and control stations toward the Evolent. Little fragger.

"I don't know. I've got something else you can have." Pik laughed. "It's down there. I'd take it out for you, but-"

Pik stopped talking as the armor around his neck constricted inward, cutting off his breath.

"That's better," the Evolent said. "Gloritant Thraven said you might be coming. I wanted to go out to the field to meet you, but he said to stay behind, so you might think you're winning."

"Do you always talk this much?" Gant asked from behind one of the stations.

The Evolent turned, moving his hands, tearing the stations away from the ground, ripping out wires and cables as he did. Gant moved with them, remaining hidden.

"Do you know what's funny?" the Evolent asked. "It doesn't matter if you did win here. The plans for the ships have already been sent back to the others. All we need to do is collect more bodies, and we can rebuild the fleet."

Gant shook his head. Of course Thraven transmitted the schematics. He would have been an idiot not to. One thing at a time.

"Do you know what I think is funny?" Gant asked.

He moved out into the room, right behind the Evolent. Thraven's man spun around, putting out his hand. Gant felt the tickle on his skin, but nothing else happened. The Evolent was suddenly afraid.

237

"Gants are immune to magic when they're angry," Gant said. "And I'm very, very angry."

He bounced forward, springing up at the Evolent, who had no idea how to fight without the Gift. He sank his knife into an eye, riding the man down as he fell backward.

Pik was released, and he reached up and grabbed at his helmet, tearing it off and throwing it aside, getting a metal finger below the neck armor and wrenching it away. He took in a few massive breaths.

"Frag. He almost killed me." He walked over to the downed Evolent and kicked him in the side, sending him across the room and into the wall.

"Just kill him," Gant said.

"He almost killed me," Pik said again.

"Okay, we don't have time for revenge. Just kill him."

"Fine." He bent over the Evolent, turning his back to Gant and removing the man's head.

Gant hurried to one of the terminals, pushing the body slumped over it from its seat. It took him a minute, but he found status reports for each of the ships on the ground.

"Jester," he said. "Three crews?"

"Roger. Four, now," Benhil said. "But we're taking heavy casualties down here."

"I'm lighting up the targets now," he said. "They're going to be tough to see from down there, but do your best."

Gant put his hands together, mimicking a human hand as he navigated to the external controls for each of the ships. They were wired to the main center so that they didn't need individual crews to run diagnostics and standard prechecks like life support and lighting. He turned all of the lights on for each of the four ships that reportedly hadn't been prepped for reconfiguration.

"I think I see one," Benhil said. "Crew one is on its way. Nerd is going with them."

"Roger," Gant said. "Brimstone, sitrep?"

"Shields are at fifteen percent," Dak said. "The Devils are engaging

The Devils Do

the Nephilim warship. Keep your fingers crossed."

"Physically impossible," Gant replied. "Use your scanners to pick out the dark ships on the ground, the ones furthest from the fighting. Start blasting them."

"You know once I do, the gloves are going to come off, right?"

"The gloves are already off. We came here to do some damage, not stay alive."

"Roger. Iann, get me some targets and align half our batteries. We're going down fighting."

"Aye, Commander," Iann replied.

"Commander," a new voice said. "We've got new targets on scanners. Six ships, four identified as Republic battlecruisers, and two unidentified. We're being hailed, sir."

"Open a channel," Dak said. "Retransmit to the surface."

"Aye, sir."

"Brimstone, this is Colonel Brink of the Ophanim. I've been authorized by General Sylvan Kett to assume command of this assault. Please transmit your active combat data immediately."

What?

"Excuse me, Colonel," Gant said. "I'm in charge of this operation."

"I don't know who this is, but not anymore. If you want to get away from Kell alive, you'll listen to me."

Gant growled softly. Who the frag did this Colonel think he was? They couldn't afford to waste time bickering over it. Not when people were dying.

"Fine. Dak, send the Colonel the data. Colonel, watch out for the enemy ships. They pack a punch."

"I've already seen it back on Azure," Brink said. "Prep your individuals for evacuation. I've got work to do. Brink, out."

CHAPTER FORTY-THREE

Phlenel rolled the Devil again, diving between two of the Shrikes as they whipped past, inverting the fighter to squeeze between them. She reversed thrust as she did, the inertia threatening the integrity of the craft while she relaxed her form to absorb the force. The Devil flipped back and she loosed a stream of fire, catching the Shrike in the rear and blasting it to pieces.

"That's five for me," she said, hitting the main thrusters to shoot forward again.

"I will even it out in a moment," Ruby said.

Phlenel found her fighter nearby, exchanging maneuvers with another Shrike. A few seconds later she got the best of it, pounding its cockpit with a mass of projectiles that broke through the shields and killed the pilot.

"We're almost there," Phlenel said, moving the Devil into formation with Ruby's.

They had made the awesome power of the Shrikes look nonexistent during the confrontation, their respective design superiority offering them attack vectors that other individuals couldn't match, and that often took their opponents by surprise. Once they had joined up and began double-teaming opponents, that superiority had allowed them to

The Devils Do

make quick work of any of the enemy ships that tried to intercede in their path to the Nephilim warship.

"Watch the lasers," Ruby warned as they streaked toward the ship.

Phlenel did, monitoring the HUD for warnings as they swooped toward the target, coming in nose-first. The dark warship started firing defensively, lighter-powered lasers and plasma bursts that filled the space around them with destructive energy. They weaved back and forth, rolling and flipping and corkscrewing unevenly around one another, remaining close together as they bypassed the top of the ship, angling past it toward the rear.

A fresh squadron of Shrikes moved to intercept, appearing out of a hangar nearby and jetting toward them. Phlenel checked her ordnance status. One hundred projectile rounds and the two heavy missiles, plus a pair of small lasers to give it at least a minor offensive capability once its tangible loadout was dry.

"Stay on the main target," Phlenel said. "I don't have the munitions to handle the Shrikes."

"Roger. Me neither. Let's disable this one and break for the Brimstone."

The two Devils raced along the hull of the warship, the Shrikes giving chase behind. They stayed as close to the surface of the ship as they dared, ducking behind extrusions and staying just above the web of energy coming from the shields. The onboard computer rained continual tones down on them, warning them of incoming fire, the rounds from their attackers coming dangerously close to removing them from the fight.

Then they burst out of the back, passing the ship and heading into space, preparing to make a tight turn to circle back and unleash their ordnance. Four heavy missiles. They could only hope it would be enough to bring down the shields and plant one of them in the reactor.

"Prepare to reverse course and acquire a lock," Ruby said.

"Roger," Phlenel replied.

She was enjoying working with the synth. Ruby's calculated motions and rigid attention to detail matched her own, and while she knew her counterpart wasn't truly alive, there were plenty of times she felt like bots and synths were better than real individuals, anyway. They could only see things for what they were, not what their emotions wanted them to be. They were incorruptible unless physically hacked. They were tireless. Who wouldn't prefer that?

The two Devils made a tight arc, coming about, weaving around the Shrikes.

A ship suddenly appeared right in front of them. It was long and teardrop-shaped, with lines of what looked like energized vines running along the hull.

"Shit," Phlenel said, adjusting her vector to get up and over it. Ruby did the same, but the appearance threw off their run. "What the hell?"

"Kett's forces," Ruby said. "It must be. There are six Longhorn-class battlecruisers as well as these two ships. They are unidentified, but if I had to make an estimation, I would say they are Seedships."

"What they are is in the fragging way," Phlenel said.

"I agree."

They cleared the top of it. The Nephilim warship was in motion, turning to get its main weapons to bear on the newcomer.

"It's going to get hammered," Phlenel said. Her HUD began to light up with dozens of new targets, both Republic starfighters and Shrikes.

"I've set a new vector," Ruby said.

Phlenel tracked it, getting into position and chasing the tail of the Nephilim ship anew. It was already starting to hit the Seedship with its smaller lasers, causing flashes of shield energy along the surface of the vessel. Ahead of it, four of the cruisers were firing on the warship, sending missiles and lasers against its powerful shields, concentrating their fire on the same spot they were going for.

"Queenie must have told them where to shoot," Ruby said.

The enemy captain was doing their best to bring the ship around. A torpedo fired, flashing and hitting one of the cruisers. It began to fall apart a moment later.

"They can't survive against this."

The Devils Do

"We're almost in position."

"I've got a lock," Phlenel said, slipping the fighter in behind the ship. "Firing."

A missile launched, following the lock to the area near the back, closest to the monstrous reactor. It detonated against the shields. A second did the same.

"Frag. Not enough."

"Firing," Ruby said, releasing her final two.

Phlenel looked back over her shoulder as she moved away from the ship. The first strike caused the shields to flicker and began eating at the armor plating. The second dug in behind it, finishing the work of the first and eating through the metal. A short burst of burning oxygen, and then the warship went dead.

CHAPTER FORTY-FOUR

"Jester, where the frag are you?" Gant said.

He and Pik were on the move, heading away from the main structure as quickly as possible. A squadron of Daedalus fighters swooped in from overhead, unleashing their ordnance on the building. Detonations shook the ground and sent a warm breeze in from behind them, along with smaller bits of stone from the building.

"I just turned my beacon on," Benhil said.

Gant checked the HUD, finding the blue icon that represented the soldier in the augmented reality of the helmet. "I've got you. We're incoming."

A pair of Shrikes crossed overhead, bearing the markings of General Kett's forces. They exchanged fire with a set of enemy fighters, taking one of them down as they went past.

"Are all of the pens clear?" he asked.

"Affirmative. We'll have to do a head count later."

"Nerd, what's your status?" Gant asked.

"Powering up and almost ready to go,' Erlan replied.

Gant could see one of the other ships already rising, escaping from the surface battle. He turned his attention to the Brimstone. It's looked battered, but it was still maintaining altitude. The attacks on it had ceased,

The Devils Do

the enemy turning their attention to Kett's forces. He didn't know how the rest of the Ophanim were doing up there, but considering the number of fighters that were destroying enemy mechs down here, he didn't have any complaints.

"Surface One, Gant, this is Brimstone. We're moving back into orbit. You have three minutes to clear the field."

"Three minutes?" Gant said. "That's not enough time."

"Sorry, Boss. That's all you get. Colonel Brink's orders."

"Fragging Colonel Brink," he muttered. "Jester, we've got three minutes to get these soldiers loaded and ships skyward."

"Are you kidding?"

"I wish."

"Are you going to make it?"

"We'll be there."

Gant and Pik continued to bounce along the surface, their suits carrying them fifty meters with each jump. The fighting was still heavy around them, the number of dead from both sides overwhelming. Thraven had left plenty of Converts here as well, and they were wandering the field, some missing arms or legs, others with half a face. They picked up nearby rifles and fired at any enemies that came close, slowing their progress as they paused to knock them down before they could get shot.

"This is Nerd," Erlan said. "We're lifting off."

Gant saw the ship begin to rise a few kilometers away. The *Brimstone* was getting smaller above them, vanishing into orbit. Another ship had come into view nearby. Two more. Nephilim warships. They were black splotches against the purple sky.

They were also getting closer.

"Dak," Gant said. "Tell Colonel Dick that he can't do this. There are still hundreds of individuals on the ground who haven't made it to a ship, and a lot of them are wounded."

"Surface One," Colonel Brink replied. "I had Commander Dak patch me into the Brimstone's comm link. You have sixty seconds to get clear. We have no way of knowing how soon Gloritant Thraven or his forces will arrive, and if they do before we're gone, we're all going to die."

"There are innocent individuals down here," Gant complained.

"Innocent?" Brink said. "From what I understand, they're all soldiers. They aren't innocent. Certainly, neither are you."

Gant disconnected the link. "Fragging son of a mother fragging whore," he cursed.

"What's going on?" Pik asked.

"I'm not sure how, but he's bringing those ships down on the field to destroy the others."

Pik looked up. "We're still under them."

"I know."

They made the last few jumps to the waiting warship. Benhil was at the hatch, refusing to let the others close it.

"Thanks for holding the door," Gant said.

"This is some fragged up shit, right here," Benhil replied.

"Tell whoever is running this boat to get us the frag out of here."

Benhil said something to one of the prisoners, who ran ahead and passed the message along.

"We don't have access to the comms yet," he explained. "Hopefully they'll see the hull is sealed and just go."

The ship began to vibrate, the reactors increasing their power output. Gant could feel the gravity inverters begin humming.

"If I ever meet Colonel Brink in person, I'm going to cut his fragging head off," Gant said.

"Let's get to the bridge," Benhil suggested.

They ran along the corridors, not entirely sure how to get to the bridge. They made it just as the craft reached the thermosphere, rising into it at the same time the two dead Nephilim warships were sinking in. He didn't need to see the impact to know it would destroy anything that remained on the ground, including all of the prisoners that hadn't made it to a ship.

"How many were still down there?" Benhil asked.

"I don't know if I want to know," Gant replied.

A dirty, ragged woman with dark hair was sitting in the command chair, barking orders to the three other crew members on the bridge. She

The Devils Do

glanced over at them for a moment.

"Ensign, see if you can contact Coalition Command," she said.

"Belay that order, Ensign," Gant said. "This isn't your ship."

"What?" the woman said.

"Ma'am, we're being hailed," the Ensign said.

"Put it up."

"Free people of Kell, this is General Sylvan Kett of the Seraphim United Defense Force," General Kett said. "Please maintain course and prepare to be boarded. You are declared prisoners of war, until you can be divested. Any efforts to escape will be met with deadly force. Any efforts to resist will be met with deadly force. We have no interest in imprisoning you again, but we do require an orderly transfer of interest. Ship's captains, please acknowledge."

"Prisoners of war?" Benhil said.

"General Kett?" Pik said. "That means Queenie is back, doesn't it?"

Gant felt a sudden coldness, his whole body going stiff. "I don't know. Seraphim United Defense Force? Queenie would never let Kett take over like this."

He looked out through the ship's forward viewport, searching. He found what he was looking for a few seconds later. The Faust, hanging close to one of the Seedships.

"I have a bad feeling about this," Benhil said.

"So do I," Gant replied, forcing himself to stay calm.

Abbey hadn't been dead the last time he had thought she was. He had to assume she was alive until someone proved otherwise.

He might do something he would regret again if he didn't.

"Why does it feel like even though we won, we lost?" Pik asked.

CHAPTER FORTY-FIVE

"THIS WASN'T PART OF THE deal," Bastion said, glaring at General Kett. "This is Queenie's army. This is Queenie's fight. The Rejects."

"Abigail is dead," Sylvan replied, his face stone. "Just like Charmeine."

"You don't know that," Jequn said. "She may have survived. We need to go back."

"Go back?" Sylvan said. "We can't go back. There's nothing to go back to. This is the way forward. The way that we planned. The way your mother wanted it to be."

"What do you mean?" Bastion asked. "You were planning this bullshit the whole time?"

"No," Jequn said.

"Yes," Sylvan said. "Cage would have been a powerful asset, but she's not a leader. She doesn't have the experience I have."

"What she has is heart," Bastion said. "What she has is courage. She was going to do this herself because you were too much of a coward to help. The only reason you're even here is because-"

Bastion grunted as the General's fist hit him hard in the gut. A moment later, an arm was around his neck, choking him.

"The reason I'm here is because I promised Charmeine I would be.

The Devils Do

The entire galaxy is in danger, Bastion, and we're the only ones who can stop it. Tactical experience has value right now. Heart doesn't. It isn't personal."

He let Bastion go. Bastion reached up and rubbed at his neck. Son of a bitch. Abbey had told him how much she respected this guy. What the hell for?

"Look General; I got you here, you won the day. Whoopee. You want the ships? You want the army? That's fine by me. Whatever. Just let me collect my team and we'll be on our way. You can stay here. We're going back to Azure."

"I'm sorry, Bastion," Sylvan replied. "I can't let you do that. We need skilled soldiers more than anything else. You're a top notch pilot. I can't let you go."

"What? Are you fragging kidding me? You don't control me."

"Right now, I do. Even if I let you go, how would you get back to Azure? The *Faust* is mine now."

"General," Jequn said.

General Kett turned back to her. "You know what will happen if Thraven wins. Is that what you want?"

"No, but we helped make Abbey into what she is. She's our responsibility."

"She's dead," Sylvan snapped. "Thraven was on the planet with her. Do you think she was strong enough to beat him?"

Jequn paled. She glanced over at Bastion. "I'm sorry."

"Yeah," Bastion replied. "Me, too."

"Colonel Brink," Sylvan said.

"Yes, General?" the Colonel replied.

"Once we've moved to a safer location, I want you to find these so-called Rejects and consolidate them on the Brimstone."

"Yes, General."

Sylvan moved beside Bastion. "This isn't up for discussion. If you want to be part of the solution, I'm happy to have you. If you want to cause problems? I can take care of those, too."

Bastion stared at the General for a moment. He wanted to punch him in his smug face, but he kept himself restrained.

"Aye, sir. I want to be part of the solution, sir."

"Good," Sylvan said. "Set coordinates for FTL. We need to get away from here before Thraven returns."

"Yes, sir," Bastion replied.

He had been in prison before. He knew how to survive. He knew how to be patient. They would figure something out. He wasn't giving up on Abbey. She had never given up on him.

And when Queenie got her hands on Kett?

There would be hell to pay.

The Devils Do

CHAPTER FORTY-SIX

OLUS STUMBLED DOWN THE TUNNEL that had been dug into the earth beneath Manhattan. His body was on fire, every nerve ending screaming out. He wasn't sure if he had been burned, or if the meds Dilixix had given him were the source of the agony. All he knew was that he needed to get back to her, to find out if there was some way to stop the pain.

The other Plixians in Little Plixar watched him curiously, most of them afraid to offer assistance. He avoided eye contact with them as he moved slowly through the passages, keeping a hand on the sides to steady himself. He probably looked drunk to them. He probably looked like a vagrant.

He had escaped the museum. He still wasn't quite sure how. He had gone out a window, landing on the lawn, miraculously away from any of the bystanders who had witnessed the blast. He had rolled over to see the flames engulf the entire space, breaking the rest of the windows and rising into the night. They were intense, inhuman flames. Nothing should have survived inside, but he knew that Ruche and Elivee had. An Evolent and a Venerant had destroyed what remained of the Council's opposition to Thraven's agenda.

It was only a matter of time before the time bomb he had been trying to disarm finally exploded, and there was nothing immediate he could do about it.

He could only hope that Abbey was having better luck.

He fell to the ground in front of the row of storefronts where Dilixix' pharmacy sat. His muscles were weak, his body shaking. He clenched his teeth and forced himself up. He had gone too far, gotten too close to collapse now. He made it a few more steps, and then a pair of hands was beneath his shoulders, propping him up. A second pair lifted his legs, putting him into a sitting position. A head leaned in beside his.

"Captain Mann?" Dilixix said, cradling him. "What happened to you?"

Olus turned his head, looking into her small eyes. "I have a feeling you already know."

She lowered her head. "I do. This is worse than we were expecting."

"You knew who I was looking for?"

"Not who. What. An Evolent of the Nephilim."

"So you know."

"Yes. I'm sorry I didn't tell you before, Captain, but we've learned not to trust easily."

"What are you?"

"A Servant of the Watchers," she said. "An employee of the Ophanim."

"Who?"

"You will find out, Captain. When you wake up."

"Wake up? The pills."

"I'm sorry, Captain. I didn't have a choice. You needed it if you were going to confront an Evolent."

"Needed what?"

"The Blood of the Shard."

"I don't know what that means."

"I know. You will find out."

"When I wake up?"

"Yes."

"I'm still awake."

The Devils Do

Dilixix made a clacking sound his translator couldn't handle. He felt something stab into his arm, and he was vaguely aware of one of her hands having moved there.

"This will not harm you, Captain. Your body will heal and recover. Everything will be explained. We have much work to do. The time has come."

Olus tried to reply, but he could feel himself fading. He considered resisting, but what would be the point? She had saved his life. Had she given him the Gift? He didn't quite understand. He supposed he would.

When he woke up.

CHAPTER FORTY-SEVEN

Gloritant Thraven looked down at the charred form of the Seraph at his feet. She was holding something in her hand. It was a small device, the front of which ended in a needle that led back to a cracked and empty reservoir behind it.

The Blood of the Shard had been spilled onto the blackened dirt. There would be no coming back for her this time.

He reached up and placed his hand against his neck. He ran his fingers over the roughness there, the remains of the damage Abigail Cage had inflicted on him.

Damage caused by the Gift.

Damage that would never completely heal.

He glanced over at the teleportation device, and the red light on its bent and burned surface. He was tired. He was in pain. He had used so much of his Gift. Cage would never know it, but if she had survived his final attack, she might have been able to kill him. That's how weak he had allowed himself to become. That's how desperately he wanted the Focus.

They couldn't return to Elysium without it. The Gate was being built, but it required the Blood of the Shard. The true Blood, not the altered copy of the Father. It didn't need much, only a single drop, but that was a single drop more than he possessed.

The Devils Do

"It will come," he told himself. "I will get it. The Father has Promised it in his Covenant. His Promise cannot be undone."

He found Airi's body on his way back to the Shrike. He paused ahead of it for only a moment, shaking his head. He had overestimated her, and she had failed him. If she weren't dead, he would have killed her himself.

He stepped over her, continuing to the Shrike, climbing into it and leaning back into the seat. He needed the Font if he was going to survive. He needed to find the *Fire* and retrieve it.

"Report," he said, activating the comm.

"Gloritant," one of his Honorants replied. He didn't know which one, or which ship. He didn't care right now. "Four of the enemy ships escaped. We destroyed six battlecruisers."

"The Seedships?"

"They escaped, Your Eminence."

He was too weak to do more than sigh.

"Any word from the *Fire*?"

"No, Your Eminence. Gloritant, we also lost Warships Three and Six to the enemy. They had some kind of weapon on board that disabled all of our systems."

"This is war, Honorant. There will be death."

"Yes, Gloritant."

"Regroup the ground units, and send two more dropships to the surface, fully loaded."

"Your Eminence?" the Honorant replied, confused.

"They're to search for remaining enemy combatants. One in particular. A woman named Abigail Cage. I want her dead. Send three dropships. She's incredibly dangerous."

"Yes, Gloritant."

"Also, send a transport to the *Fire*."

"Yes, Gloritant. It will be done."

He disconnected the link and closed the canopy, bringing the Shrike into the air and ascending into the storms. He could sense the Font, and he altered course, crossing the hundreds of kilometers of distance, his body growing weaker by the second. He had almost gone too far. He had almost used too much.

He came upon the *Fire*. It was mostly intact, at the end of a massive crater of its own that had dislodged tons of dirt and rock. It was still dark. Still dead. He expected that none of the crew would be alive.

The hull was buried under the churned earth, so he landed the Shrike on top of the ship and peeled away the armor until he had a path to the inside, using the last of his strength to do so. He hobbled along the corridors almost peacefully, praying to his Father for strength as he made his way through the ship, passing dozens of corpses on the way.

His Immolent was standing at the entrance to his quarters, brought back to life by the Gift and still defending the Font. It didn't react to his sudden appearance other than to move aside and allow him to enter.

He made his way to the pool. It was sealed over the top, the Blood contained within. He put his hands on the control pad, opening it once more. Then he climbed in still clothed, submerging himself and feeling the strength immediately begin to return.

He had hoped his conquest would be easier than this. Then again, nothing worth having was ever easily obtained. The Republic would be under his control within the coming weeks, and the rest of the galaxy would follow. There was nothing that Sylvan Kett could do about that.

He had lost more than he had won today. He had lost more than he expected. But he also knew the defeat was temporary.

He had been waiting thousands of years for the Great Return. He could wait a few weeks more.

CHAPTER FORTY-EIGHT

ABBEY DIDN'T KNOW HOW LONG she spent sleeping. It hadn't been a conscious decision. She remembered turning off the teleporter. She remembered crying. She didn't remember anything else.

She was starving. She had never been so hungry before. She had woken up in a room made of stone, an unlit room with only a sliver of light pouring in from beneath a crack in one of the walls, betraying it as a hidden door. Not that there was anything to see. The room was empty.

She realized she had to be under the crater. There was no other way the teleporter could have reached. Had Jequn given it to her knowing she might need an emergency escape hatch? How could she? If she had planned it, why the hell hadn't she put any food in the damn room?

Charmeine. She felt sadness at the loss of the Seraph, now that she had time to be sad. She felt anguish when she thought about the Rejects, too. Gant was going to be beside himself, and she had left her newly established force without their Queen. At least they had General Kett. He would help them continue what she had started.

Besides, she was going to find her way back to them. No matter what.

She stood up, approaching the false wall. She was still tired. She couldn't feel the Gift. It was nearly expended and required food to be able to replicate. Her body was sore. She reached back, putting her hand on the small bump over her rear. The tail. It felt a little larger. She shivered as she ran her fingers through hair that had grown nearly six centimeters while she was sleeping. She could feel the ridges along her scalp, the beginnings of the bone protrusions she recalled from Phlenel.

She needed the damn Serum.

She didn't want to be a monster.

She put her hands on the fake wall. She couldn't use the Gift to open it. She needed something else.

The ceiling above her shook slightly, dumping small bits of debris on her head. She glanced up at it. If she was underground, then someone was above her. Thraven? She doubted he would stick around just for her. He had other things to do, but he might have left some units behind. Maybe an entire warship. With the Republic Council soon to come under his control, he would have all the ships he needed.

If they were here and couldn't find her, that meant she was well hidden, wherever she was. A single room, or a whole complex? The Ophanim had been on this planet for a long time. This had to be part of their original compound.

She felt along the seam of the wall. She had to get out. She had to get off Azure. She had to get back to the Rejects. Once she made it out of here, where was she going to get a ship?

From whoever was above her, maybe? She would figure it out.

She was the fragging Queen of Demons, damn it.

She would survive.

Printed in Great Britain
by Amazon